INFRINGEMENT

A Novel

BENJAMIN WESTBROOK

Visit Benjamin Westbrook's website at
www.benjaminwestbrook.com

Follow Benjamin Westbrook on Twitter: @BKWestbrook

Infringement

Cover design by Andrew Figel.

Scripture quotations taken from The Holy Bible, New International
Version, ® NIV. ® Copyright © 1973, 1978, 1984, 2011 by
Biblica, Inc. TM Used by permission of Zondervan. All rights
reserved worldwide. www.zondervan.com

ISBN 978-0-9862136-2-5

For My Family
Above all else, trust God,
and never, never, never give up

Preface from the Author:

When I began writing this novel, my purpose was twofold. First, utilizing a fictional medium, to examine an array of current events through the lens of biblical prophecy and, in some cases, introduce the reader to the Bible more generally. The second purpose, again through a fictional medium, was to try and come to an understanding of what it truly means to put one's trust in God.

During the course of the year, my life experienced a jolt that I never saw coming in the form of a cancer diagnosis within my immediate family. Needless to say, my life and the lives of my family members, changed forever in an instant.

Prior to cancer invading our lives, trusting in God was something I *wanted* to do. Trust was a concept I was interested in putting into practice. It sounded great, but I was always holding something back from God. In short, I really didn't understand what "putting one's trust in the Lord alone" really meant, although I was attempting to write a novel about that very thing.

While I certainly wouldn't have ever volunteered to take the road my family and I are now traveling, I do view it as a blessing in many ways, because, through cancer, I finally came to know faith and trust. I came to see that the only aspect of one's life he or she truly has control over is his or her faith. Because I simply had no other choice, I came to understand that putting my trust in God meant holding nothing back. It meant giving myself and my life over completely to God, never doubting, even during the toughest times, His faithfulness to His Word. It meant counting on His strength and His peace, because my own paltry strength was totally inadequate, and I had no peace on my own. Ultimately, trust meant being joyful in all circumstances, even the most seemingly dire, and knowing, beyond any doubt that God is faithful and trustworthy because of who *He* is, not because of who I am. This is the lesson cancer has taught me this year, and for that lesson, I am grateful.

My main character, Declan Parker, finds himself on a similar path in this story. Declan's times are dark, his circumstances difficult. There is evil in the world, even at his front door, but with trust in God, there is joy and peace.

Maranatha.

Benjamin Westbrook

PART I

"They had as king over them the angel of the Abyss, whose name in Hebrew is Abaddon and in Greek is Apollyon (that is, Destroyer)"

Revelation 9:11

Chapter 1
December 15th

He worked deliberately and meticulously atop the short ladder in the dark, quietly screwing into place the last of the four bright red "Exit" signs to be replaced. As far back as he could remember, he'd been a night person. He enjoyed working in the darkness, amid the silence and solitude one typically found during the late night hours when most were asleep. There were fewer distractions at night, no people to get in his way or take up his time with their generally meaningless chatter.

He turned the last screw firmly into place, quietly, one rotation after another until the metal screw squeaked against the metal bracket and it could go no further. After he'd finished, he scanned the sign to be certain it was perfectly even, gave each of the four screws another quick turn to verify they were tight, and gently nudged the "Exit" sign from each side to be absolutely sure it was securely in place. Satisfied with his work, he then turned the power switch to "On" and removed his night vision goggles to see the four red letters glowing in the darkness above the doorway. He stepped slowly and quietly down from the ladder, careful not to misstep, and walked to the center of the semi-circular sanctuary where he had a clear view of each of the four "Exit" signs he'd installed. As he'd planned, the new signs looked, in all respects, exactly like the four he'd replaced, except for the tiny HD video camera in each. The camera, located just to the right of the "T", was totally indiscernible from a distance, unless someone knew to look for it.

Eager to test the new signs, he made his way toward the last row of pews nearest the main entrance of the sanctuary, where he'd left his laptop. He opened the laptop and deftly pulled up the admin page of his website, which was still under construction and hadn't gone live yet. He clicked on the "Live Webcams" link, which took him to another page split into four window panes, one for each video camera in the "Exit" signs he'd installed. Three of the panes were completely dark, which was expected given the darkness of the sanctuary. The fourth pane, which showed the video feed from the camera in the sign above the main entrance, featured the dim light of his laptop. He couldn't test the camera views completely until he could return during the day, but he knew, together, they should stream a full 360 degree live view of the sanctuary to his website.

Unable to wait until morning, he decided a small test was in order, so he took his iPad out of his backpack and pulled up his website there as well. Once he'd again accessed the page showing the live webcam feeds from the four "Exit" signs, he walked slowly to the center of the sanctuary, holding his iPad close to his face in order to illuminate it slightly. As he walked toward the main pulpit area, he watched each of the camera views on his iPad, to see when each camera picked up the dim light and his faint silhouette. Although not ideal, it was a sufficient test for the time being, and just seeing his dim silhouette from the cameras' views gave him a distinct and very pleasing sense of excitement.

Once he arrived at the pulpit area in the center front of the sanctuary, he stepped up the few small marble steps to the main stage, and saw each camera feed had picked up the light from his iPad. From anywhere on the pulpit, he'd be perfectly visible to all four cameras in full light.

He shut down his iPad, leaving the sanctuary pitch black again but for the red light from the "Exit" signs, and slid his night vision goggles back on over his eyes. The pews fanned out in a semi-circle from the large stage, thirty rows deep. He stood in the center of the pulpit, where the preacher typically gave his sermon and prepared communion, and enjoyed an unobstructed view of the entire sanctuary. With his goggles on, he carefully scanned each section of the empty and otherwise dark pews, beginning with those on his left side, until he'd gone through them all one by one. Then, he again removed the goggles and closed his eyes, letting the perfect darkness clear his mind.

He stood facing the pews directly in front of him with his eyes closed tightly, his breath slow and measured. His mind began to focus, his imagination came alive, and one by one the pews were populated with faces. Soon, the faces, some familiar and others not, filled every corner of the almost bursting sanctuary. From the pulpit, he watched them talking to one another, greeting and hugging each other. He heard them chattering back and forth before services began, joking with one another, and laughing. He sensed their warmth, their excitement, their joy. His eyes still closed, he turned slowly and deliberately from his left to his right, watching them intently and letting their faces burn into his memory. He wanted to remember them, to know the joy on their faces down to the very smallest detail, so that when he finally raised his rifle and began spilling their blood onto the glittering marble sanctuary floor, he'd be able to recognize the precise instant when the careless joy in each face turned to horror and fear.

Chapter 2
December 17th

"Hey Kev, are you heading out soon?"

"Another hour or so probably. You?"

"On my way out now," Declan responded. "I'm meeting my buddy Dan over at McNulty's for a few drinks and to watch the game for a bit. You want to meet us over there?"

"Sure, I'll come by when I finish up here."

"What are you working on?"

"Just my report on the Slater matter. Nothing major, but I want to get it put to bed before we get into full-on holiday mode."

"Gotcha. Alright, I'll see you at McNulty's," Declan said as he finished buttoning up his coat. He made sure his computer had powered down, picked up his backpack, and headed toward the elevators, when his desk phone rang.

"Damn…I'd better get it," he said, and reluctantly backtracked to his desk. "This is Special Agent Parker."

"Agent Parker, this is Detective Norman, Roger Norman."

"What can I do for you Detective?"

"Well, we received an anonymous call a little while ago expressing concern about a David Timothy Stanton. Are you familiar with the name?"

"No, I don't think so. Should I be?"

"Probably not. I only ask because this is the second call we've received about him. The first call came in, anonymously, a few weeks ago. Per protocol, I contacted your field office and passed the info on to another agent. Let's see, my notes say I spoke with Special Agent Costello."

"I know Agent Costello."

"Good. Well, like I said, I gave the info we received on Stanton to Special Agent Costello and never heard anything back. I didn't even really think about it again until a follow up call came in tonight. One of our desk officers took the call."

"What's the nature of the complaint?"

"The caller says he thinks Stanton has some radical and dangerous political leanings."

"Such as?"

"The caller was pretty vague, but essentially said Stanton has some of the standard wacko political views. I think his exact words were something to the effect that the country is rotten and morally corrupt and disease filled, plagued with a cancerous government and brain dead populace who should basically be eradicated."

"Well, that makes him about one of a million or so other nut jobs out there. Frankly, it doesn't sound like anything out of the ordinary so far. Just another disgruntled misfit with a big mouth."

"I agree. I ran Stanton through our system and he came back clean, no record at all. But, since we've received two calls now, and, things being as they are lately with the new legislation and Homeland Security mandates, we're required to pass along anything and everything of a potential terrorist nature to the Feds, so that's what I'm doin'."

"I understand. Like I said, it doesn't sound like anything based upon what little info the caller provided, but I'll run a check. You said this guy's name is Stanton, David Timothy?"

"That's right. His date of birth is July 22, 1982, and his address is 9292 Parkside Ave., Apartment B."

Declan wrote down the information. "Do you know whether it was the same caller both times, Detective?"

"That's my understanding."

"Did the caller leave a call back number or any way to contact him, or her?"

"Him," Detective Norman replied, "and no, nothing."

"Did he say what his relationship to Stanton is?"

"Nope. He just gave us what I've given you and expressed his concern about Stanton's general disdain for congress, the president and essentially everything related to the government. I suspect he's a neighbor or co-worker. Like I said, I'm passing this to you guys because we're required to, but I'd be surprised if anything comes of it."

"I'll run him through our systems and records anyway, and talk with Costello. Because of the first call, we should at least have a report in our system. I'll look into it and get back to you tomorrow."

"Sounds good. Have a good night."

Declan set his notes from the call on top of his computer keyboard, again picked up his backpack, and headed out for the night.

But for the blue screen on the high definition monitor, Stanton's apartment was pitch black. He inserted a homemade black video game DVD into his computer and waited for the program he'd developed and programmed to boot up. After ten seconds or so, the blue screen turned black and the title "ABADDON – The Destroyer" appeared on the screen in an intentionally ominous red font. Below the title was the word "Play", which he clicked on and picked up his game controller.

The title screen graphically faded completely into red, which gradually dripped off the screen, like blood, revealing a digitally animated black Ford SUV slowly driving into a busy parking lot. The driver of the SUV, the game's hero, parked and sat for a few moments, watching the last few well-dressed animated characters hurry through the lightly falling snow into a large white stone building. The sound of chiming bells came through loudly over the muffled chatter of the other game characters remaining in the parking lot.

The clock on the console of the hero's SUV read 5:00, then 5:01, then, a minute later, 5:02. The digital hero simply sat in his car, watching the snow fall outside, until the clock finally read 5:10, at which point he stepped out of the car. The game's hero was a tall, buff, imposing figure, dressed in a sharp black suit. He was ruggedly handsome, and, by design, very reminiscent of Daniel Craig's James Bond.

Using the game controller, David Stanton took control of the game's hero, Abaddon, and walked him to the back of the SUV, where he clicked a button on the controller which prompted Abaddon to open the rear door. Three black duffle bags sat in the back. With a click, the character opened one. Another insert screen popped up, featuring a timer, which the digital hero set to 5:26, and then zipped the bag back up. With another click of the controller, Abaddon reached in and quickly slung the other two black bags over his shoulders, and closed the back of the SUV.

He walked briskly across the parking lot to the rear of the church, where he waited until 5:17. At that point, Stanton's hero made his way to easternmost of the three main building entrances, removed a key from his pocket and locked the deadbolt from the outside. He then looped a chain through the door handles, and locked it. Abaddon then moved swiftly to the entrance on the opposite side, repeating the same process, and went back to the main double door entrance at the building's center. Stanton clicked the controller again, and Abaddon locked the deadbolt to the center doors and threaded a third chain through the two door handles and locked it together with a padlock.

Abaddon quickly made his way to the back of the church. When he reached the back entrance, he removed his coat and opened the bag, from which he took out a black tactical vest, loaded with four ammunition magazines and a 9 mm semi-automatic. After putting on the vest, he pulled out two AR-15 semi-automatic rifles, one with a 60 round magazine and the other loaded with a 100 round drum magazine. Finally, he removed a black magazine belt, containing four additional 60 round magazines, which he strapped on below the vest.
Finally ready, he opened the rear door slowly and quietly,

then slipped inside and locked the door behind him. The sounds of a choir singing "Oh Come All Ye' Faithful" came clearly through Stanton's computer speakers. Digital Abaddon stood in the hallway directly behind the main sanctuary, a few feet away from a closed door which provided direct access to the pulpit.

Stanton's fingers caressed the controller as he consciously steadied his excited breathing. He felt the adrenaline surging through his body, until he finally maneuvered his digital hero through the door and onto the pulpit in the midst of the service. He quickly spotted the pastor and his assistant and with a flurry of taps on the controller and "rat-tat, rat-tat, rat-tat", took them both down. The sound of gunfire rang through the sanctuary and he immediately turned his full attention to the congregation in the pews and opened fire indiscriminately. The animated congregation scrambled in all directions, falling left and right while a red counter in the upper left of the screen, which had begun at zero, kept count of fatalities. Stanton deftly moved Abaddon from side to side, shooting down the men who tried to rush him on the stage. He moved from one side to another, firing in a semi-circle at the characters rushing for the locked exits. Screams flowed out of Stanton's computer speakers, mixed with the "rat-tat, rat-tat, rat-tat" of his assault rifles. The fatality count quickly reached 38 and continued to climb with each round fired: 39, 40, 41, 42.

Stanton tried his best to look at the faces of the people as Abaddon mowed them down, but in his zone he saw them merely as targets, which when hit, raised his fatality count. He didn't care who they were, he took aim and fired at anything moving whether man, woman or child. As he manipulated the deadly and menacing Abaddon down the main aisle of the sanctuary, firing at those lying on the floor between the pews, he looked at the fatality count and realized he was close to his record. He intensified his focus and fired to his left, hitting a running adult male in the back of the head, 88. He fired at two teenage girls in colorful dresses trying to run ahead of Abaddon in the aisle, 89 and 90. A man tried to grab his hero from behind, but Stanton quickly turned him around and hit the man with the butt of the AR-15, knocking him to the floor. "Rat-tat, rat-tat", fatality 91 and a new record.

Chapter 3
December 18th

Declan woke up with a slight headache and looked at his alarm clock to see that it was already ten minutes past seven. After a quick shower and a brief stop for his daily coffee, he made it into the Bureau field office about an hour later. He briefly looked over his notes regarding David Stanton from the night before and set them aside while his computer booted up.

Once his system was up, he checked his emails. Finding nothing pressing, he looked over his scribbled notes on David Stanton again. Declan ran Stanton's name through the FBI's National Crime Information Center, or NCIC, database which turned up nothing. He then accessed the FBI's Terrorist Screening Center, or TSC, system and found no records on a David Timothy Stanton.

Declan picked up his phone and called an inside extension. After a few rings, a voice on the other end answered, "Costello."

"Costello, hey, it's Declan Parker."

"What's up, Parker?"

"Nothing, just following up on a call I received last night before I left. It was about an anonymous complaint on a Stanton, David Timothy. Ring a bell?"

"A bit."

"The detective said an earlier call was made and info given to you. Something about radical ideology and the potential for domestic terrorism."

"Yeah, I do remember that. It was an anonymous call about some alleged right-wing wacko or other."

"Something like that," Declan replied.

"I ran the guy through our systems and he came back clean. Nothing in TSC or NCIC, so I let it go."

"I just did the same thing and he came back clean again."

"There you go. I wouldn't waste much time on this one, Parker. You're not going to uncover the next Unabomber or anything here."

"Wasn't expecting to, but thanks."

"No worries. By the way, if any other calls come in on this guy, just direct them to me. I'll deal with it."

"Will do."

After hanging up with Special Agent Costello, Declan thought for a few minutes, looked over his notes again, and wanting to be sure he'd done a diligent job before determining nothing was there, decided to check and see if any background checks had been run for Stanton within the past two years. He typed Stanton's name and date of birth into another system, which then checked them against yet another FBI database for prior searches in the NICS (short for the National Instant Criminal Background Check System), the nationwide system used for conducting criminal background checks on individuals attempting to purchase firearms.

After a few seconds, his search came back with two matches. An NICS check was run on David Timothy Stanton, DOB 7/22/82, on December 22, 2012 and again on April 19, 2013. Declan then ran a search through the FBI's national database of registered gun owners and quickly located Stanton as the registered owner of two Colt AR-15 Tactical Carbine semi-automatic rifles, purchased and registered in December 2012 and April 2013, respectively.

"Interesting," Declan said to himself.

"Good morning, Pastor."

"Good morning, David. How are things today?"

"No problems so far."

"Looking forward to the holidays?"

"Very much."

"Excellent. It's a wonderful time of year. Have a

good day."

"You too, Pastor."

Stanton carefully maneuvered his dull gray janitor's cart into the men's restroom just outside the sanctuary and took his time, meticulously cleaning the sinks and mirrors and disinfecting the urinals. He slowly and methodically mopped the tiled floor, careful not to deviate from his left to right, back to front pattern.

Almost two hours later, after knocking politely to verify it was unoccupied, he rolled his cart into the women's restroom and followed the same deliberate routine, first cleaning the sinks and mirrors, then the toilets, and finally mopping the floor. When Stanton had finished with the women's restroom, he parked his cart out of the way in the main foyer, and walked back to the parish office to pick up his sack lunch and his iPad.

As was his habit, Stanton sat on the plush ivory sofa next to one of the two large windows in the main reception area. He ate his lunch slowly, watching the bundled up children playing on the small playground at the church elementary school across the parking lot. He watched the children intently, listening to their laughter and the joy in their voices. He envied their energy and carelessness and, without being entirely cognizant of the feeling, he longed to be one of them. When had he ever felt that type of freedom, that type of joy? In truth, he acknowledged that he never had, particularly not when he had been a child. Stanton sat staring at the school kids, who looked to him so filled with joy and so blissfully unaware of the miserable painful lives led by so many other children in the world. He remembered such kids from his own childhood, the ones he would have given anything to trade lives with in order to escape the hell in which he had been forced by God to dwell in each day. He both hated and envied their happiness and longed to try again, to go back and live a life untouched by suffering; however, life was what it was. Stanton was who he was, and there was only one way back, which was, ironically, to move forward.

When he'd finished his lunch, Stanton turned on his iPad, logged onto the administrator's page of his still offline website, and walked quietly into the church sanctuary. Once inside, he clicked on the "live feed" link and in a few seconds saw the four high definition camera views of the sanctuary fill his touch screen. He initially saw himself in two of the camera views and was very pleased. The clarity and color of the picture in each frame was excellent. The buffering was sufficient to stream a consistent and fluid video feed. Stanton walked throughout the sanctuary, being sure to avoid his "stage", the pulpit, and was thoroughly satisfied with the camera angles and quality. With his test finished, he turned off his iPad, put it back into his backpack in the church office, went back to his plastic gray janitor's cart, and resumed his work.

After a group meeting on another matter headed by John Bleeker, the field office's Special Agent in Charge, Declan grabbed a quick bite to eat and refocused his attention on David Stanton when he got back to his desk. He wasn't entirely sure where to look next, but due to the fact that Stanton owned two AR-15's, which wasn't in itself illegal as they were purchased prior to the federal semi-automatic weapons ban, he just couldn't let the matter go as nothing.

Declan pulled up Stanton's motor vehicle and drivers' license records and photo. The face in the photo looked familiar, but he couldn't place where he would have seen it before. He printed a copy of Stanton's drivers' license: David Timothy Stanton, Height: 5'7", Weight: 190 lbs., brown hair, brown eyes, no restrictions, not an organ donor. A black 2004 Ford Explorer was registered to David Stanton, license plate HRW 247.

Declan thought for a few minutes, then heard the familiar voice of Kevin Cameron, a career agent in his early fifties who was Declan's friend and de facto mentor, pop up behind him, "Whatcha working on?"

"Uh, I'm trying to get some information on a call I got last night before I left. Costello looked at it before and nothing comes up in TSC or NCIC, but I did find two grandfathered pre-ban AR-15's registered to this guy."

"What else are you looking for?"

"I'm not really sure. I guess I want to know why he would want not one, but two semi-automatic rifles. I just don't know where else I can look."

"I do, rookie."

"Okay, spill it."

"It's easy, put in a PRISM request with the regional fusion center."

"That's a great idea."

"Of course it is. They'll be able to tell you anything and everything you want to know about your boy. Where he works, where he shops, who he emailed this morning and what he said."

"How about ammo purchases?"

"That's easy. Unless he's bought ammo on the underground market, or stolen it, they'll be able to tell you exactly how much he's bought, when and from where, even going back to pre-ban purchases."

"Sweet," Declan replied. "That's exactly what I need."

"Glad I could help."

Declan accessed the fusion center request protocol, made sure he had the necessary information and credentials in front of him and placed a call to the regional fusion center. After providing his credentials and various information and passwords verifying his security clearance, the representative asked for his request.

"I need a history of all ammunition purchases for a

subject."

"Subject's name?"

"Stanton, David Timothy."

"Date of birth?"

"7/22/82"

"Current address?"

"9292 Parkside Ave., Apartment B."

"Hold please."

"Okay," Declan replied.

A few seconds later, the representative said, "I'm sorry, but your security clearance isn't sufficient to obtain the requested records on Stanton, David Timothy."

"What?"

"Information relating to Stanton, David Timothy has been classified SCI. You don't have SCI clearance for this compartment."

"I'm not even certain I know what SCI clearance is, but why would his records be SCI?"

"SCI means Sensitive Compartmented Information. Essentially, additional controls have been placed on the dissemination of certain records and information relating to this subject."

"By whom?"

"I don't know and couldn't tell you if I did, without SCI clearance of course."

"You said certain records and info are SCI."

"Correct."

"Can you tell me what info I can access?"

"Not without a request."

"Fine, I'm requesting all information and records on the subject available to my clearance level."

"That's very vague."

"Agreed, but it's my request."

"I'll forward any information at your clearance level to your secured email address."

"Thank you."

Chapter 4
December 19th

Unable to sleep for much of the night, Declan finally gave up trying. He'd stayed at his desk until close to 10:00 the night before, hoping a response to his fusion center request would come back; however, nothing had been sent to his secure email account. He'd been up throughout the night unable to shake the nagging question of why someone who checked out clean in all the FBI's databases had been classified SCI. It made no sense.

Sometime around 4:00 a.m., determined to begin a serious investigation into Stanton, Declan got out of bed and headed to the gym. He worked out until 7:00, showered, stopped to grab a bagel and coffee, and headed to Stanton's building on Parkside. By 7:42, he was parked half a block or so from the small four unit building, with a good view of the apartment door and Stanton's parked black Ford Explorer.

As was his custom on his off days, David Stanton slept until nearly noon. After making a small breakfast, he hopped on his computer and spent an hour or so making detailed adjustments to his website. He tinkered with the graphics, layout, fonts and font colors, trying hundreds of options in his search for the most suitable combination to effectively convey his intended message to a global audience.

After working on the site's aesthetics, Stanton decided to focus on what, along with the live video feed, would become the site's content. He pulled up a Word document saved as "Abaddon's Message – Draft 16".

"Tonight, on this eve of the celebrated birth of the Zionist Messiah, Jesus Christ, you shall witness the power and rage of the Destroyer, Abaddon, the Angel of the Abyss. Tonight, in defiance and justice, I, Abaddon, shall rise and wreak destruction and death upon the so called Bride of Christ and upon the people of this most sinful and depraved generation. In so doing, I shall usher in the Beginning, the ultimate destruction of the old order. Tonight, those who have eyes to see and ears to hear, shall witness a rebirth of our world, accomplished through the destruction of those still clinging to doctrines of oppression and falsity. Abaddon, the Destroyer, shall bring death, and with it, ultimately, life for a new, untarnished, generation. Tonight, the work of ages shall finally culminate in the passing of the falsity of religion and the long awaited birth of Truth. The blood of the sheep, shed in the sanctuary of lies, shall pay the price of Truth and usher in a new era, a new order, a world which will not tolerate the sins of the past. Eternity begins tonight. Witness this Beginning and stand in awe of Abaddon's cleansing and righteous power. Abaddon, the Destroyer, is AT THE DOOR!"

Chapter 5
December 19th

"Declan, is that you honey?"

"Yes, mom."

"Oh, hi honey. Here, let me take that." Declan's mom took the bottle of wine he'd brought for her, along with the twelve pack of Fat Tire beer he'd brought for himself, his brother, and sister-in-law. "I'll put these in the fridge. Do you want me to open one of the beers for you?"

"Thanks, mom. That would be great."

"Would you like it in a glass?"

"No, the bottle is fine. How's your marathon training coming along?"

"Great," his mom responded. "I did sixteen miles this morning."

"You continue to amaze me. What is this one, your tenth or eleventh?"

"Twelfth. I'm gonna go open your beer, and get a glass of wine for myself. I think I've earned it today. I'll be right back."

"Okay."

Declan took off his coat and dropped it gently on the familiar upholstered bench in the foyer, just as he had for as long as he could remember. He walked into the family room and warmed his hands in front of the fireplace, rubbing them together slowly and taking in the crackling aromatic warmth radiating from the slow flames. His focus turned to a small framed photo on the mantle. It was a picture of himself, his older brother Evan, and their dad, taken outside of the family's small rustic lake house three days after Declan's tenth birthday.

The joy and energy in his dad's eyes struck Declan. His dad's glowing prideful smile as he stood between his two boys, each holding a fish so small it would scarcely feed a mouse, typified the understated steady peacefulness Declan remembered so clearly about his dad. Nothing rattled the man, not even the cancer which took his life a mere 362 days after that photo, on Declan's eleventh birthday. Declan looked into his dad's eyes, into everything he remembered, loved and missed about the man.

"Here, honey," his mom said coming up beside him.

"Thanks," he replied taking the open beer from her. "I was just looking at the picture of us with dad at the lake house that summer before he got really sick."

"That's my favorite picture of you three."

"Mine too, I think. He just looks so strong still, so happy."

"He was. He loved taking you boys up to that house."

"I remember he'd sit there on that little pier fishing with us for hours, just waiting for someone to get a bite. He didn't really seem to care if we caught anything."

"He didn't. Your dad was just happy to be out there with you and Evan, to have time to talk with you both. He loved you boys more than anything or anyone, except God. I know he's still proud as can be of both of you."

"I hope so."

"Of course he is. You following in his footsteps in the FBI and your brother being a doctor? We're both extremely proud of you boys. You've turned out as well as any parents could pray for."

"I still miss him."

"I do too, honey. Every single day, but I know I'll see him again someday, relatively soon perhaps."

Declan paused for a second, then, wanting to avoid the subject of God and heaven, asked, "Are Evan, Michelle and the kids on the way?"

"They should be. You know they never really get anywhere on time these days."

"Trust me, I know. Evan even has trouble getting places on time when he doesn't have the family in tow. What are we having for dinner?"

"My lasagna with salad and garlic bread."

"I was hoping that's what I smelled. Do you need help with anything?"

"Since you ask, it would be great if you'd help me set the table."

"Of course."

"What do you think of the new amendment?" his mom asked as they went to set the dinner table together.

"Hmm?"

"The constitutional amendment, you think it'll get passed?"

"It wouldn't surprise me. There was plenty of push for it toward the end of the last administration. I think it has a good chance."

"What do think about it? You think it's a good idea to have the same president for more than two terms?"

"I don't know. I know what you think of it, but I'm not really sure yet. I mean, if it passes, it doesn't mean the president would be re-elected, it would just allow for that possibility. That doesn't seem so horrible. Besides, we're essentially talking about a person who is my boss, so I can't or shouldn't really say anything negative. Neither should you really. We've talked about that before."

"Yes, of course, we shouldn't criticize the president, or the vice president, or the speaker, or any of our self-serving so called leaders. We know all too well these days that nothing we say is private."

"Mom, we've been over this and you know I can't talk about this stuff, except to tell you what I've told you before, which is that we all need to be really careful about what we say, what we write, or what we look at and do online. Things aren't the same as they were before. People can't just go around saying whatever they want about our leadership."

"Sadly, I never thought such a thing would ever be said about this country in my lifetime. I just think it's another huge step in the wrong direction. Too much power in the hands of one person who already has way too much power to begin with."

"I know, mom. I know you and Evan think we're headed to a dictatorship, the fall of America, a one world government and all that, but I just don't see it. I'm surrounded by this stuff every day, and while there is some truth in some of the conspiracy theories, and we admittedly are under substantially more surveillance and scrutiny, it's a necessary evil so to speak. It's a necessary tradeoff in order to keep us all safe. Trust me, there are lots and lots of bad people in this world."

"I don't doubt that my dear boy. I'm just afraid most of them are running our country."

"Mom, c'mon, you can't say stuff like that. Technically, under Bureau and Homeland regs, I should report and investigate a statement like that as a possible domestic terrorism threat."

"That's absolutely ridiculous."

"Granted, but it's also reality. I've seen surveillance details issued for nothing more than comments just like that one."

"We'll have to agree to disagree, honey, and leave it at that."

"Thanks, because I know I'll be having this same conversation with Evan and Michelle when they get here."

"I just wish you could see what we see."

"I know, I know, we're near the end of the world and all that stuff," Declan replied with moderate sarcasm.

"Not the end of the world, but the end of the age and America isn't mentioned specifically in any of the end times' prophecies. You'll see, all of this is happening according to an agenda. Just like the UN small arms treaty we signed and the global carbon tax that was passed, this amendment will pass too. Then, the presidency will eventually become essentially a lifetime appointment, and we'll be one giant step closer to a dictatorship and, ultimately a single global government. The structure is already in place for a single currency, and with our national debt and the moves other nations are taking to replace the dollar as the reserve currency, that can't be far off."

"What, you mean the IMF currency thing?"

"Yes, they've had this plan in place and ready to replace the dollar for years. All we need is another major crisis, financial or otherwise, which I suspect we'll see soon, and we'll see that agenda rolled out."

"Right, the global elite plan to control the world."

"Don't mock me, Declan Parker. This will happen. God told us how the story ends and Jesus himself gave us the signs to look for at the end of the age."

"Sorry, mom, but seriously, where does the Bible talk about this stuff? Where does it say we're going to have a one world government?"

"Revelation 13, and everything we're seeing now, from this move to allow the President additional terms, to the bigger role of the UN, to the various financial and economic issues the world is still going through, to the problems in the Middle East, to the concerted push for even more gun control; it all falls right into place with what the Bible tells us about the end of the age and the generation leading up to the Tribulation."

"Honestly, mom, I pretty much gave up on the Bible when dad died."

"I don't know why your dad had to die when he did, honey, but turning away from God isn't the answer. We just have to trust God's plan and our place in it."

"I'm sorry, but I don't see any plan."

"You will. I just pray you see it before it's too late."

Chapter 6
December 19th and December 20th

After leaving his mom's house, Declan again stopped and sat in his car down the street from David Stanton's apartment building. He waited for a little over two hours; however, as had been the case that morning, there was no sign of, or movement by, Stanton.

As he waited, Declan's thoughts turned back to dinner and to his older brother Evan, who, as expected, had brought the conversation back around to the state of the country and the Bible. Declan had grown used to the topic over the years and could generally let the words pass through one ear and out the other without any trouble. He'd grown up, for the most part, in a strong Christian house and remembered loving God when he was a boy, but after watching his dad die he'd lost whatever faith he'd had. Initially, Declan hated God for taking his dad from him. He couldn't fathom how a loving God could take a good man like his dad off the earth so early in life. Over time, his hate had subsided into a general antipathy toward God and religion.

However, for whatever reason, his mom's words that night hadn't just passed through his ears, but had hung on somewhere in between, occupying his thoughts in an annoyingly consistent manner. As much as he hated to acknowledge it, Declan did see her point about people's rights and privacy being degraded. He'd seen it at the Bureau and with the new Homeland regulations. He didn't necessarily believe that would inevitably lead to the types of things she and Evan purported, but, for the first time ever, for whatever the reason, his mom had gotten a small part of his attention, if for no other reason than a childish desire to prove her wrong.

When he finally made it home, Declan looked through his boxed books and found the Bible his parents had given him for Christmas one year, which he hadn't looked at or touched in years.

"Let's see where it actually says everyone in the world will follow one guy," he said to himself.

Declan flipped through the onion skin pages quickly scanning the words and came to Revelation 13.

"[1]And the dragon stood on the shore of the sea. And I saw a beast coming out of the sea. He had ten horns and seven heads, with ten crowns on his horns, and on each head a blasphemous name. [2]The beast I saw resembled a leopard, but had feet like those of a bear and a mouth like that of a lion. The dragon gave the beast his power and his throne and great authority. [3]One of the heads of the beast seemed to have had a fatal wound, but the fatal wound had been healed. The whole world was astonished and followed the beast. [4]Men worshiped the dragon because he had given authority to the beast, and they also worshiped the beast and asked, 'Who is like the beast? Who can make war against him?"

Declan read the passage again, admittedly bewildered by many of the words, but then he read it a third time, focusing on the sentence, "The whole world was astonished and followed the beast."

"The whole world will follow the beast," he said to himself somewhat astounded. "The whole world will follow him."

Declan read further:

"[5]The beast was given a mouth to utter proud words and blasphemies and to exercise his authority for forty-two months. [6]He opened his mouth to blaspheme God, and to slander his name and his dwelling place and those who live in heaven. [7]He was given power to make war against the saints and to conquer them. And he was given authority over every tribe, people, language and nation. [8]All inhabitants of the earth will worship the beast – all whose names have not been written in the book of life belonging to the Lamb that was slain from the creation of the world. [9]He who has an ear, let him hear."

The words burned into Declan's mind as he read them again and again. "And he was given authority over every tribe, people, language and nation.... He who has an ear, let him hear. He who has an ear, let him hear."

Chapter 7
December 20th

With each passing day, David Stanton grew more excited about his imminent entry into world history. The path chosen for him was, admittedly, nothing new or novel. People had been shedding the blood of others since the beginning of time. Certainly, others had come before him, and his relentless research had made him as intimately familiar with his various predecessors as possible. However, while Abaddon wouldn't be the first, he would be the only one to invite the whole world to witness the fulfillment of his destiny, judgment and wrath, live on the web and through social media.

Stanton had always viewed his endeavor as having four essential stages. The first stage, setting up the technical mechanisms to broadcast what was soon to come to the whole world, he'd already accomplished. The second stage was his virtual training, which he engaged in daily. While he acknowledged the value and essential nature of his virtual training, no matter how realistic the simulation, it could never substitute for killing a real flesh and blood human being. David Stanton had never killed anything substantial before and he couldn't leave such an important detail to chance. He couldn't run the risk of freezing when the time came to seize his glory, and risk the humiliation of failing in front of his anticipated world audience. Quite simply, Abaddon had to know, beyond the shadow of any doubt, that David Stanton could kill and, more importantly, would kill without hesitation. Thus, stage three of his plan.

In the early evening Stanton double checked his equipment, then dressed in a shabby, intentionally dirty, second hand military jacket, nondescript black t-shirt and worn jeans he'd picked up for $1.00 at Goodwill. The outfit hadn't been washed in two months, despite multiple wears, intentionally carrying the strong distinctive scent of body odor. Once dressed, Stanton stuffed a shabby unkempt high-quality brown wig and a dirty faded baseball cap into a small brown paper bag and headed out.

He walked over a mile from his apartment to a bus stop he'd scouted and knew to be generally deserted most nights. Most importantly, the bus stop featured a covered partially-enclosed seating area, which was only dimly lit at night. Stanton ducked inside, took the wig out of the brown paper bag and applied it over his own closely-shaved hair. He put the baseball cap on over the wig and threw the paper bag into a trash can. A few minutes later, the No. 202 bus, which was headed downtown, stopped and let Stanton board.

The downtown streets were frigid and mostly deserted. Stanton walked deliberately through the biting cold, being sure to take in anything happening around him. Generally, things were quiet and still, but every so often a car would pass a bit too slowly or he'd notice another pedestrian moving about. Whenever he saw signs of life, another person out on the streets, he paid close attention and quickly assessed whether the situation fit his various conditions. In most instances, for one reason or another, it didn't.

After walking for about thirty minutes, Stanton decided to veer off onto a small side street when he heard someone sneeze. He walked slowly, looking around for the source of the sound, until he finally saw a single silhouette leaning over a trash can about a hundred feet in front of him. Stanton stopped and watched the silhouette for a few seconds, then looked around the rest of the street to see if any lights were on in the surrounding buildings or whether there was any other movement on the street. Seeing nothing, he slowly approached the silhouette, still leaning over the open trash can.

"Anything good in there?"

The startled silhouette jumped slightly and turned around quickly to face Stanton. "You scared me to death, man. What the hell?"

Stanton looked over the man standing in front of him. He was young, maybe in his early 20's, but with an already worn-down and rugged face. He had a full light-brown beard and dirty matted hair which seemingly hadn't been cut in quite a while. "Sorry," Stanton replied. "I didn't mean to startle you."

"Dude, you should know better than to come up from behind somebody like that. That's not cool."

"Sorry. Forget I asked."

"Whatever. Why don't you just move the hell along?"

"Fine, I'm moving along."

Stanton turned around and began walking back in the direction from which he'd approached. The man watched him until he reached the end of the block and turned back onto the main street. A few seconds later, Stanton discreetly peeked around the corner to see the man's silhouette once again leaned over the trash can. Looking around the street again and still seeing no lights or other signs of life, he moved slowly toward the man again, staying in the shadows close to the building facades.

He stopped and ducked into an unlit doorway about 60 feet away from the man, took out a pair of black leather gloves from one of his coat pockets, and put them on. Next, he gently removed the perfectly polished and sharpened hunting knife from the inside pocket of his military coat. The 12 inch metal blade glistened ever so slightly in the night. Stanton closed his eyes and readied himself. He breathed in slowly, he breathed out slowly. He breathed in again, even more slowly, more measured, then let his breath out again, controlled and calm, but with a quiet fury burning deep within him. With each breath, his mind focused more pointedly on the scum digging through the trash, on the dirt-ridden and matted excuse for a human being who'd had the audacity to tell Abaddon's servant to move the hell along.

Stanton felt his limbs tightening, steadying

themselves for battle, preparing his body to release the just and righteous fury building to a crescendo within him. He gripped the knife tightly in his hands and closed his eyes to envision the long metal blade sliding smoothly into its victim.

"Abaddon, great one, give your servant the strength to fulfill your mission," he whispered into the cold. "This, the first blood I'm about to shed, the first fruits of my coming harvest of blood, I dedicate to you, the Destroyer, Abaddon the mighty."

Stanton ducked deftly back onto the street, immediately locking his eyes like a killing machine onto the silhouette now standing erect in front of him, unwrapping something he'd apparently found in the trash. He moved swiftly toward the man, feeling as though he was practically gliding. When he was within about five feet, the man either heard or sensed that he was no longer alone and turned around to see Stanton bearing down on him. A second later, Stanton was upon him and immediately thrust the hunting knife deep into the man's stomach, dropping him to the sidewalk instantly.

Stanton swooped down onto his knees above the man, who was writhing on the concrete, and looked into his eyes, which, to Stanton's great joy, were an indisputable mixture of terror, pain and disbelief.

"Take solace in that you are blessed to be the first among many," Stanton whispered into the man's ear.

Then, with one fluid precise left-to-right movement with the hunting knife, David Stanton slit the man's throat, and sat above him watching the last warm breath wriggle meaninglessly from him into the cold night air. Where seconds before, the man's eyes had been overflowing with emotion, they were then completely void in every respect. This change fascinated Stanton to no end. He stared into the lifeless eyes below him, fully cognizant of the fact that he had taken the life and emotion from them. An unexpected sense of pride and power came over Stanton. He was worthy of the task before him, truly he had been born for it.

Sensing it was time to move before someone happened by, Stanton pulled out his iPhone and quickly took a close up picture of the man's blank eyes. He then collected some of his blood in a small plastic medicine dosage cup, and held the full cup up to the night sky.

"I pray that you now find your servant worthy," he said still looking to the sky. David Stanton took the cup to his lips and, with great satisfaction, drank the man's blood. The salty taste on his tongue and lips only whet his appetite for more.

Chapter 8
December 21st

"Declan, are you ready? We're going to be late for our range time."

"Yeah, I'll be right there," Declan replied while locking his computer.

"So, what did you think of Bleeker's initiative this morning?"

"It seems ambitious," Declan responded. "I'm not really sure how it's going to play out in practice, but it is ambitious."

"That's not surprising really. Bleeker's an up and comer."

"Didn't he graduate from Yale?"

"Yep. He has big time family connections. I'm pretty sure his grandfather served as an ambassador to somewhere in Europe and his dad is connected to Wall Street somehow. I know for a fact that he's friends with the Director. Bleeker's biding his time here, working to make a name for himself in the Bureau, but I wouldn't be surprised to see him at Langley soon or taking over the New York or L.A. field office."

"You think?"

"Count on it. He has a pedigree and this is just a brief stop on his way up the ladder."

"Must be nice. Hey Kev, I have a question for you."

"Shoot," responded Kevin as they entered the shooting range.

"Funny. Anyway, last week after we talked about the guy with the two registered AR-15's."

"Which guy?"

"The guy I got a call about. I ran him through TSC and NCIC and he came up clean, but when I ran him through NICS he came up with two AR-15's registered to him."

"It's ringing a bell. What's the guy's name?"

"David Stanton."

"Gotcha."

"You told me to put in a PRISM request on him, which I…"

"I did?"

"Yes, you did, which I did, but he came back SCI and I didn't have proper clearance."

"Really?"

"Yeah. What do you think that means? I mean, it seems kind of strange to me."

"I don't know, Declan. It could mean any number of things. Maybe there's something Homeland, the CIA, or the NSA has in relation to the guy that got him tagged SCI."

"Is there any way to get around the clearance?"

"Probably, if you want to end up in the federal pen. He really came up SCI?"

"Weird, huh? I mean with that kind of required security clearance to get info on him, you'd think he'd show up somewhere on our systems."

Kevin thought for a minute as he loaded and checked his 9mm pistol. "My suggestion is to leave this one alone, Declan. There's no telling why he's SCI, but I know they don't just dole out SCI clearance requirements on every Tom, Dick and Abdul. If he's SCI, it came from somewhere well above us."

"From where?"

"Who knows? For all I know he could have been tagged SCI by the Homeland Director or even the president. The point is, this sounds like something way above your pay grade and, obviously, your clearance level. You've done your due diligence on this one. I'd let it go here."

Declan raised his sidearm, squared to his target, and fired five quick rounds, each of which found the innermost kill circle of the target. Taking off his headset, Declan replied, "I don't suppose I have a choice."

Kevin put his shooting glasses and ear protection on, raised his Sig Sauer P226 and eyed the target 50 feet in front of him. "No, you don't," he said as the sound of his weapon firing echoed through the range.

Chapter 9
December 21st

Under the pretense of conducting field work in a developing meth-cooking case, Declan left the bureau office around 2:30 and headed home. David Stanton was still gnawing at him and, despite what he'd said to Kevin, Declan knew he wouldn't be able to leave it alone. He needed to know about Stanton, to know why he'd been classified SCI, and as much as he both dreaded and hungered for the call, Declan knew the one person who could, and would, get him the information he wanted. Unfortunately, that person was Megan Neary, whom, until about eight months earlier, had been his fiancée.

Megan came from an old-money Massachusetts family with substantial connections which, coupled with her general brilliance, she'd parlayed into a position at the Department of Justice right out of law school. Within a few months after joining the DOJ, Megan caught the attention of the kind of people whose attention an up and comer welcomes. One of those people moved into a Deputy Directorship at Homeland Security a year or so later and took Megan with him. Not long after Megan moved to Homeland Security, Declan had completed his training at the Bureau and was transferred out of Washington D.C., back home. Shortly after that, Megan became his ex-fiancée, a status he had trouble coming to grips with.

He had only talked with Megan twice, very casually and friendly, since they'd split. It wasn't his favorite option, but Declan knew Megan was an insider at Homeland, and she had the type of security clearance that could get him the information he needed on Stanton. Plus, it was an excuse to hear her voice again, which was something Declan missed dearly. He somewhat reluctantly and nervously dialed her cell phone.

"This is Megan Neary," she answered after a few rings.

"Megan, it's Declan. How are you?"

"I know who it is, and I'm good. How are you stranger?"

"Fine, just keeping busy. Something I'm sure you're familiar with."

"You have no idea. I barely have time to breathe and I'm supposed to be home for Christmas tomorrow night. It's insane. I'm going to be working on the train the whole way up tomorrow and probably the whole time I'm home."

"They're keeping you that busy eh?"

"It's ridiculous really, but, it is what it is. Too many bad guys. What about you? It must be nice to be back home and not have to do the whole TSA-groping holiday travel thing."

"One of the few perks of being out of D.C. and back in the sticks."

"So are you getting together with your mom and Evan, Michelle and the kiddos?"

"Yeah," Declan replied. "We do the same thing every year. You know the drill."

"I sure do. Your family Christmas is so much more laid back than mine."

"That's an understatement."

"I really miss it sometimes. I miss your mom too. Is she doing well?"

"She's doing great. She's training for her twelfth marathon. You know her. What you see is what you get."

"That's one of things I love most about her."

"Well, you should come down sometime," he said hesitantly. "I know she'd love to see you."

"What about you? Would you love to see me?"

"I thought that went without saying."

"After last year, I don't take anything between us for granted, Declan."

"Well," Declan paused, "I think we both wish that had gone better. The long-distance thing…well, I guess it just doesn't work too well sometimes."

"I've actually been giving that a lot of thought lately," she replied.

"You have?"

"I have."

"And?"

"I think the determining factor in whether a long-distance relationship works or not is the amount of work the people in the relationship are willing to put into it."

"I tend to agree with you."

"So…"

"So what, Megan?"

"How much work are we willing to put into it?"

"After the way things were left the last time I saw you, the time when you insisted I take your engagement ring back, I wasn't under the impression there was any relationship left for us to work on."

"If, hypothetically, after having sufficient time to reach the conclusion that she didn't put enough work into her relationship with a certain guy, and to regret her decision, a girl said she hoped there still might be something to work on, what would the guy say?"

"Hypothetically?"

"Well, maybe not entirely hypothetically," she responded.

"I suppose he'd ask why the girl regretted her decision."

"Because she now realizes what she had and what an idiot she was to give it up…to give up the man who knew her better than anyone else in the world and, despite knowing her deep dark secrets still loved her and could always make her laugh, just because of a thousand or so stupid miles."

Declan couldn't speak for a moment. He'd hoped for that moment, for her to say those words in one form or another, since the last time he'd seen her.

"Declan, are you there?"

"Yes, I'm here."

"So…what would the guy say?"

"He'd say...he'd say that he never stopped loving the girl and as far as he's concerned no amount of miles in the world could keep him from her."

"He sounds like a bit of a romantic."

"He is a bit of a romantic."

"So, should the girl call her family and tell them she can't come home for Christmas this year after all and, instead, buy herself a plane ticket to come see the guy tomorrow."

"Absolutely."

Chapter 10
December 21st

Declan had been so overwhelmed by Megan's unexpected change of heart that he'd hung up without asking her to look into David Stanton's file, and had to call her back. Megan took Stanton's name and social and said she'd see what, if anything, she could come up with.

In the meantime, Declan did the dishes and began cleaning up his apartment in anticipation of Megan's imminent arrival. When he'd finished cleaning, he sat down on the sofa and turned on the news. The news anchor was asking a female correspondent, who was apparently somewhere in the Middle East, if she could confirm earlier reports that the Israelis had launched a unilateral attack against various military and nuclear facilities inside Iran and that, in retaliation, missiles had, in fact, been fired from Gaza, Lebanon and Syria into Israel. "At this point, we've received no official confirmation, but various unofficial sources have confirmed numerous explosions at different locations in Iran, including near the Fordow and Arak nuclear facilities. I've also received confirmation that a number of missiles were fired at Tel Aviv, Galilee, and other Israeli towns earlier this evening. Early indications are that the missiles originated in Gaza, Lebanon and Syria. Again, we're still awaiting official word from the Israeli government on both points, but if true, this attack would mark a critical turn in Israel's position with respect to the Iranian nuclear program and its relations with both Syria and Iran, not to mention Hamas, Hezbollah and its other neighbors in the region."

Declan's phone rang and he looked to see Evan's number on the display. "Hey, Ev. What's up?"

"Have you been watching the news at all today?"

"I actually just turned it on. Do you think the Israelis really hit Iran?"

"It appears that way, and if so things over there are

just about to get really interesting. All the pieces finally seem to be lining up."

"Lining up for what?"

"What mom and I have been telling you about all this time, the further fulfillment of God's Word," Evan replied. "If Israel hit Iran unilaterally, that's a big deal. The Iranians certainly aren't going to take it sitting still and this could be the match that leads us into the Psalm 83 battle and the complete destruction of Damascus, just like Isaiah told us would happen thousands of years ago, especially with The Islamic State now looking toward Israel as a new target."

"Isaiah?"

"Isaiah 17, Declan."

"Right, of course. What does it say again?"

"It tells us of the complete destruction of Damascus overnight."

"Hasn't that already happened, like thousands of years ago?"

"Nope, Damascus is the oldest continually inhabited city in the world, so we know that the Isaiah 17 prophecy still hasn't been fulfilled. That's what I'm saying, Declan. We could be seeing the beginning of its fulfillment right now."

"Gotcha. I guess that would be a big deal if it actually happened."

"You guess? Just do me a favor and read it. Read it now while the news still has your attention. Do some investigation Special Agent Parker and let me know what you think."

"Alright, I will Dr. Parker. I will."

"Excellent. I'll talk to you later little brother."

"Okay, later."

Declan hung up and focused on the aerial news feed images coming in from Tel Aviv, then he reluctantly picked up his Bible and eventually opened it to Isaiah. Finding Isaiah 17, he read:

"[1]An oracle concerning Damascus: 'See, Damascus will no longer be a city but will become a heap of ruins.

[2]The cities of Aroer will be deserted and left to flocks, which will lie down, with no one to make them afraid. [3]The fortified city will disappear from Ephraim, and the royal power from Damascus; the remnant of Aram will be like the glory of the Israelites,' declares the Lord Almighty."

Half-interested, Declan read the passage a few times and realized, aside from the part saying Damascus would no longer be a city, but a heap of ruins, that he really had no idea what or where the cities of Aroer and the fortified city of Ephraim were. He shrugged and closed the Bible, when his phone rang again.

"Hey," he said. "Can't get enough of me?"

"We have to make up for lost time," Megan replied.

"No doubt."

"I wanted to tell you that I bought my ticket. My flight gets in at 6:05 tomorrow evening."

"Perfect. I'll pick you up at the airport."

"You'd better," she said with a sly laugh. "Also, I ran this David Stanton guy you asked me about."

"And?"

"Like you said, he's SCI, and despite my security clearance, which doesn't suck, I'm not on the authorized list."

"So you couldn't access his file either?"

"No, I couldn't. However, I was able to call in a small favor and find out who placed him on SCI."

"Who?"

"John Bleeker."

"Did you say John Bleeker?"

"Yep," Megan responded.

"John Bleeker is my Special Agent in Charge."

"I figured that out too. See how smart I am?"

"That was never even a question, my dear. So, John Bleeker tagged Stanton SCI? Really?"

"Apparently."

"But why?"

"That I don't know, but I can tell you that this is no

ordinary SCI. Only John Bleeker, the FBI Director, the Homeland Director, and the White House Chief of Staff have access to David Stanton's file. That's ridiculously high level clearance."

"Seriously? Bleeker's on the same list as the White House Chief of Staff and the Director. Doesn't that seem strange to you?"

"I will say, based on my experience, it's at least a bit unusual, although not entirely unheard of. Who is this Stanton guy anyway?"

"That's what I'm trying to figure out."

"Well, be careful, Declan. Whoever he is, he has some extremely high level interest and we could both be in big trouble for even looking into this."

"I will. I'll meet you at baggage claim tomorrow. Call me when your flight's about to leave."

"Will do. I love you, Declan Parker."

He let those words sink in for a second. The three words which, only a few hours earlier, Declan thought he'd never hear Megan say to him again. "I love you too."

Chapter 11
December 21st and December 22nd

David Stanton had spent the day at work, preparing the church for the annual Christmas influx which would take place a few short days later. His thoughts returned throughout the day to the successful completion of his first bloodshed and he was compelled to sneak numerous peeks at the photo he'd taken of the dead man's eyes. He was still absolutely fascinated by their blankness, their total absence of anything.

The transition he'd watched in those eyes the night before, the passing of life into death, replayed over and again in his mind and he wanted desperately to see it again, but in a more controlled environment. Stanton ached to kill again, but not to be rushed the next time. He wanted to watch the next victim and to record his or her eyes close up in order to try and capture the exact second when life left the eyes.

A little after five in the evening, Stanton left work in the early winter darkness, drove through McDonalds to pick up dinner and headed home. After dinner he made some minor changes and upgrades to his website, killed an hour or so watching "It's a Wonderful Life", then spent a few hours on his simulator, which after tasting the experience of truly killing, left Stanton entirely unfulfilled.

When the night had finally progressed enough for most people to be home and off the streets, Stanton put on a fresh shirt, sweater and jeans, grabbed his jacket, as well as a brown wig trimmed to look like a man's haircut, and headed to his black SUV. He drove out onto the street in front of his apartment building and passed Declan, who was sitting fifty feet or so down the street in one of the FBI's unmarked Ford Mustangs. Long enough after Stanton passed not to be conspicuous, but still keeping his taillights in view, Declan fired up the Mustang and began to tail the black SUV from a safe distance, careful to keep a few cars between them.

Stanton took a few turns, stopped at a convenience store, where he purchased gas, and hopped on the highway headed away from downtown toward the suburbs. Declan followed, keeping the SUV's taillights in sight a few hundred feet ahead. The highway traffic wasn't heavy, but as it was a major interstate, stayed consistent, giving Declan plenty of cover.

After driving for almost twenty minutes, the SUV finally exited the interstate and headed along the access road until it turned into the parking lot entrance to one of a few gentlemen's clubs in the area. Declan slowed down a bit and watched the SUV roll slowly through the parking lot, but instead of turning in behind Stanton, Declan continued along the access road to the next intersection. Eventually he turned around and approached the club from the opposite direction.

Stanton's SUV was parked in one of the last rows, well away from the club entrance, in a barely-lit parking space. Declan drove to the opposite side of the parking lot and backed into a space between two cars, but where he still had a clear line of sight to the SUV. In the darkness, it was difficult to tell if Stanton had left the vehicle and gone inside. It looked like someone was sitting the driver's seat, but the image was only a dim outline and Declan couldn't be certain if it was Stanton or just the shadows and play of what little light there was.

Another car pulled in and drove past the SUV to park a few spaces away. The car's headlights illuminated the inside of the SUV for just a second or two, but it was enough for Declan to make out Stanton's shadowed face behind the steering wheel.

"So he's just sitting there," Declan said to himself. "Well, we'll just sit here too and see what he's up to." Declan looked at his watch, which read 11:27.

Patrons and cars came and went until 2:00 a.m. finally rolled around and the club closed, leaving only twenty or so cars in the parking lot. Declan stayed low in the small backseat of the Mustang, keeping out of sight and watching Stanton, who had simply sat in his SUV for two and a half hours. Not once had he gone into the club, or even moved much really.

Around twenty minutes later, a couple of girls, whom Declan presumed worked at the club, came out with a heavy-set guy, who looked like a bouncer. The girls walked to their cars as the heavy-set guy watched from the club's entrance. The first girl got into her car, which was parked a few spaces from Declan's, started it up and drove through the parking lot, and out onto the access road. Declan glanced over to Stanton's SUV, but nothing moved.

A moment later, the second girl, an attractive brunette who looked like she was in her early twenties, reached her car, which was parked under a light in the center of the lot.

"Goodnight, Quentin," she yelled to the heavy-set guy still in the doorway.

"Goodnight, Nikki," he responded.

Once Nikki was in her car and had turned on the ignition, Quentin went back inside the club and the door closed behind him. Nikki put her car into gear and proceeded toward the access road. When she'd just about reached the access road, Stanton turned on his SUV, but not his lights initially, and began to follow her, just as the door opened again and Quentin came out with three more girls.

Declan quickly hopped back into the front seat of the Mustang and readied himself to follow Stanton, who had finally flipped his headlights on once Nikki's car had turned out of the parking lot. Quentin noticed Declan's movement in the Mustang and went quickly toward the car in a very protective manner.

"Hey, you're not supposed to be out here," Quentin yelled as he approached the Mustang.

Declan turned the ignition and rolled down the window as he began to pull the car out, not wanting to lose Stanton and Nikki.

"It's okay, I'm FBI," he said, flashing Quentin his badge.

"Yeah right. Get your ass out of here before I kick it all over this parking lot and call the real cops, pervert."

Declan drove quickly out of the parking lot and turned right onto the access road, hoping he hadn't lost Stanton. He saw two sets of taillights sitting at a red light at the intersection, both with their left turn signals blinking. As he neared the intersection, it became clear the two vehicles were Nikki's and Stanton's.

The light changed to green just before Declan reached the intersection. Nikki turned left, crossed over the interstate and waited to turn left at the next light, in order to get on the highway heading back toward the city. Stanton followed her and Declan reluctantly followed him, fully cognizant of the fact that he was no longer exactly inconspicuous, but unwilling to lose Stanton.

The light finally changed and Nikki merged onto the interstate. There was enough traffic on the highway that Declan was able to fall back a bit and blend more comfortably into the background.

Chapter 12
December 22nd

Stanton stayed focused on Nikki's taillights like a laser, so much so that he hadn't once noticed Declan's Mustang behind him. He'd never seen Nikki before and knew nothing about her. In fact, he'd only barely caught a glimpse of her before she'd gotten into her car, but who she was or what she looked like were of no concern to him. Nikki fit the profile he was looking for, which was a woman (whom he could presumably easily overpower) who was alone. The basis for his decision to follow her had truly been that simple.

A hunger had been growing inside Stanton since he had taken his first life only two short nights earlier. He'd tasted blood, literally, and longed to taste it again before making his presence known to the world. Since watching Nikki step into her car, he'd envisioned himself taking her somewhere quiet and private, someplace where he could take his time with her and take her life artfully, with the patience and deliberation befitting his labor.

The hastiness of his first kill was Stanton's only regret. While successful, it had been messy and rushed. Yes, he'd tasted the blood of life, but he hadn't had time to truly savor its texture and flavor. He hadn't had time to enjoy the kill to the extent he'd hoped.

The kind of satisfaction he sought would take time, which meant privacy and a person whom, hopefully, nobody would miss for a few days. That's why he'd chosen a girl, any girl alone, from the gentlemen's club. Stanton figured, to be working in a place like that, to subject oneself to that environment, a girl had to have some issues. Maybe, hopefully, she lived alone. Maybe she'd be drunk or high, or just jaded enough to make her vulnerable for the 30 seconds Stanton needed to take her captive. Maybe.

After roughly fifteen minutes, the right turn signal on Nikki's car began blinking and she exited the interstate onto 45th Street, which was only a few exits north of Stanton's neighborhood. Stanton followed a few seconds behind, and Declan exited shortly after Stanton, still far enough back so as not to be too obvious.

A few blocks and turns later, Nikki's car pulled into the driveway of a small apartment building and parked in one of the open spaces near the front. Stanton slowed down and pulled his SUV over to the side of the street where he could see Nikki getting out of her car. Declan drove past Stanton and past Nikki's apartment building and, after seeing Nikki enter one of the first floor units in his rearview mirror, turned at the next intersection, which was less than a block away from the building.

He quickly parked his car on the street and hurried on foot through an empty parking lot to a bushy shadowy spot where he could see both Stanton's SUV, with Stanton still sitting inside, and Nikki's first-floor apartment. A few seconds later, the lights in Nikki's apartment came on.

Stanton sat in his SUV, in the dark, watching the lights in Nikki's apartment come on. His eyes patiently followed her slim silhouette as she moved behind the drawn shades. He waited and focused on the apartment until he was relatively certain Nikki was alone inside, although he knew he couldn't be absolutely sure of that until he'd committed himself by going in.

When he was finally ready, Stanton turned on the ignition again, drove slowly into the driveway and parked in a space on the side of the apartment building, only ten feet or so from Nikki's front door. He picked up his 9mm handgun and slid it into his jeans, where it would be concealed under his jacket. Opening the glove box, he took out a small bottle of chloroform and a white hand towel and stuffed them into one of his jacket pockets.

"Abaddon, master, look upon your servant with favor and again bless my work," Stanton whispered. "More blood will flow tonight in your name."

When Declan had seen Stanton pull into the parking lot, he quietly moved from his position in the bushes, around the back of a neighboring building and crept along in the shadows until finally crouching low behind a parked car not far from Stanton's. From that position, he was ready to intervene if necessary. When he saw Stanton step out of the SUV and approach Nikki's front door, Declan's pulse began to race faster.

Stanton slowly approached the first-floor apartment. It wasn't evident from his blank expression, but he was teeming with energy and excitement. His mind ran through his plan again, which was to simply knock on Nikki's door and quickly force his way inside when given the opportunity, however brief it may be. He'd subdue her with the chloroform, carry her to his SUV, and be out of there in under three minutes. The real fun could begin when he got her home.

As he approached the front door, Stanton could hear music coming through a slightly open window to the left of the door. It wasn't anything he recognized, something with a peppy pop sound, which wasn't the kind of thing he liked. Just outside the door, Stanton stopped and readied himself. Deep slow breath in, long slow breath out, deep slow breath in, long slow breath out. Finally, he closed his eyes and envisioned one last walk through. In and out in under three minutes, he thought again. No problem. With that, Stanton knocked on the door, just as two headlights appeared in the parking lot heading in the direction of Nikki's building.

"It's open babe," came Nikki's voice from inside. "Just come in, I'm too tired to get up again."

The headlights drew closer and Stanton froze, not sure whether to go in or abort the mission. A second later, his decision made, Stanton bolted back down the walkway, jumped into his SUV and shot out of the parking lot, just as the headlights came to a stop in the open space next to Nikki's car.

Chapter 13
December 22nd

The morning sun rose and traces of its light slowly penetrated David Stanton's apartment, each ray illuminating his utter shame and undeniable failure. Stanton stood naked in the growing light, staring at his wretched miserably inadequate face and body and watching the blood trickle from the self-inflicted gashes on his arms, chest and legs. How could he have failed so pathetically? At the moment of truth, he'd frozen and allowed himself to be scared away by the arrival of a pathetic mortal, whom he should have simply sliced open and left for dead. Abaddon had gifted him with an unlocked door, a veritable open invitation, and yet he'd failed.

Stanton's shame was amplified by his fervent knowledge that, had he only trusted Abaddon, no obstacle would have stood in his way and the girl would have been his. Instead of staring at his own pathetic bleeding nakedness, he'd be looking into hers at that very moment, quenching the undying lust for blood that had built up within him.

"Master Abaddon," he wailed into the mirror. "Please, forgive your servant's ineptness. Forgive my failure and grant me the opportunity to redeem myself in your eyes, to bring myself back within your favor. Please, forgive me. Please."

Stanton's lips and tongue were desperately dry, but he didn't deserve to quench his thirst. How could he move forward with the ultimate work, the final phase of the mission that was before him when he was a picture of failure? His confidence was lost. He stared into the mirror, desperately searching his own eyes for an answer, for a way to rectify his failure and regain his rightful place at Abaddon's table.

"Damn you, you worthless piece of crap. Damn you. It was there for the taking and you froze, you froze you miserable undeserving fool. How could you freeze? How could you screw it up? It was so easy, it was perfect. It was perfect and a real man wouldn't have run away like you did. No, if you were truly worthy you would have exerted your power, the power your master has provided, and you would have taken that girl, whatever the cost. Look at you, you're still as pathetic as you've always been, still the boy who did nothing and just allowed them to torment you."

Looking deep into the reflection of his own bloodshot eyes, intently following the tiny lines of blood running through them, Stanton slowly came to know what he had to do. Abaddon didn't tolerate failure. His ultimate task still lay ahead, but if he was to have any hope of success, his pathetic debacle had to be rectified and the only way to satisfy Abaddon, and restore his place at the table, was a sacrifice, a blood sacrifice. Abaddon had sent Stanton for blood, and blood he would deliver.

Declan awoke from a meager two hours of sleep on his sofa, thoroughly exhausted. He showered, made some strong coffee and left for the Bureau field office intent on finding whatever he could on Stanton. Megan's flight was due in the evening and he planned to pick her up at the airport and spend the next few days with her, but Declan was convinced Stanton had very bad intentions and he had to get a surveillance detail in place.

Stanton exited the No. 86 bus a block from Nikki's apartment complex and cautiously, but deliberately, made his way back to her ground-floor unit. The car which had prompted him to abort his mission in the dark hours earlier that morning was still parked outside, yet Stanton's determination didn't waver. There was only one way back into Abaddon's favor. Turning back was not an option.

It was still early enough that very few people were out and about. Stanton approached the front door, keeping his eyes peeled for an open or seemingly unlocked window. He assumed Nikki and her companion would still be sleeping and hoped to find a way into the apartment that wouldn't wake them. In the event no such path existed, he'd have to knock on the door and force his way in without making too much noise and commotion.

Seeing no open window on the front-side of the apartment, Stanton walked quietly to the front door and, fully expecting to find it locked, gently turned the knob. To his absolute amazement, the unlocked door opened. An enormous grin appeared on his face as he very quietly and quickly slipped through the front door into the warm dark apartment and gently closed and locked the door behind him.

The apartment was still and quiet, and Stanton could hear the heavy rhythmic breathing of two people coming from the bedroom. All the shades were drawn shut, letting very little morning light into the living room. Stanton scanned the tiny living room and the adjoining small dining area and kitchen. Nikki's apartment struck him as being very much like his own, which gave him a certain sense of comfort and ease.

He put down the backpack he'd brought with him and quietly removed his boots, so that he stood in his thick white socks, which would make substantially less noise. Stanton put on a pair of latex gloves, removed the small bottle of chloroform and white hand towel from his jacket pocket, and pulled the large hunting knife from its sheath.

He crept noiselessly down the dark hallway, past the bathroom to the open bedroom door, where Nikki and a male companion lay naked, sleeping next to one another. On a nightstand next to the bed were four empty beer bottles and a small pipe, with a lighter and an empty Ziploc baggie next to it. He stood in the doorway, taking in the scene and listening to the rise and fall of the slumbering couple's peaceful breaths.

Again, Stanton closed his eyes and said a silent prayer. Then, he moved swiftly to the sleeping male, who looked to be in his very early-twenties. Stanton jumped on top of his torso, while at the same time forcefully pushing the companion's head into the pillow, which startled the man awake, with a violent but tardy shake. Within seconds, before there was even time to scream or realize what was happening, Stanton drove the hunting knife directly into the man's exposed throat, killing him instantly, and causing his blood to spray wildly from the wound.

He immediately shoved the dead bleeding body to the floor and turned his attention to Nikki, who had woken in a haze, not entirely comprehending what was happening. Before she could make sense of it all, Stanton had straddled her body, with his knees pressed firmly into each of Nikki's arms, and shoved the chloroform-doused hand towel into her mouth, muzzling her until her eyes finally closed again.

Chapter 14
December 22nd

The sound of music woke Nikki the second time, who despite her technical state of consciousness, was still in a haze. Her head throbbed and her vision, at least initially, was blurred and glassy. She couldn't move her mouth, as it was held tight by something uncomfortably stuck to her face, forcing her to breathe through her nose. She was still naked, but sitting upright in what she recognized as one of her dining room chairs. Nikki tried to move her hands, but like her slightly open legs which were tied firmly to the front two chair legs, they were bound tightly behind her and she felt a heavy metal object, which she suspected to be handcuffs, squeezing each of her wrists.

Initially, the music, which sounded like some sort of opera, filled most of Nikki's dulled senses. It was a man singing, with a very deep voice, but she couldn't understand the lyrics or even make out what language was being sung. As she slowly became more and more cognizant, she began to recognize and understand the depths of her exposure and vulnerability. This realization was accompanied by an immediate sense of fear and terror.

Nikki looked around, as her head seemed to be free, and realized she was still in her own bedroom, apparently alone and bound to the dining room chair which had been placed next to her bed. To her left, on her dresser, she saw what appeared to be a video camera on a small tripod pointed at her. She looked to her right, towards the bedroom door, and saw another video camera, standing atop a tall tripod, watching her. When she looked down at the bed and saw her boyfriend's blood which had sprayed onto the white hotel-style sheets, she tried to scream and began to shiver in panic and cry uncontrollably.

Nikki violently shook her body, trying in vain to free her arms. The panicked rocking motion only served to knock the chair, and therefore Nikki, over sideways onto the floor.

The new position did nothing to loosen her bindings or improve her situation.

Upon hearing the chair fall over onto the floor, Stanton came back into the bedroom, with a third video camera in hand. The video camera was on and filming Nikki, who startled when she saw him walk into the room and jostled even more furiously against the carpeted floor trying to free herself. Stanton set the rolling video camera onto the dresser for a second and went toward her. He leaned over, picked up the chair with Nikki in it, and reset it to an upright position.

"Shhh," he whispered to her, which only served to make Nikki tremble more fervently. "We're here to help each other. So, shhh, no crying."

Stanton set Nikki back up in her chair and scooted her back to her previous location, next to the bed. Then, he walked over to the HD video camera mounted on the small tripod on her dresser, and readjusted the camera such that it was zoomed in on Nikki's still tortured face, and her terrified light brown eyes filled the frame. He walked past her over to the other mounted camera, and checked to make sure that camera was zoomed out enough to be filming a fully body view.

He picked up the third, un-mounted, HD video camera, and left the bedroom for a minute or so, only to return with another dining room chair which he placed directly in front of Nikki, and sat down opposite her. Nikki sat trembling and confused, waiting for Stanton to say or do something, but for what seemed like an eternity, he simply sat across from her with his camera focused on her face.

In truth, Stanton sat in complete silence watching her through the camera's monitor for just over ten minutes. Nikki's eyes were filled with tears, panic and total confusion. Stanton relished every emotion so purely expressed in her deep brown eyes, so much so that he quite completely lost himself in bliss. He was fixated on the undeniable terror rushing through her body, which mixed flawlessly with the confusion and lack of understanding that spoke through her eyes. That silent, uninterrupted time, the chance to look so deeply into Nikki's soul through her eyes, to revel in the range of emotions he'd brought forth in her, thoroughly erased every memory of Stanton's prior failure and the shame that had accompanied it. He was finally, ever so slowly, becoming Abaddon.

Still holding the camera in one hand, Stanton slowly moved the hunting knife toward her face with the other. Nikki shuddered and jerked her head away.

"Don't do that," Stanton said softly, as he reached out further with the knife, pressing the razor sharp tip against the center of her forehead. "Just be still and keep your eyes open. Don't close your eyes."

Very slowly, Stanton followed the contour of her face with the knife, softly tracing the outline of her cheeks and lips. He guided the knife tip over her chin and down the length of her throat, careful not to press so hard as to break skin. As Stanton maneuvered the knife down, along her nervously heaving chest and the contour of her breasts, he could feel her body tremble beneath the touch of steel. He kept his eyes on her eyes the entire time, never looking at the rest of her body even as he slowly guided the knife over her hips and pelvis. Nikki continued to look up or down, never wanting to hold Stanton's disconcerting gaze. Tears were streaming from her eyes. Her body began to tremble violently as the knife made its way back up her torso and stopped again against her pounding chest.

Finally, Stanton pulled the knife away from her skin and asked, "Do you know what we're listening to? Just nod yes or no."

Nikki tried to focus on the music, the singing she had only been partially cognizant of a second earlier. She nodded her head side to side, to say no.

"This is 'Faust', composed by Gounod. Not to be confused with 'Doktor Faust', which was the one composed by Busoni. Frankly, I enjoy them both, but I find this one more beautiful. Just listen for a moment."

Stanton put his finger to his lips and silently watched her through the camera monitor again. "What do you think? Do you like it?"

Nikki didn't know how to respond. Her entire body still trembled uncontrollably, but she tried to gather herself enough to communicate with Stanton, which she suddenly thought, and hoped, might provide her with some way out of her situation. She nodded her head slightly up and down.

"A little, maybe? Good. It is a beautiful opera. Do you know the story?"

Nikki, gaining a bit more control of herself, nodded no.

"Well, let me give you the abridged version. Dr. Faust is an older man, a man of science, who's dissatisfied with his life. One night, he curses God and calls on the devil, Mephistopheles, who of course appears. He's real you know? The devil, he's real. Did you know that?"

Nikki again nodded to say no.

"Well, he is, and so is God, but we'll come back to that later. Back to the story, Mephistopheles appears and offers Faust riches, power, whatever he wants in this life, in exchange for Faust's soul. But, all Faust wants is to be able to return to his youth, which Mephistopheles gladly grants him. Faust goes back and eventually seduces a beautiful young maiden, much like you, named Marguerite. He impregnates her and leaves her, but she still loves him. Later, Mephistopheles speaks to Marguerite, telling her she's damned in part for causing the death of her brother, and she goes insane and is put into prison for infanticide. It's a sad opera in many ways, but in another way it offers hope. Do you know how?"

Again, Nikki nodded, no.

"This is where what I told you about the devil and God being real becomes relevant. Faust wanted the innocence of his youth, he wanted to relive his youth, to be young again, and Mephistopheles gave him that. I'll tell you a little secret…he's giving that to me too. Let me ask, did you have a happy childhood?"

Nikki nodded yes.

"Really? That's somewhat surprising, given what you do for a living. I've always thought girls in your profession probably had screwed up childhoods, but what do I know. Well, my childhood was not happy or pleasant. I won't bore you with the various sordid details, but my childhood, from my earliest memories, was full of pain. Mostly, it was my father, but my mother never raised a hand or voice in my defense. Neither of them ever loved me and then, when I was thirteen, they both died. I didn't kill them, though I wish I had. When they died, I went to live with my grandmother, who didn't love me either, but at least she didn't hurt me. That, in a nutshell, was my youth."

"If that story makes you feel bad for me, you're not the first, but it doesn't matter. I couldn't tell you how many times I prayed to God when I was growing up. How many times I pleaded with him to make me someone new, put me somewhere new. He never did. No words or pity or prayers to God ever helped me, nor will they bring back my youth or erase all the crap I dealt with. But Mephistopheles, or more accurately, the devil, can and he is. I've struck my own bargain so to speak. When God stayed silent, I called out to his antagonist and he answered my call. I've given myself over to his servant, to Abaddon. Do you know of Abaddon?"

Nikki forced herself to nod no again, but listening to Stanton, she was beginning to lose any hope of escaping unharmed and began to tremble visibly again.

"He's one of the devil's most powerful servants. He's described as the 'Angel of the Abyss' or the 'Destroyer', and, to make a long story short, very very soon, we'll be one."

Stanton put the video camera down on the bed and pointed it toward Nikki. He sat atop Nikki, straddling her trembling body. "You're a very beautiful girl," he said. "Would it surprise you to know that I've never been with a woman, never touched a woman's skin as I am with you now? In truth, that's one of the reasons I was chosen. I've never defiled myself with a woman."

His hand gently caressed Nikki's cheek and traveled slowly down to her neck and then to her bare shoulder and slowly down along her left arm. He felt the softness of her trembling skin, as he stared directly into her panicked eyes, but the suppleness of her body did nothing for him.

"This is truly a blessing," he said. "I am truly in my master's favor again and rewarded with this opportunity to look into you and to understand you before you're gone."

Nikki let out a muffled squeal and shook back and forth, desperately trying to escape. The terror surged through her eyes, which only heightened Stanton's awe and enjoyment of the situation.

"No, don't close your eyes. Keep them open wide and I'll make this part quick. I owe you that. Like me, you're one of Abaddon's chosen. I won't make you suffer. This is part of my debt, part of giving myself to Abaddon, to becoming one with Abaddon."

Stanton reached around his back and removed the hunting knife he'd stuffed into his belt. He gently grabbed Nikki's struggling head and, taking a firm grip of her dark-brown hair as she tried again to free herself, tilted her head back to expose her neck and throat. The hunting knife in his other hand flashed across her line of sight and two seconds later she felt the cold steel as it moved swiftly from the left side of her neck to the right side.

Blood began to rush from the wound down her neck and onto her chest. Still straddling Nikki, Stanton dropped his head slightly and leaned in, kissing Nikki's neck and letting the blood flow onto his lips. The flavor was even sweeter than before, like a vintage wine perfected by patience and time.

Finally, Stanton stepped back, picked up the video camera from the bed and filmed Nikki's last breathes as they gasped laboriously from her blood covered body. He watched as the terror and pain, which had been so plainly visible only seconds before, gently diminished in unison with each fading breath until, finally, with the last breath no sign of life or spirit was left in Nikki's eyes at all.

David Stanton turned off the video camera and stood for a moment, peering into Nikki's lifeless eyes, no less in awe by the transformation than he had been with his first kill. He put the camera down, leaned over Nikki's slumped lifeless body and, with the already bloody hunting knife, surgically pried each of her light brown eyes from her face and placed them into a small clear plastic freezer bag. His sacrifice to Abaddon was complete and the fulfillment of his mission, his destiny, his complete oneness with Abaddon lay less than seventy-two hours away.

Chapter 15
December 22nd

"Is Special Agent Bleeker available?"

"I believe he is, Declan," responded John Bleeker's secretary, Ellen. "How are you doing today?"

"I'm good. How about you? Any plans for the holidays?"

"I'm fine. My husband and I are leaving later this afternoon to spend Christmas with his family."

"Are you driving or flying?"

"Driving, but it's only five hours or so. I'll ring Agent Bleeker and let him know you're here."

"Thank you," Declan replied.

"Special Agent Bleeker, yes, Special Agent Parker is here and has requested a few minutes," Ellen said into the phone. "Of course, I'll send him in."

Ellen hung up the phone and looked at Declan again, "He's ready for you."

"Thank you, Ellen. Enjoy the holidays."

"You too, Declan. Merry Christmas," she replied with a smile.

"Merry Christmas."

Declan walked into the large office of Special Agent in Charge, John Bleeker. While Declan had been in Bleeker's office countless times as a kid, when it belonged to his dad and Ellen was his dad's secretary, he hadn't been back inside during his relatively short time since being assigned to the field office out of the academy. Bleeker impressed Declan as all business. He was congenial and usually pleasant, but one didn't have to dig too deep or pay too much attention to realize Bleeker wasn't particularly interested in making good friends with the agents underneath him, many of whom, like Kevin Cameron, were older and had substantially more service time with the Bureau than he did.

"So, what can I do for you, Parker," he said as Declan

closed the door behind him. "Please, take a seat."

Declan looked thoughtfully around the office, trying to remember what it had looked like when his dad had been the Special Agent in Charge years earlier. Bleeker noticed Declan taking in the surroundings and said, "I guess you haven't been in here to see me before have you? We always meet in one of the conference rooms."

"No, I haven't," Declan replied. "But I used to come in here all the time when I was a kid."

Bleeker thought for a second. "Oh, that's right, your father headed up this field office at one point, didn't he?"

"He did."

"Special Agent Ron Parker, correct?"

"That's right."

"He was responsible for some pretty big cases during his career. I've heard he was a very good agent."

"One of the best," Declan responded.

"So, what can I do for you, Parker?"

"Sorry, I won't take up much of your time."

"Not a problem, Parker. You have my ear."

"Well, I received a call a few days ago through local law enforcement, based on a 'See Something, Say Something' tip they got. I ran the guy through our systems and he came back clean. No big deal, but I did find two grandfathered pre-ban AR-15's registered to him through NICS."

"I see."

"Like I said, not seemingly a big deal as I know there are still plenty of pre-ban AR-15's out there, but I wanted to get more info on him, like ammo purchases, internet search records, etc., you know, the basic stuff."

"Of course."

"So, I put in a PRISM request through the regional fusion center and he came back SCI."

"SCI?"

"Sensitive Compartmentalized..."

"I know what SCI means, Parker."

"Of course, sir. I'm sorry. Anyway, he's SCI and the fusion center won't give me anything on him at all because I'm not authorized. It just seems strange that someone who comes up clean in our various databases would be classified SCI by the NSA or Homeland or whomever. It makes me wonder if we're missing something."

"Doubtful. He could be SCI for any number of reasons," Bleeker replied.

"That's what Kevin said too."

"You've discussed this with Special Agent Cameron?"

"Only briefly. He was around when I took the call and he recommended that I put in the PRISM request."

"I see."

"I think there's something here. I tailed this guy Stanton…"

"Stanton?"

"Yes, sorry, that's the suspect's name, David Timothy Stanton. I tailed Stanton late last night for a few hours."

"You've set up surveillance on him?"

"Not exactly," Declan replied. "I was able to obtain his address, vehicle type, registration, DL photo and most of the standard stuff through our systems, so I've been staking out his apartment for a few nights. Late last night, after I'd already been outside for an hour or so, he came out, so I followed him to one of the strip clubs just outside of the city. He never went in, just sat in his truck for two hours or so until the place closed down, then he followed a girl who came out back to what I believe was her apartment."

"Did he do anything?"

"No, but I think he planned to. He followed her from the club to her apartment. I have the address and her plates and plan to run both when I'm finished here. But, he followed her, watched her go inside, then he walked up to the front door. I think he got spooked when another car pulled into the complex and he bolted."

"So, he didn't actually do anything?"

"Other than follow her home? No."

"Do you know whether he, what's his name again?"

"David Stanton."

"Do you know whether Stanton knew the girl?"

"No. At least not yet, but I'd like to look into it further and set up a full surveillance detail. Something just doesn't seem right. I'd also like to see if you can contact someone at Homeland or the NSA and see about the SCI classification. Maybe see if we can get access under the circumstances."

"I tell you what, Parker. I'll call a friend from Yale who's now over at Homeland and see what I can find out about the SCI classification. I'll do that today and see if there's anything to it. In terms of a surveillance detail, in that you didn't see Stanton really try anything, I think it's premature at this point. At least until we get additional intel."

"Okay, but what if Stanton just got spooked last night and goes back tonight? He was definitely up to something; that I know."

"Maybe, but at this point you don't know what. This girl could be an ex-girlfriend or a harmless infatuation he was trying to ask out, but chickened out at the last minute. He could just be some kind of pervert, or a peeping tom or something. I don't think a full surveillance detail is justified at this stage. Let's give it a few days and get some more information before we commit the man hours and Bureau resources."

"If that's your decision, sir."

"It is."

"Can I at least continue to keep an eye on him, until you've had chance to speak with your friend and gather more intel?"

"Of course, I'd expect nothing less."

"Thank you."

"But, take tonight off. If there is something there, I don't want him to catch onto you and get spooked."

"I've been using different vehicles and locations."

"As I would expect, but that doesn't mean he hasn't noticed. You did say you followed him outside of town and to this girl's apartment last night, right?"

"Right," Declan answered.

"Do you acknowledge the possibility that Stanton could have noticed you following him?"

"I suppose, but I don't think so."

"Regardless, brief Costello and take tonight off. We'll touch base on this thing tomorrow after I've had a chance to talk with Homeland. Let's say, 10:30."

"Will do, sir."

"Excellent. And, Parker, I'm serious about tonight. Costello will cover it, understood?"

"Understood."

Chapter 16
December 22nd

Megan's flight from D.C. had been delayed over an hour and wasn't expected in until sometime closer to 7:30. Declan was a walking bundle of anticipation, which rendered him unable to just sit at home waiting for a reasonable time to head to the airport, so he left as if her flight was on time and figured he'd kill some time in the main terminal. At least he'd be there, and he was hopeful some diversion or other would occupy the time.

Upon entering the airport, Declan immediately checked the Arrivals board only to discover Megan's flight had somehow suffered an additional delay and wasn't expected until 8:10. After browsing the various bookstores and sundry stores in the main terminal, Declan made his way to the "Runway Bar & Grill" and nabbed an empty seat at the crowded bar, which was bustling with holiday travelers.

After a few minutes, one of the bartenders brought him a draft beer and put in his food order. Declan drank his beer and watched the news coverage on the latest escalation of events in the Middle East. Israel had begun exchanging heavy rocket fire and targeted air strikes with the Syrians, Hamas, Hezbollah, and Islamic State fighters operating just over the Jordanian border. The Israelis had suffered civilian casualties from Syrian missiles fired into Tel Aviv the day before, using missile technology provided by the Russians. They had responded with a substantial air strike on various military and government sites in and around Damascus. Those air strikes prompted, or depending on one's point of view, provided an excuse for Hezbollah and Hamas to engage Israeli Defense Force, or IDF, soldiers in the West Bank, Gaza, and the border area between Lebanon and Israel, as well as for the Syrians to launch another flurry of missiles into Israel, many of which had been intercepted by the Iron Dome. Islamic State fighters had begun engaging IDF troops along the Jordanian and Syrian borders.

"It's quickly becoming a mess over here," the man sitting next to Declan said as they both sat watching the news.

"It definitely looks that way," replied Declan, happy to have someone to talk to, if only to kill some time. "I wonder how long until we get our troops involved."

"We won't get our troops involved this time, not to help the Israelis. No one will. This administration certainly hasn't shown any love for the Israelis, and particularly not for the Prime Minister. They went out on their own against Iran, and will likely have to go it alone on this too."

"You don't think the U.S. will just sit on the sidelines, do you? I mean, despite some obvious tension with the Israelis, they're still our main ally in the region."

"I think if the administration were going to get involved directly and come to the Israelis' aid, they'd have done it by now," the man responded. "I think Israel is on our own this time."

"Are you Israeli?"

"No, I live in Philadelphia, but I am Jewish and I have family living in Jerusalem, including both my sons and their families. I'm Joseph Steinman."

"Declan Parker," said Declan, introducing himself.

"A pleasure to meet you. Declan is an Irish name isn't it?"

"It is. I'm told that it was always one of my mom's favorite names. She couldn't get my dad to go for it when my older brother was born, but by the time I came along she'd worn him down."

"Are you Irish, I mean of Irish descent?"

"Irish on my mom's side, and English on my dad's."

"An interesting combination."

"Yes, it is. It made for an entertaining childhood at times."

"I can imagine. Where are you heading?"

"Nowhere. My girlfriend is coming in from D.C. for Christmas, so I'm here to pick her up, but her flight is delayed."

"Aren't they all," replied Mr. Steinman.

"Are you traveling?"

"I am. I'm headed home to Philly. I was out here for business this week. My oldest son and his family are supposed to fly in from Jerusalem tomorrow. I'm hoping they are still able to get out okay."

"Has Jerusalem been hit with any of the missile attacks?"

"Nothing major so far, but with the attacks on Tel Aviv yesterday and what's happening today, I'm obviously concerned."

"Understandably. It has to be difficult to have family in the midst of all that fighting."

"It is, and I fear it's only going to get worse. Blowback from the Iran strike was expected, but with this escalation, and an absence of international support for Israel, I fear that things in the region are going to get really ugly really quickly. I don't think we're too far from seeing Syria employ chemical or biological weapons of some sort."

"I didn't think the Syrians had any left. I thought they had to give them all up at one point quite a while ago."

"Trust me, they still have them. That was a bit of a debacle. Regardless, with all the chaos in that country since the civil war began and with ISIS holding areas of the country, who knows where all the chemical weapons went or to whom they went."

"If that happened, if Syria, ISIS, or someone else used chemical weapons, do you think Israel would respond with chemical weapons of their own?"

"No, I think their response would, eventually, be nuclear. Israel has always been very clear that a chemical attack will be viewed in the same light as a nuclear attack and treated as such. My guess is that if the Syrians, or anyone else, launched a chemical attack, the nuclear option, for the first time, would truly be on the table. If that happened, if things escalate to that point, I think we could very well see the prophet Isaiah's words regarding Damascus come to pass in the near future."

Somewhat surprised by the comment, Declan replied, "That's what my brother said yesterday too. He told me about the destruction of Damascus in Isaiah something…I can't remember the chapter right now."

"Isaiah 17, the prophecy is found in Isaiah 17."

"I read it yesterday afternoon, but wasn't entirely sure what it meant."

"It means that Damascus, the oldest continually inhabited city in the world, will be reduced to a heap of rubble in one night and will never again be a city. That sounds to me like something a nuclear strike would accomplish."

"I agree," said Declan, taking a sip from his beer. "But, do you really believe the prophecy? I mean, do you really think Isaiah could know about something that was supposed to happen thousands of years after he lived?"

"If you'd asked me that question when I was younger, when I was your age, I'd have said no. But, over the years, as I've come to know God's word through the Torah and the Bible I'm absolutely certain in its truth. I've specifically studied the Old Testament prophecies concerning the Messiah and cannot deny that each and every one of the three hundred plus prophecies addressing his first coming was fulfilled just as God told us it would through His prophets. Do you know the odds of even ten or eleven of those prophecies being fulfilled by one man?"

"Not really."

"They're truly staggering. To put it in perspective, you'd have a better chance of winning Powerball three times in a row. God is the ultimate, unrivaled mathematician."

"So, and I hope I'm not overstepping by asking this, but do you believe in Jesus as the Messiah?"

"Absolutely," Mr. Steinman responded.

"But you're Jewish?"

"I am, but I'm also a believer in Jesus, much like the

Apostles and many of the early church. I guess you'd call me a Jewish Christian or a Messianic Jew."

"Interesting. And you believe this Isaiah prophecy is yet to be fulfilled, like my brother said?"

"I certainly do. It's the word of the God of Israel. God tells us that He gives us the end from the beginning, as only He can, and one of the things that distinguishes God from the world is that He never lies. His words are, quite simply, truth. Anyone who undertakes a serious, honest study of Biblical prophecy can only reach one conclusion, which is that God's word is one hundred percent accurate, one hundred percent of the time. The prophets, whether Isaiah, Ezekiel, Jeremiah or Daniel were truly speaking God's word, telling us about things that would happen in such detail that they could only have come from the supernatural. Would you like a wonderful example, something that will truly blow your mind?"

"Sure, I mean, if you don't mind talking about it. I don't want to hold you up or anything."

"Not at all. My flight isn't supposed to leave for another three hours and I've spent far too many years avoiding or ignoring opportunities to speak with people about the things of God. Are you familiar with Jewish history?"

"Somewhat."

"Alright, Babylon's rule over Judah began in 609 B.C. Jerusalem and Judah fell to the Babylonians, specifically to Nebuchadnezzar, in 586 B.C. This was prophesied by Isaiah, who lived from roughly 740 B.C. to 681 B.C., as well as by Jeremiah and Ezekiel later. I forget the specific verses in Isaiah, but look at Isaiah 2, Isaiah 5, and Isaiah 6 to see for yourself. But, that's not the most impressive part. In Isaiah 44 and 45, he tells the Jews, over a hundred years before they've even gone into Babylonian captivity mind you, that they will be returned to the land, to Jerusalem, by Cyrus. Isaiah specifically gives the name of Cyrus."

"Okay," Declan responded with evident interest.

"And, sure enough, in 538 B.C., Cyrus the Great, King of the Medo-Persians, who conquered the Babylonians a year prior, issued a decree allowing the Jews to return to their homeland, to Jerusalem and Judah, just as Isaiah said would happen over a hundred and fifty years earlier, long before Cyrus the Great had even been born and before the Medo-Persian empire had come to prominence. Is that not amazing?"

"It is."

"And that's just one of hundreds of examples," Mr. Steinman said as he raised his glass. "So, as I said before, I believe without hesitation in God's word."

As the night slowly gave way to the freshness of a new morning, Declan sat up in bed unable to sleep. The rhythm of Megan's breathing, soundly asleep next to him, danced over the silence of the fading night. He took in every inch of her in the dim blue moonlight, lying beside him in the place he'd feared she'd never be again, and for the first time in a long time he knew, for whatever reason, he'd been blessed. There was no accounting for why; no earthly explanation for her sudden unexpected change of heart. Less than 48 hours earlier Megan had no place in his life, or, more precisely, he'd no longer had a place in hers. Yet, there she was, glowing beside him again, filling his miniscule world with the overwhelming light found only amid love.

As Declan thought about it, it was the reemergence of Megan into his life, as much as anything he'd heard from his brother or his random encounter with Joseph Steinman earlier that night, which guided him to the prospect that, maybe, just maybe, God really did still exist.

Chapter 17
December 23rd

"So you're leaving me for the day," Megan said, playfully pulling the sheet over her chest.

"Not for the day. That would be impossible. Actually, if it weren't for this meeting with Bleeker, I wouldn't go in at all."

"It's fine, babe, for a few hours anyway. It'll give me a chance to get a few things done and off my mysteriously always full plate."

"I promise, I won't be long. I'm meeting with Bleeker at 10:30, and should be home by noon. Then we can go grab some lunch and do a little Christmas shopping."

"I'm not entirely certain I'll be dressed for lunch by noon," she replied.

"I certainly hope not."

"You're making me blush, Special Agent Parker."

"Good."

Declan leaned over the bed to kiss Megan goodbye. "I love you," he said.

"I love you too."

"See you soon?"

"I'll literally be right here where you left me."

David Stanton stood bathed in the deep cobalt light being dispersed through one of the towering stained glass images of the Apostle Paul, his mop gliding from left to right over and again across the last section of shimmering marble floor. Once he'd finished mopping, Stanton went through each row of pews, making sure each had sufficient hymnals and Christmas programs, and that they were properly placed and aligned.

With that task complete, Stanton took his iPad out and accessed the live feed on his website. He walked slowly through the sanctuary, beginning from the podium and checked to make sure each camera feed was picking him up and that the picture quality and buffering were still superb, with no hitches or delays from the camera feeds to the images online.

"Soon," he whispered to himself. "Soon this place will be known to the whole world. Soon I'll be known to the world, never to be forgotten or discounted again."

Stanton walked slowly, almost triumphantly though the sanctuary, taking in the silence and peacefulness around him, the play of the sun's light through the stained glass windows, imagining what it would look and sound like when he finally made himself known to its patrons.

"It looks wonderful, David," came a voice behind him.

"Thank you, Pastor," Stanton replied as he turned around.

"Seriously, David, I can't ever remember the church looking better. You've outdone yourself."

"Thank you."

"It's a truly fitting atmosphere for celebrating the birth of our Lord."

"I agree, Pastor. I wanted it to be perfect."

"Well, you've certainly succeeded."

Chapter 18
December 23rd

"Come in, Parker. I'm on my own today. Ellen took off yesterday for the holidays. Are you going anywhere?"

"No, sir. All my family is here."

"That's beneficial this time of year, if no other," replied Bleeker. "I always hate dealing with the holiday travel routine."

"Are you heading home, sir?"

"No, not this year. Frankly, I just couldn't do it again this year," Bleeker replied as he took a seat behind his meticulously organized desk. "It's too much hassle. Anyway, let's get down to the business of David Stanton, shall we?"

"Of course."

"Unfortunately, at this point I don't have much new information. I had Costello watch his place last night, and he witnessed no movement."

"What about your contact at Homeland and the SCI?"

Bleeker leaned well back in his leather chair and looked up toward the ceiling. "Believe it or not, I was getting to that. My classmate at Homeland was already out for the holidays, in Europe somewhere apparently. I left him a message on his cell to call me. I didn't say what it was in reference to. So far, no response. I did put in a call to the regional fusion center, like you did, and confirmed that Stanton is, in fact, SCI by putting in my own PRISM request. Unfortunately, I'm not on the access list either, so I didn't make any progress there."

"I see."

"So, at this point I know about as much as you."

"Which is to say, not much," Declan replied.

"Well, not much yet; however, I'm hoping I can get some additional intel from my contact. I just don't know that I'll have it today."

"So what do we do in the meantime? Have you

reconsidered a surveillance detail, or maybe a drone surveillance unit?"

"Actually, I'm still of the mind that we hold tight for a few more days."

"But, sir,…"

Bleeker stood up again and began slowly pacing behind his desk. "We've already been through this and I understand your position, Parker; however, from what I've seen so far, there doesn't appear to be an imminent threat here. Further, if someone has tagged this guy SCI, then in all likelihood that someone is already watching him. Adding our own surveillance detail, aside from being duplicative, could end up actually being detrimental to whatever type of investigation is possibly already underway."

"But we aren't certain there is an investigation underway. I've watched Stanton's apartment for a few nights now and I've never seen any indication that anyone else was watching him too."

"Look, Parker, I appreciate your enthusiasm and determination on this, but if the guy is SCI, he's SCI for a reason. Call me crazy, but I'm willing to make the educated assumption that whoever tagged him knows what they are doing, and I'm not willing, nor do I think it's necessary at this point, to get my field office officially involved."

"In other words, leave it alone?"

"Well said. Yes, leave it alone, at least until I hear back from my contact at Homeland and have more intel to work with."

Chapter 19
December 23rd

Declan had no intention of simply leaving David Stanton alone. His dad certainly wouldn't have let it alone. While he'd only been with the Bureau, outside of the Academy, for just over a year, his gut knew enough to know something wasn't right with the whole situation. Initially, he was absolutely certain that car in the parking lot two nights prior scared Stanton away from whatever he'd had in mind.

More importantly, Declan couldn't figure out what reason John Bleeker would have for pretending he didn't have access to Stanton's NSA and Homeland files, when Declan knew otherwise. If Stanton were a suspected domestic terrorist or somehow involved in or part of an NSA, CIA or Homeland operation or investigation, why didn't Bleeker just say so? Something about the entire scenario didn't sit well, and Declan couldn't just sit aside and trust Bleeker to follow up, particularly when Bleeker was clearly lying about his access to Stanton's files.

After leaving Bleeker's office, Declan headed down to the field office supply division, where he checked out various pieces of remote audio surveillance equipment under the auspices of using it for his ongoing investigation into an interstate methamphetamine ring he'd been working on. The equipment was relatively small and could be used from a car or other vehicle. One piece of equipment would allow Declan to pick up any cellular transmissions and conversations within a 200 foot radius, and the other was capable of obtaining and recording live audio from Stanton's apartment, provided Declan could get within 50 to 70 feet, which was exactly what he planned to do later that night.

David Stanton finished up his morning work and took his lunch and iPad out to his SUV, where he turned on the engine and heater to warm things up. The day had turned dramatically colder, with the temperature dropping down to 20 degrees F throughout the morning.

Stanton was both exhilarated and exhausted, given his lack of sleep the two previous nights. He took a few bites of his turkey sandwich and a couple sips from his can of diet soda. The cold soda fizzed around the roof of his mouth, providing a pleasant tingling sensation. He laid his head back against the driver's headrest and closed his eyes. The time of his complete surrender to Abaddon was nearly upon him. He'd made all the necessary preparations, had polished and perfected his equipment, and had proven himself worthy of the task that had been set before him. It was, quite simply, a matter of execution from that point forward. Stanton knew he needed a good sleep, along with sufficient nutrients and fuel to prepare his body for Abaddon's arrival. After that, it was simply a matter of maintaining his focus and letting his master use him to accomplish the ultimate goal.

It was so close, Stanton could finally taste it. The years of planning, pain and frustration had finally brought him to the verge of earning his due, his reward for staying true and obedient to his master's plan and direction. At the end of the rainbow, so to speak, Stanton's second chance sat waiting. The blood that had flown, and was to flow still, had purchased him redemption, a new life free of the misery and scars he'd carried for the majority of his years. Soon, very soon, David Stanton would cease to exist. He'd die the death he'd so often prayed for as a little boy and be reborn as Abaddon, the all-powerful Destroyer. In destruction, he'd finally find rebirth.

———————————

"So, Bleeker didn't say anything about having access to Stanton's files," Megan said. "Why do you think he's not sharing that info with you? I mean, it seems pretty innocuous."

"I'm really not sure," Declan replied. "It just doesn't make any sense. Why lie and tell me he doesn't have access to the SCI when he does? Why tell me he's waiting for a call back from his friend at Homeland for information he can access on his own?"

"You didn't let on that you know he has access, did you?"

"Of course not, because how do I explain how I came across that information. Honestly, I figured he'd tell me once I brought up the name, but he didn't. It's just weird."

"I agree."

"I wish I could see what's in this guy's records that's so flippin' top secret. Is he a Homeland or NSA asset or something? He doesn't show up on any of our terror watch lists, so he's got to be something else."

"Maybe he is an asset, NSA, CIA, Homeland, who knows."

"Exactly, who knows?"

"John Bleeker for one, I suppose," she replied. "So what are you going to do?"

"Well, I can't run an official surveillance op, but I can run my own small scale op and keep an eye on the guy for the next few days until Bleeker tells me his friend at Homeland has gotten back to him. I'm not going to just sit back and twiddle my thumbs."

"Can I come with you tonight?"

"I don't know, Megan. I'm not sure it's a good idea."

"Why? We're just going to be sitting in a car listening."

"What if he moves again tonight? What if he goes back to that girl's apartment? What am I supposed to do with you then? I don't think it's safe."

"If something like that does happen, then we'll deal with it. I won't get in your way. Besides, I do have a higher security clearance than you."

"You're a lawyer, not an agent."

"Haven't you heard the things people say about

lawyers? We're nothing but ruthless mercenaries. Trust me, I'll be fine, Special Agent Parker," she responded with a smile Declan was unable to refuse. "Besides, if it looks like we're too conspicuous or if somebody comes by the car, I can kiss you and we can pretend we're just two love-crazy kids making out."

"That really only happens in the movies."

"But it always works in the movies, doesn't it? Not to mention the other obvious benefit."

"What's the other obvious benefit?"

"It's fun."

"Of course. Alright, fine, you've worn me down, counselor."

"And I didn't even break a sweat."

Chapter 20
December 23rd

Declan and Megan parked amid other cars in a dark corner of the parking lot outside David Stanton's apartment building shortly after 10:00 p.m. Based on his previous stakeouts, Declan knew Stanton to be a night owl, and figured the later evening hours to be his best chance to observe Stanton moving again or pick up some insightful audio. He set up the audio surveillance equipment and aimed the device directly at the darkened apartment, sixty or so feet away.

"Alright, I think we're up and running," he said to Megan. "Here's an earpiece for this one."

"What does this one do?"

"This one should pick up sounds from inside his apartment. The other will latch onto any cellular signals in the immediate area and allow us to listen in. It shows a little red light right here when it picks up a call."

Megan slid the tiny earpiece into her left ear, and was immediately surprised by the clarity and power of the transmission. "He's listening to music," she said.

Declan inserted his earpiece as well and immediately heard what sounded like symphony music.

"It's classical," Megan stated. "Actually, it's…"

"It's what?"

"Hold on. I've heard this before. It's an opera. Just wait, in just a second you should hear a woman's voice, a soprano." They both sat silently for a few more seconds, then, just as Megan had predicted, came the pleasant sound of a female soprano.

"I know this opera, I've seen it before," Megan said. "The girl, her name is…her name is Marguerite. That's it, this is Faust. He's listening to Faust."

"I thought that was a book."

"Well, it is, but there's also an opera adapted from the original story by Goethe. There are a couple actually. I saw it performed at the Metropolitan Opera a few seasons ago with my parents. I can't be totally certain yet, but I think that's what he's listening to."

"It's got something to do with selling your soul to Satan, right?"

"Essentially. Faust makes a deal with the devil to regain his lost youth, which the devil grants him, but, as one would expect, it doesn't go well. Faust meets and finally seduces Marguerite, that's the girl singing now. After seducing her, he leaves, not knowing she's pregnant with his child. The devil torments her and she eventually kills the baby and winds up in an asylum. Faust is wracked with guilt and pity when he finds out what became of her, and gets the devil to take him to try and save her, but she's even more terrorized by the sight of the devil and ultimately dies. He damns her, but is seemingly overridden by angelic voices proclaiming she's actually saved. It's really a very sad and dark opera."

———————————

David Stanton lay naked on his living-room floor, facing the ceiling with his body spread out in the shape of Da Vinci's Vitruvian Man. His body was surrounded by a circle of burning black candles. At the tip of each hand and each foot, and just above his head, a red candle burned. He was perfectly still, eyes closed, breathing gently and rhythmically in time with the music as it washed over him like surf on the beach. The instruments and voices filled his entire being, Marguerite's lamenting tone accounted for the whole of his world, blocking out all distraction and every ounce of the various white noise typically filling one's ears.

The music slowed then gradually built up again, string over string, word over word, effortlessly working to a crescendo, to the complete expression of grief on its path to madness. The sounds caressed and tortured Stanton's senses, taking him back to places he'd tried so many ways to forget and leave forever in the tucked-away black corners of his mind. Initially, he tried to resist, to fight hard and mercilessly against the memories which had so twisted his world into the unrecognizable, yet inescapable, mass of suffering he'd known.

He fought to push back the humility, shame and sadness which had arrived with the scent of alcohol in the dark of each night, but, as was so often the case, his fight, fierce as it was, proved fruitless. David Stanton's sense of himself, forever defined in the darkest hours of nights too numerous to count, couldn't be denied. His pale naked body shuddered on the floor, aching for something that couldn't ever be recaptured though human effort.

"FILL ME," he screamed suddenly. "FILL ME WITH YOUR SPIRIT!"

Stanton's words shot out, piercing through the music. They burned quick vicious holes through the photos of his past which played through his mind. His words, he knew were powerful.

"I give myself over to you. TAKE ME! USE ME TO BREATHE LIFE INTO YOUR RAGE!"

Megan shuddered at the sudden unexpected sound of Stanton's shout.

"Do you hear that?"

"He's shouting," Megan answered. "But I can't make out exactly what he's saying."

"It sounds like he's yelling cage or rage or something like that."

"Is there any way to filter what he's saying from the music?"

"Not really. It will pick up whatever's audible in the apartment, but I can't filter live. I'd need to record it and then run the digital audio through one of our filtering programs to focus only on what he's saying."

"Are you recording this?"

"No. Technically I'm not even supposed to be here, much less conducting audio surveillance. Wait...there he goes again."

"I got that one," replied Megan. "He yelled 'fill me'".

"I got that too....there it is again."

"That's really creepy."

Stanton's shouts continued until his rage overcame his pain and he finally felt worthy of taking the final necessary step before the culmination of his mission: the death of his old powerless self. He focused his thoughts on one name, and slowly and repeatedly chanted that name, "Abaddon..., Abaddon..., Abaddon..., Abaddon..." His chant began simply as a thought. It slowly and meticulously evolved into a whisper, then into a statement, and finally into a summons. The chant grew louder and more authoritative with each utterance, "Abaddon..., Abaddon..., Abaddon..."

An almost imperceptible chill began to filter through the apartment and it grew slightly more palatable with each chant. "Abaddon..., Abaddon..., Abaddon..."

The chill slowly enveloped David Stanton, reaching into every part of his naked body, touching every extremity like frost on grass, but he didn't shiver. He continued to chant the name of Abaddon, his thoughts focused solely on that name. "Abaddon..., Abaddon..." His breath soon became visible through the cold with each word. The candles flickered ever so slightly, wavering back and forth as if in a gentle breeze. "Abaddon..., Abaddon..."

Suddenly, a flash of light, like lightning, and a powerful surge of energy filled the room. A violent icy wind rushed through the apartment, blowing the candles out as if in a rage and shaking the entire room like an earthquake. It descended furiously upon David Stanton from every direction. When it hit him, Stanton's body started and convulsed uncontrollably, and then, fell back down again into silence and stillness on the floor. It was done.

Listening outside, Megan and Declan each felt the chill and it sent shivers down their respective spines. Declan pulled the earpiece out and asked, "What the hell just happened?"

"I'm not sure, but whatever just happened was freaky," Megan answered, her hands trembling. "It sounded like a hurricane blew through his apartment or something."

"It literally looked like a lightning strike, but inside."

"I saw that. What do you think he's doing in there?"

"I have no idea, but whatever just happened, whatever we just heard and felt, I don't think it's good."

"No," Megan replied. "I'd even say evil."

"I think it's time to get going."

"Declan, look."

Declan looked up from the car to see the man he recognized as David Stanton standing, completely naked, on his balcony in the frigid December night air.

"Is that him?"

Despite the fact that there was something very different about him, almost like looking at a different man than he'd watched a few nights prior, Declan whispered, "That's him."

At that moment, despite the cold darkness, Declan caught Abaddon's cold glare staring directly at him, eye to eye, through the black night. His lifeless gaze impaled Declan, as if he knew exactly who he was and why he was there. An instinctual chill shot up Declan's spine and he shivered suddenly, unnerved and visibly shaken. Abaddon simply smiled wryly and looked back up to the glowing stars, as though Declan no longer existed.

Chapter 21
December 23rd – December 24th

The dim light from a blood moon hung amid the otherwise total blackness enveloping Declan. He raised his hands toward his face, trying desperately to see something, anything, in the darkness, but could only make them out when they were practically touching his eyes. Screams pierced the night, so many that it was impossible for Declan to determine whether they came from a particular direction.

He walked blindly, not knowing where or why, but looking up to the blood moon for perspective and to try and keep his bearings. The screams grew louder and more desperate, but no closer. There were so many voices, so many different pitches and moans that they overwhelmed Declan until he finally stopped in his tracks, unable to maintain any sense of place or direction. There must have been thousands of them, each crying out in the dark for help. They formed an air of hopelessness that filled Declan's entire being, forcing him down, first onto his knees, then into a total collapse on the cold, hard, damp ground hidden in the blackness surrounding him.

Tears poured from his eyes and he finally called out into the night for help, for mercy from the deafening screams that filled his ears. His own howl joined the horrid harmony of the other sad suffering souls whom he could hear, but could not see, and, like their cries in the night, his own cry went unanswered.

He writhed on the ground for what seemed like days, until he sensed a hint of distinction among the voices, an understandable call from a recognized voice which had somehow managed to distinguish itself from the others. This hint of the familiar prompted Declan to sit up and focus all his energy and senses on that single voice in the black night. The voice became ever so slightly louder, and he could just make out her calling his name, "Declan...Declan...", then "Declan, help me, please, Declan, save me."

He focused more intently, pulling himself up from the ground. Soon her voice rose above all the others, until finally, Declan heard only her cries, "Declan, help, please", then she screamed, "No, no, leave me alone!"

"Megan, I'm coming," he called out. "I'm coming!" But, where was she? He tried to follow her voice, still unable to see anything except the foreboding blood moon hanging in the darkness above him. He moved left, then right, then turned in a complete circle, trying to determine the source of her voice.

"Declan, Declan," she called again, the fear in her voice rising. "Declan, please, I'm scared. Please, help me!"

"Megan, where are you? Where are you?"

"Declan, please, he's coming for me. No, no!"

He ran desperately in every direction, gasping for breath and unable to determine in the dark whether he'd actually gone anywhere.

"No! No! Leave me alone," she screamed, her voice filled with fear. "Declan!"

Declan raced toward her, determined to find her in the darkness, to save her from whatever monster was tormenting her. He ran as fast as he could, yelling, "I'm coming, Megan, I'm coming," until he suddenly tumbled over something in the darkness, falling hard and painfully, face first, onto the ground again.

The voice had gone silent. Declan struggled to shake off the pain radiating from his head and chest and regain his senses. "Megan, where are you? Where are you?"

His calls went unanswered. A cold bitter stillness fell over the night and permeated the darkness around him. Declan rose to his knees and groped along the ground trying to find whatever he'd fallen over. His blind hands moved along the hard ground, slowly probing for the object, when he finally felt the softness of her hair beneath his fingers.

"Megan," he screamed. "Megan!" Declan's fingers quickly found her breathless body and followed the contour of her beautiful face.

"No! No! Megan, Megan, come back! No!" Declan's own cries were the only thing breaking the insufferable stillness of the night.

He sat holding her lifeless body, sobbing into the darkness, pleading with God to bring her back. He gently caressed her face and kissed her forehead, but she didn't stir. Finally, Declan slunk down beside Megan's lifeless body, exhausted and defeated. He'd failed her.

The black night hung all around him, quiet and still. Declan laid next to her, listening to the rhythm of his breathes, when, as with her screams amid the thousands of others, he slowly picked up on the rhythm of another breath. He shot up, and felt her chest. It was perfectly lifelessly still, yet the breathing of another person became even clearer. He was not alone.

Unlike Megan's earlier screams, Declan had no trouble determining that the breathing was coming from behind him and was getting louder and closer. He turned quickly, unable to see anything in the dark, but the sound still came from behind him. He jerked around again, flailing his hands aimlessly into the darkness to try and fend off whatever or whoever the slow rhythmic breathes belonged to, but, again, he heard them behind him. Regardless of which direction he turned, the breathing came from the total blackness behind him, and continued to grow louder until he finally sensed that whoever it was, quite literally, was right behind him.

A wave of cold air rushed over Declan as he tried to gather himself, and he could feel the slow steady breathes on the back of his neck. With a rush of adrenaline, he whipped around to see the lifeless blank eyes of David Stanton only inches from his own in the darkness.

Declan shot up in bed, sweating and breathing hard, as if he'd just run a forty-yard sprint. He looked to his left to find Megan sleeping peacefully next to him.

Chapter 22
December 24th

Declan got out of bed and tried to gather himself, to shake off the nightmare and the uneasy feeling that had been with him since seeing David Stanton out on the balcony earlier that evening. He was certain he and Megan had listened to, and witnessed, something extraordinarily evil, but was uncertain what. Unable to go back to sleep, Declan reached down beneath the headboard and removed a 9mm Glock 19, then went out to the living room.

He got his gun-cleaning kit out of the hall closet, sat down on the sofa, and began cleaning the Glock 19, which had belonged to his dad. His dad had named the gun "The Lone Ranger" after his favorite TV show when he was a kid. Declan couldn't count the number of Lone Ranger reruns he'd watched with his dad and Evan growing up, or the number of times he and Evan had played Lone Ranger and Tonto with their own toy guns; going after bad guys and rescuing the townspeople, not to mention one another, when things went wrong. They'd vowed as "blood brothers" to always be there for each other.

"The Lone Ranger" was the only possession of his dad's Declan had wanted when he died. His mom finally gave it to him on the day he'd graduated from the Academy, and he'd kept it in perfect condition. For whatever reason, holding it gave him a sense of calm and he often resorted to cleaning the gun when he felt out of sorts. As he cleaned "The Lone Ranger", Declan turned on one of the cable news channels.

"The retaliatory strikes continue here in Israel as the situation here in the Middle East seems to be quickly spiraling out of control," the reporter began. "It began earlier in the week when Israel unilaterally, and without provocation, struck Iranian nuclear facilities. Almost immediately, rocket and missile fire began coming from Gaza, Lebanon and the Syrian border. Syria then initiated prolonged missile fire into Israel, inflicting serious damage on outlying parts of Tel Aviv, and ISIS fighters based in Syria and Jordan began engaging in skirmishes with Israeli Defense Force troops along the borders. Reportedly, two Israeli soldiers have been taken captive in the fighting. With no end in sight to the ongoing Syrian civil war, some have speculated that the Assad regime saw an opportunity to deflect the attention and recent momentum of the various rebel groups, if only temporarily, and draw the Israelis into a wider regional conflict."

"The Syrian government's assault began when a series of Tishreen medium range missiles were fired from a location near Damascus into Israel. The initial missiles were intercepted by the Iron Dome missile defense system, but were quickly followed by other Tishreen's and, reportedly Iranian made Shahab 3 medium range missiles, many of which reached parts of Tel Aviv and Hebron, inflicting some casualties and serious damage."

"The Israelis have responded with precision air strikes on military targets in and around Damascus, which, instead of quelling the conflict, appear to have prompted quick retaliation in the form of numerous, apparently coordinated, rocket and missile attacks from Gaza, Lebanon, the West Bank and ISIS held areas in Jordan. The United States, the EU and Russia have all condemned Israel's unprovoked attack against Iran."

"As I stand here on the roof of my hotel, the rocket and missile barrage, seemingly from all sides, continues into the day, as do Israeli Air Force strikes into Gaza, Lebanon, the West Bank, and Syria. Sources tell me that IDF troops have been deployed on the Golan Heights and the Jordanian border and are on the ground in Gaza as well. In addition to the reports of skirmishes with ISIS fighters, we've received reports of firefights between IDF troops and Hamas fighters in Gaza. It appears that Israel is literally coming under attack from all sides."

"Just over an hour ago, the Prime Minister released a

brief but pointed statement saying, 'The Israeli people will not succumb to the attacks currently being directed at us from all sides. As we've stated on numerous occasions, Israel will not tolerate a nuclear Iran, whose leaders have repeatedly called for the destruction of Israel and the total eradication of the Jewish people. We will continue to defend our nation and, if necessary, will meet aggression with aggression and force with force. Be warned that any use of chemical or biological weapons of mass destruction against Israel will not, I repeat, will not be tolerated. Any such act will be treated as an attempt to fulfill the stated goal of eradicating us and shall be responded to accordingly. Again, to be absolutely clear, the use of weapons of mass destruction against Israel will leave us with no choice but to employ any and all means at our disposal to protect our nation and our people.'"

"The not-so-subtle implication being that Israel's nuclear weapons would be on the table as an option in the event of chemical and biological attacks against it, which, despite a prior agreement requiring Syria to surrender and destroy their chemical and biological weapons cache, Syria is believed to possess."

Declan got up and took his Bible from the bookshelf, turning the pages until he again reached the 17th Chapter of Isaiah and reread the first two verses:

"¹An oracle concerning Damascus: 'See, Damascus will no longer be a city but will become a heap of ruins."

Chapter 23
December 24th

Early the next morning, as the sun began to rise, Declan woke up on his sofa, sore and tired, but with a sort of renewed mental energy. He looked at his watch and, knowing his brother would be awake despite the early hour, picked up the phone to call Evan.

"Declan, is everything okay?"

"Everything is fine. I need to talk with you and wanted to see if you're up for an early breakfast or some coffee or something."

"Sure. Do you want to come over or do you want to meet me somewhere?"

"I'm starving. Let's meet over at the diner dad used to take us to on Sunday mornings."

"Kempton's?"

"Yeah, Kempton's. Does thirty minutes or so work?"

"I'll see you then," Evan replied.

Declan hung up, rinsed his face and brushed his teeth. He wrote out a quick note for Megan, who was still sleeping peacefully, and headed out.

The waitress brought Evan's pancakes and Declan's country breakfast to the table and refilled their coffee and water. Declan watched as Evan closed his eyes and made the sign of the cross followed by three quick kisses to the index finger on his loosely-balled right hand. Evan opened his eyes to see Declan staring at him and asked, "What?"

Declan was silent for a second, then answered, "Nothing, I was just thinking about how dad did that after every prayer."

"Where do you think I picked it up?"

"Oh, I know. It just reminded me of him. What did he used to say about the three kisses?"

"A kiss for the Father, the Son and the Holy Spirit."

"That's right."

"I remember adopting it shortly after he passed. I guess it's just stuck with me. Doing it just gives me a feeling of peace, like still having a part of dad in this world and a reminder to myself that it will all be okay in the end, that I'll see dad again one day standing next to Jesus."

"I can see that."

"So, what would you like to talk about?"

Declan hesitated, and said, "I saw something last night, Evan, something evil. The feeling it gave me, coupled with all the things you and mom have talked about lately, have prompted me to start thinking about the world. I just feel like the world is beginning to spin out of control. A part of me feels like there's more going on than I'm seeing."

"That part of you is absolutely right. What did you see last night?"

"I'm not entirely sure. It seemed almost demonic, like a man overtaken by a force I wanted nothing to do with. I had a dream about it, a nightmare really, and couldn't go back to sleep so I sat up watching the news and everything that's going on in the Middle East right now. It's just crazy to me, but you and mom don't seem surprised by it at all."

"As we've talked about before, God's told us all what's coming."

"The Isaiah 17 thing right?"

"Among others," Evan replied, dipping a piece of sausage into some syrup.

"I've read it, but how does it relate to what's happening today?"

"Isaiah 17 tells of an event that hasn't happened yet. We know this because it speaks of the ultimate destruction of Damascus, specifically that it will no longer be a city but a heap of ruins. Damascus is widely considered the oldest continually inhabited city in the world, so this battle, this prophecy, is clearly still to come."

"And you believe we're seeing it take place now?"

"I believe we're finally witnessing the early stages of the event described in Isaiah 17, along with the battle described in Psalm 83. I've studied this stuff for a long time now, and I've always been of the opinion, like many prophecy scholars who know way more than I do, that the two battles will be related."

"What's Psalm 83 say?"

"Psalm 83 tells of a war between Israel and her immediate neighbors, which, like Isaiah 17, has not taken place yet. Israel defeats its neighbors, but is badly damaged in the process. Given the events taking place in the region right now, these things could happen at any moment."

"It just seems crazy. I mean I see it and agree that what I'm seeing appears to correspond with what you're telling me the Bible says, what I've read for myself, but it's hard to really believe. I just have trouble taking the Bible literally, trouble believing there's a God at all after watching dad die the way he did and seeing all the evil in the world. It all just seems like a fairy tale, all the stuff about the whole world following one man and the mark of the beast and all that stuff. I know you believe in God, but do you really believe all that stuff is to be taken literally?"

"Without a doubt."

"Do you really believe the world is going to end soon?"

"Absolutely not," Evan replied. "However, I am confident that we're living in the last days before Jesus returns. The signs are all around us and increasing in frequency, duration and intensity, just like Jesus told us they would."

"So you really believe the whole world is going to eventually follow one man?"

"That's what we're told in Revelation and in Daniel. This man, the antichrist, will appear on the world scene offering peace to all, but particularly Israel, and deceiving many. In truth, he'll be exactly the opposite of what he says. But, before this happens things have to be put into place. I mean a world government, and all of the systems, mechanisms and infrastructure can't just pop up overnight. We've been witnessing this shift for a long time now and the plans by a very small elite group have been in play for hundreds of years to bring it about."

"Assuming there is a God, and that all this prophecy stuff is real, my question is why? That's what I don't understand. Why would anyone want to rule the world?"

"Honestly, I really don't know. I'm sure power, greed, and control play a large part. I also think, in many cases, there's a knowing and intentional worship of Satan. That's what all this stuff we've seen is about. The federal government has been selling us out to the globalist elite for decades now, and the ironic thing about it, through all this additional taxation, and the squeeze on the middle class we've been experiencing, is that 'We The People' have been funding our own demise."

"I don't know, Evan. I work for the federal government and I don't see it that way necessarily."

"Declan, look at me and tell me, honestly, that our rights in this country haven't been systematically decimated since at least 2001. I mean, you know from experience that the government tracks everything people look at online or say on the phone and every email they send or thing they buy with their credit cards. What's worse, since the whole NSA whistleblower thing, they aren't even trying to hide it anymore, and, sadly, the bulk of the population doesn't really seem to care. The IRS has been used to harass those who dissent or oppose the agenda, the media is either bought-out or too scared to print the truth, and the government is even telling people how much soda they can drink and what kind of medical procedures and treatments they are allowed to have."

"Fine, some of that is true, but the data thing and other aspects are necessary for security."

"Whose security? This stuff isn't random, it's intentional and every day they find another excuse to take away more and more rights. The end result is going to be the loss of our sovereignty and, ultimately, a world government, with a single world currency and economic system, and a single world religion, which will eventually morph into worshipping the antichrist. These are some of the things John described in Revelation, the things revealed to him by God."

"Okay, maybe we are moving in that direction, but maybe it isn't a bad thing. Maybe it will actually turn out to be good thing. How do we know the bad stuff in Revelation is all true, Evan? I mean, I get the parts of the Bible that talk about love your neighbor and all that. I even understand Jesus dying on the cross to pay for our sins, even though I'm not certain I believe it. But, some of the rest of it just seems so unreal, so far-fetched."

"We know it's true because it's given to us in the Bible, which is God's word. Think about it this way, Declan. If God is perfect and sinless in all respects, which I believe He is, He cannot lie."

"If that's true, then I agree."

"So, if the Bible is God's word and God is incapable of lying, then the entire Bible, down the very smallest word must be the truth. There's no exception. That's why we can't believe or accept certain parts and deny or disregard other parts. He didn't give us that option. To do so would mean God is lying to us, and, quite simply, He never lies. It's either all true or it's all false. There's really no in between."

"That's essentially the same thing a Christian Jewish guy I met at the airport the other day said."

"He's right. God's not trying to hide anything from us. In fact, He's put it all there in the Bible. God tells us the end from the beginning, and He's the only one who can."

"So, what if I don't believe it all? What if I don't believe God exists at all? I mean, you saw him too, Evan. You saw dad go from being this vibrant wonderful man to a sickly shell of himself and finally to a corpse in less than a year. How could a supposedly-loving God allow that to happen to someone? How could he take a father from his kids, who needed him? Why would he?"

"Declan, losing dad hurt us both. It hurt mom too, but God didn't take him from us and dad surely wouldn't have wanted his death to cause any one of us to doubt our faith or turn away from God. God isn't responsible for all the ills in the world."

"If he isn't, then who is?"

"How is everything?" the waitress interjected.

"Great, thank you," Evan replied.

"Can I get those plates out of your way?"

"Yes, please."

The waitress cleared away the plates and left. Evan picked up the conversation again, "Honestly, sin is. In a way, we are because of our sin. The world isn't a wonderful place. It's a place filled with selfishness and evil and glimpses of love. That's why Jesus said that while we have to live in the world, we shouldn't be of the world. Do you remember what dad always used to say?"

"What, you mean about running the race to win and all that?"

"Exactly. Do you remember where that came from?"

"Not really."

"Do you know what he meant?"

"That we should approach life, everything, like we want to win, to do things the best we can."

"Not exactly. He was paraphrasing the Apostle Paul's words from 1st Corinthians, Philippians, and 2nd Timothy. Paul essentially said that every believer runs his or her own race and we shouldn't run it aimlessly, or not run it at all, but run it with the goal of finishing or running it to the very end. That's what dad did. That's how he lived his life and that's what he wanted for us, which is why he harped on that expression so often. Belief in Jesus as our Savior, or, in other words salvation, is only our entry into the race, it's not the finish line. The finish line is to grow in faith. It's to put our trust in God alone in all circumstances, to trust Him to bring about good when, to us, everything looks horrible. That's what dad was talking about and that's how he lived. To the very end, his faith was strong and he never wavered. He never questioned God's existence or why he was sick, why he wouldn't get to grow old with his wife or watch his sons grow up. That's biblical faith, trusting God in the face of every challenge and giving up one's self and selfish interests to follow the Lord."

"What if I just don't believe that, Evan? What if I want to, but I just can't?"

"Honestly, this may sound harsh, but whether you or I believe is totally irrelevant to everyone but us."

"What do you mean?"

"Tell me about something that happened this week," Evan said.

"Like what?"

"Anything. Tell me something that took place this week."

"Megan came into town," Declan replied.

"I don't believe you."

"What?"

"I don't believe you."

"That's stupid. I told you this earlier. She's at my apartment now."

"I don't believe you."

"What are you talking about?"

"I'm proving my point, Declan. You told me the truth, which is that Megan is here in town. Does my disbelief change the truth in any way whatsoever?"

"No."

"Exactly. It doesn't matter whether I believe it or not, the truth is that Megan is at your apartment. It's the same with God. He gave us His Word in the Bible. His Word is the truth, and whether we believe it or not, it remains the truth. In other words, my belief or disbelief is only relevant to me. Likewise, whether you believe or not is, ultimately, only relevant to you. It's between you and God."

"I see what you're saying," Declan replied.

"I'll say this too, which is that if you're blaming your disbelief on dad's death, I can't think of a worse way to honor him. That's truly the last thing in the world he'd have wanted, Declan."

"I just can't see how a loving God would allow that to happen. I don't understand why."

"It happened when sin entered the world, it's that simple. That wasn't God's doing, it was ours or, more specifically, our ancestors. The thing is, God in his love for us gave His Son's blood, innocent blood, to pay the price for our sin, for our selfishness. That's the truth, that's the depth of His love for us."

"I'll give that some thought."

"Do, and pray about it. Ask God to show Himself to you. He will, I guarantee it. You and I grew up together. Mom and dad taught us the same things and, to this day, I remember how much you loved the Lord before dad died. Seek Him again, Declan. His word is never false and the proof is all around us in signs He told us about that we see increasingly every day now."

"You've talked about the signs before, but what are they again?"

"The wars, the earthquakes, the disease, famine, strange weather patterns, the move toward a one world government. Even gun control, the federal push into education, the Middle East, Israel, the world economic crisis that's essentially been ongoing since 2008. It's all interconnected and it all plays into the Biblical prophecies about the end times. All you need to do is know what you're looking at. There's a guy online named Scott Sykes who has a great blog and gathers prophecy related news every single day. The blog is called "Prophecy Update." You should check it out. It's easily one of the best sources out there for keeping up with what's going on in the world and understanding how what's happening relates to Biblical prophecy."

"Maybe I'll take a look."

"I'll send you the link, it's on BlogSpot. It's truly amazing to look at the news each day. Thanks in large part to our government, the Israelis were forced to deal with the Iranian situation alone and now appear to be dealing with the blowback on their own. Israel is now literally alone, increasingly despised by the world as a warmonger, surrounded on all its borders by those who want to obliterate her from the face of the earth, and being bombarded with rockets and missiles."

"I saw that on the news last night."

"Declan, Jesus gave us the signs to look for to mark the end times in Luke and Matthew, specifically in Luke 21 Matthew 24, not to even get into the Old Testament prophets. They aren't vague or open to interpretation. If you're paying attention, you can see them all around each and every day, and what's more, He described them as being like birth pains."

"Meaning?"

"That they would only get worse in frequency, duration and intensity. Just like what we're seeing in the world today."

"Hmm."

"If you know what you're looking at, you can't miss the signs all around us each and every day now."

"And you really think all of this is taking place now, before our eyes?"

"I know it is. I know it is because it's all part of God's word and His word is Truth. Again in Luke, I think its Chapter 19 and in like Verse 40 or 41 or something, toward the end of that chapter, it says that Jesus wept on Palm Sunday when he rode into Jerusalem to the praise and jubilation of the crowd. Do you know why he wept?"

"Why?"

"He wept because their eyes were blind and they didn't recognize the time of God's coming to them. They didn't recognize that their long sought Messiah was right there in their midst, precisely when God had told them He would be. They didn't see that it was Jesus of Nazareth, and it made Him weep because He knew the consequence of their blindness. I believe it's the same today. The signs leading up to Jesus' second coming are all around us and most of us don't recognize them. Like the people in Jerusalem on the first Palm Sunday, most of us, sadly, do not recognize the time of God's coming to us and our blindness, like theirs, will have profound eternal consequences, particularly for the unsaved."

"So, how does someone become saved?"

"Confess with your mouth, 'Jesus is Lord,' and believe in your heart that God raised him from the dead, and you'll be saved."

Chapter 24
December 24th

"Good morning, my love," Megan said as Declan walked back into his apartment. "You were up early this morning. Did you go workout?"

"No, I met Evan for breakfast. Here, I brought you something back."

"Thanks. How's Evan doing?"

"He's good."

"Are we still meeting them this afternoon?"

"Yeah, they're going to pick up my mom and meet up with us at 4:00."

"Excellent." Megan took a bite of the breakfast burrito Declan brought home. "This is awesome. Thanks, babe. This is exactly what I needed. I was starving. How'd you sleep by the way?

"Truthfully, I didn't. I had this awful nightmare that involved us and David Stanton. I woke up around 2:15, and couldn't go back to sleep. I sat up watching the news, until I finally crashed on the sofa around 4:30, then got up early and called Evan."

They walked into the living room and sat down on the sofa together, while Megan continued eating. The local morning news was on, but muted. "So, why'd you call to meet Evan? Is everything okay?"

"Yeah, it's fine. I think I was just freaked out a bit by whatever we saw and heard at Stanton's apartment last night. Then, couple that with the dream I had, and, I don't know, I guess I just wanted to talk. I know he's usually up early."

"That was really weird last night. It was creepy seeing him out on the balcony, just standing there naked in the cold like he didn't even feel anything. There's definitely something off about that guy."

"I agree, I've just got to find out what." Declan leaned back into the sofa and closed his eyes. "I'm exhausted," he said.

"Go back to bed. You're not planning on going in today are you?"

"I don't know. Aside from Stanton, which I'm not supposed to be doing anything on anyway, I don't have much happening that can't wait a few days. Maybe I will go back to sleep for an hour or so. What do you want to do today?"

"Honestly, I just want to relax and read a book."

"That sounds good."

"It does, but I probably need to logon and see what's going on at Homeland first."

"Well, maybe I can sleep for a bit and you can relax, and then we can hang out before we meet my mom and everyone."

"That works."

Declan got up slowly, yawning, and walked into the kitchen to pour a glass of water. When he came back into the living room, he leaned down and gave Megan a kiss. "Alright, goodnight again, darling."

"Get some sleep."

"I wi…," Declan stopped mid-sentence, suddenly focused on what he saw on the television screen. "Can you turn that up?"

"Sure. What is it?"

"I know that place," he replied as he looked at one of the local newscasters standing outside Nikki's first floor apartment. Megan hit the mute button, and the volume came back on.

"The victims were found earlier this morning in the apartment directly behind me. I've been informed that they have both been identified, but the homicide investigators have not yet released their names. My understanding is that the victims are a male and a female, both in their early-twenties, and that both appear to have been stabbed and sliced with what investigators believe was a large knife of some sort. In speaking with neighbors earlier, I've learned that the apartment belonged to a young woman in her early-twenties. It's assumed that she is one of the victims;

however, this hasn't been confirmed by investigators. More details on the double murder here at the Willows Apartments are expected to be released soon, including the victims' identities and relationship."

"Damn," Declan said. "Damn, I knew it."

"What? What is it?"

"I've been to that apartment. I followed Stanton there a few nights ago, just before you came into town. I followed him from his apartment to a strip club outside of town. He just sat in his truck. He never went inside. A girl came out of the club a little after it closed, around two in the morning, and he followed her to that apartment."

"Are you sure?"

"I'm positive. I followed him and hid to see what he did. He approached the front door, but then he seemed to get spooked or something when a car pulled up. When Stanton saw the headlights, he ran, jumped in his truck and left. I stayed for a few minutes longer and saw a younger guy get out of the car and go into the apartment. The next morning I talked to John Bleeker about Stanton."

"Do you think Stanton had something to do with the murders?"

"Absolutely. He had to have gone back. I knew it. I knew he was up to no good, but I listened to Bleeker and now two people are dead."

"Declan, you don't know this was Stanton, and you don't know that there was anything you could have done. He could have gone back right after you left, if it was him."

"It doesn't matter," Declan replied. "I know he's got something to do with this and I absolutely have to get access to his PRISM files."

"How are you going to do that?"

"Bleeker should be out this morning. You said he has access."

"So?"

"So, I'm going to have to try and hack his computer, or find his password or something."

"That's crazy, Declan. You can't hack his computer, even if you knew how."

"I don't have a choice. Maybe he or Ellen keep his login and password info somewhere. If I have to I can break into his office and look through files and drawers. I can't just sit here and do nothing, and even with this he's not going to give me anything." Declan threw his shoes back on, grabbed his coat and keys, and headed toward the door. "I'm sorry, but I've got to go."

"Wait," Megan said.

"Babe, I've got to do this. I don't know why, but I know Stanton is involved with this. You saw him last night. There's something about him that just isn't right."

"Declan, there's something I…," Megan paused. "There's something I didn't tell you about Stanton's PRISM data. There's someone else on the access list."

"Who?"

"My boss at Homeland, the Deputy Director."

Declan stood silently for a minute. "Why didn't you say anything?"

"Because, I didn't think there was any need. I could get fired, or worse, for the information I did give you."

"I understand that, and I would never want to put you in a bad spot. You know that, don't you?"

"Of course."

"So why tell me now?"

"Because you're about to run out that door and ruin your career, and probably get yourself arrested in the process."

"I don't know what else to do? I need to see those files."

"I know, and I can help." Megan picked up her DHS laptop, which was sitting on the coffee table, and began logging into the secure Homeland internal server.

"What are you doing?"

"I'm logging on as the Deputy Director."

"Megan, don't do that."

"Too late, it's already done. Logging in as the Deputy Director, in and of itself, isn't a big deal for me. He's the one who gave me his login info, and I do it all the time for one reason or another. That won't send up any flags, but pulling up Stanton's PRISM files, if I have them open for too long, may. So, you're only going to have a few minutes to look them over and see if anything jumps out at you. Any longer and, if asked, I won't be able to play it off as a mistake."

"Okay. I'll make it quick."

Megan's fingers swiftly typed in keystrokes, pulled up various security screens and finally, pulled up Homeland's internal PRISM searchable database, which housed data collected by virtually every security and law enforcement department, bureau or agency on just about every U.S. citizen. She typed in Stanton's full name, and waited a few seconds. "Hmm," she said quizzically.

"What?"

"Nothing. Hold on, let me try it again." She typed in the full name again. "What the hell?"

"What is it?"

"Nothing, there's nothing."

"What do you mean?"

"Come look," she replied and Declan looked over her shoulder at the screen."

"It says no entry found," he said.

"Exactly, there's nothing there."

"That's impossible. Try it again."

"I've already tried it three times. Here, watch." Megan typed the search terms in a fourth time with the same result.

"You and I both looked him up earlier and he was SCI," Declan said. "How could he be SCI if there was no data on him?"

"He wouldn't, he couldn't."

"So where'd the data go?"

"It had to have been deleted from the system."

Chapter 25
December 24th

David Stanton carefully loaded the last of his equipment into a third black duffel bag and placed the bag gently beside two identical bags by the front door. He then sat back down on his sofa, and pulled his laptop within reach. Within a few seconds, he'd accessed the main email account for his website, which still hadn't gone live, but was finally ready to do so. Going to his contacts, Stanton clicked on a list serve that included email addresses for all of the major local and national news stations, as well as for all of the significant online news sites and publications.

He typed the words "Breaking News" into the subject field, and began to type his message:

"Dear Media, the beginning of the end is upon us. Our fate, the just and deserved fruits of our wretched works, is finally upon us, as the Destroyer who has been biding his time amid the darkness that shrouds the horizon, has this day come. He has been loosed upon us, upon our decadent, obnoxious and perverse generation. Today, he comes to mete out the first of many deserved penalties for our repulsive sins. The Angel of Destruction has arrived and the blood of the unrighteous hypocrites shall be the first to fill our rivers and flow to our seas, beginning NOW. Witness…
                                                                    Abaddon

www.fearAbaddon.com"

Stanton looked over the email, set it for a delayed delivery later in the day, and hit send. He pulled up his website one last time from his laptop. The home page featured the four live HD video feeds from the sanctuary and they were all working perfectly. Finally, Stanton clicked on "Publish", and his site went live. Leaving the laptop open to his website, Stanton got up and checked himself out in the mirror once more, making sure his tie was straight and his shirt still crisp.

"It's time," he said quietly.

He picked up his coat and the three large black duffle bags, stepped outside into the cold clean air, and closed the door behind him.

Chapter 26
December 24th

Declan assessed his options, which were rather limited, while his system booted up. He'd called the police investigator and obtained details about the victims and what forensics estimated as the time of the murders. The female victim, Declan had been informed, was Nicole McIver. She was twenty-two, and lived at the apartment. The other victim, the male, was twenty-four year old Robert Larson, Nikki's boyfriend.

As he saw it, since two murders had actually been committed, and he had witnessed David Stanton following one of the victims to the murder scene, Declan could try taking his case to John Bleeker again. However, for reasons he couldn't entirely pinpoint, his level of trust in Bleeker was minimal.

Another option was to contact the federal prosecutor's office to try and obtain a search warrant for Stanton's apartment based upon his presence at the scene prior to the murder. That would take a showing of probable cause, which Declan thought he had; however, the process required the warrant be issued by a federal judge and, given that it was Christmas Eve, that could take time.

Declan's final option was to simply forego a search warrant and access Stanton's apartment on his own. He could come up with an excuse, such as investigating a complaint in the area, to knock on the door and talk with Stanton, and if he saw anything suspicious inside the apartment, could then enter under the auspices of probable cause.

As he pondered which course to take, he heard Kevin Cameron say, "What the hell are you doing here today? I thought you weren't coming in so you could spend the holiday with Megan."

"Hey, Kev. I uh…something came up."

"What?"

"Have you seen anything about that double homicide over at the Willows Apartments?"

"No, what happened?"

"These two kids, both in their early-twenties were knifed up. The police forensics guys think it happened a couple days ago. The thing is, I tailed my SCI guy, David Stanton, to that very apartment the night of the 21st. He followed the girl from one of the strip clubs to her apartment. I watched him approach the front door after she'd gone inside, but he got spooked and bugged out when a car pulled up. It turns out the car belonged to the girl's boyfriend and they were both found dead earlier this morning, each with their throats sliced wide open. They were found on her bed, completely naked, on top of one another in a sexual position."

"That's really messed up."

"That's not everything. They'd both had their eyes removed from their faces, and each had 'The Destroyer' written in blood, seemingly their own, across their foreheads. It was written in Greek on the guy and in Hebrew on the girl."

"What?"

"That's what I said at first too."

"That's seriously deranged."

"No kidding," Declan agreed. "And, I'm positive David Stanton is the one who did it."

"Because you followed him there a night or two prior?"

"Yep."

"Do you have anything else?"

"Not yet, but I know he had something to do with it. I saw him again last night, on the balcony of his apartment, standing stark naked in the cold, and there was something very off putting about him. It was like being in the presence of evil."

"Have you talked to Bleeker yet?"

"I talked to him the morning after I followed Stanton

to the apartment. I wanted to see what he could do about getting Stanton's PRISM files, since they were classified SCI, and asked about putting Stanton under a surveillance detail."

"What did he say?"

"He said no to a surveillance detail, and that he'd check with a classmate at Homeland to see what he could find out on the PRISM thing. The thing is…," Declan stopped unsure if he wanted to complete his sentence.

"The thing is what?"

"The thing is, I know for a fact that Bleeker himself is on the SCI authorized list.

"How exactly do you know that?"

"That's not important."

"Actually, it is. How'd you find out who's on the access list?"

"Kevin, I'm not going to go into how I know. I just know. What's important is that Bleeker played it as though he'd never heard of Stanton before I mentioned him. When I talked to him again the next day, he told me that he hadn't been able to get any information and, basically, to back off and leave it alone until he did."

"Which you did?"

"Essentially, but now two people are dead and I know Stanton had at least something to do with it. Leaving it alone doesn't seem like an option anymore, with or without Bleeker's go ahead."

"Declan, I'm going to give you a piece of advice that you'd be wise to take," Kevin said very seriously.

"Okay."

"I like you. You know I worked for your dad when I started out. He taught me a lot and I respect him more than almost anyone else I've ever known. You're a good kid, a good agent, and you've got the makings for a stellar career with the Bureau. My advice is for you to listen to Bleeker on this one and leave it alone until he says otherwise."

"But why? Two people are dead, Kevin. If he'd

allowed me to put Stanton under surveillance when I first requested it, they might still be alive. If he'd told me he had SCI access and obtained the files for me, they might be alive. Why sit back and do nothing just because Bleeker says so?"

"Because the Bureau is, among other things, political. There are things going on, decisions being made, at levels we don't need or necessarily want to know about."

"Are you saying there's something political about Stanton being SCI?"

"I actually have no idea. What I'm saying, is that Bleeker isn't your run-of-the-mill Bureau agent. He's extremely well connected and he's on the rise, and you don't want to cross him, Declan. If Bleeker says leave it alone, my advice is to go back home to Megan, enjoy the Christmas holiday, and do just that."

"I really can't believe you're telling me this. You're saying to bury my head in the sand and ignore a double homicide just because my elitist Ivy League boss wants to be Director someday."

"I'm saying to follow orders, Declan. I know that's not what you want to hear, but it's just that simple sometimes. If you don't want to see your career go up in smoke, or worse, just follow orders."

Chapter 27
December 24th

David Stanton pulled into the church parking lot shortly after one in the afternoon. He parked his black SUV well away from the main building, next to the church school, where he had a perfect vantage point of the church and, eventually, the rush of congregants who would be arriving for service.

He sat back in his seat and closed his eyes. It had been over thirty hours since he'd last slept; however, to Stanton's surprise, he wasn't tired. His time for requiring sleep to function had passed. Soon, he knew he'd pass from the flawed, weak mind and body he'd been confined in and hated for so many years, to a rejuvenated perfect body that nobody could ever harm or abuse. His memories would be wiped clean and his new life would begin, the second chance he'd asked for so many times.

Stanton's thoughts focused on the countless digital simulations he'd run. He visualized himself stepping from the SUV at exactly 5:10 p.m., and slowly and casually walking around to the back. As the service began at 5:00, the traffic in the parking lot would have died down, but for the stragglers. He saw himself opening the back of the SUV and gently arming the explosive device inside one of the black duffel bags, setting the timer for 5:26 p.m. Once the explosive, which should blow both the SUV and a large hole in the left side of the school, was armed and set, he'd zip up the duffel bag and close up the back of the SUV again.

Stanton watched himself checking his watch, which read 5:12:00. At that point, he picked up the other two, larger bags, and walked slowly toward the back entrance of the church, where none of the congregation would be entering, and waited out of sight, listening to the opening hymns. His email would be sent to the various news organizations at 5:15, then again at 5:16, then again at 5:17.

His watch finally read 5:17:01, and he left the back of

the church, jogging quickly to the east entrance, which was clear. He used his janitor's keys and locked the east doors, then quickly looped the chain through the two door handles and locked it tight. Stanton moved swiftly around to the west entrance and repeated this process, locking the west entrance tight. Finally, he made his way to the front entrance, the main entrance, arriving at 5:20:02, and locked those doors with his keys. Again, he looped the chain through the door handles and locked it up tight. All entrances, but the back, were secure.

Stanton watched himself arrive back at the rear entrance at 5:22 p.m., right on schedule. He quickly and quietly opened the first bag, he put his tactical ammunition vest on over his suit coat, and strapped the loaded up ammunition belt around his waist. He removed the first AR-15 from the bag, inserted a 60 round clip and slung the rifle onto his back. After taking the second AR-15 from the second bag, Stanton inserted a 100 round drum magazine, and checked to make sure the weapon was ready to go.

Stanton's watch read 5:24:22. He walked calmly through the back door, to the rear sanctuary entrance, where he stood silently, just outside the sanctuary. Pastor Kellen's Christmas sermon had begun, his words about the magnitude of Jesus' birth reaching Stanton's ears.

"Lord Abaddon," he whispered, "I am yours and, together, we shall not know failure."

His watch read 5:25:50…, 5:25:51…, 5:25:52…, 5:25:53…, 5:25:54…, 5:25:55. Stanton closed his eyes and tightly gripped the weapon in his hand, squeezing the cold metal as if he were clinging to the edge of a tall building he was trying desperately not to fall from. Then, suddenly, the viciously loud boom from the explosive shattered the silence of the sanctuary. David Stanton watched himself spring from the rear hall into the sanctuary behind the lectern. His left index finger squeezed the trigger over and over, directing his aim and the rifle's deathly projectiles at anyone and everyone moving in his sightline. Screams mixed with the "rat tat, rat tat, rat tat" of the rifle to fill the sanctuary. He towered ominously over every person he came into contact with, and their bodies quickly fell on all sides of him, one after another after another in what seemed a never ending sea of death.

Stanton opened his eyes and sat up slightly in the driver's seat, rolling his head in a gentle circular clockwise motion. He looked down at his watch, which read 2:02:22.

Chapter 28
December 24th

Declan stood silently in front of the mirror in his bathroom buttoning the last few buttons of his shirt, while trying to untie the meaning of Kevin Cameron's "advice". Of all the agents he worked with, Kevin was the one Declan had always been certain had his back. When he'd first arrived at the field office, Kevin had taken Declan under his wing and acted as his de facto mentor. Kevin had consistently played it straight with Declan and had taught him the ins and outs of being a good FBI agent.

In truth, Kevin was the last person Declan expected to advise, or better yet threaten, him to back off something that was clearly not on the up and up. What Kevin had told him earlier contradicted everything he'd taught Declan during his first year with the Bureau. It simply made no sense, and Declan's sense of frustration and disappointment with the Bureau, and Kevin in particular, had defeated his desire to fight back and get to the truth.

He thought about the numerous conversations he'd had with Evan and his mom about the corruption of the federal government and the indefatigable push toward the elimination of personal freedoms and, ultimately, a global totalitarian state. While not naïve, Declan generally had a high degree of skepticism for such conspiratorial notions, but he slowly, reluctantly, began to look at John Bleeker's actions and Kevin's advice through such a prism as a last ditch effort to find some sense in the seemingly unexplainable situation.

Why would David Stanton's data files be classified as SCI when he didn't show up with any red flags in any other systems? Why would Bleeker pretend he had no access when, in fact, he did, and why push Declan to back off until he could supposedly obtain information he already had?

"Hey, are you ready almost ready to go?"

"Yep," Declan replied, as he finished buttoning his

shirt.

"You've been a bit distant since you got back," Megan said. "Is everything okay?"

"It's fine. I'm just...I'm just not sure what to do next."

"Give it a little time, babe. It'll come to you."

"I suppose."

"Trust me, you'll figure it out. C'mon, let's get going."

Chapter 29
December 24th

As Declan and Megan pulled up, they saw his mom. Declan drove up next to his mom, so Megan could get out of the car and walk with her. "Here, babe, why don't you go in with mom and I'll be back soon."

"Aren't you coming in?"

"In a bit. We're not too far from Stanton's apartment and I need to go over there and check it out. I'll be back in twenty or thirty minutes, tops. Just tell everyone I had something to do for work and I'll be right back. I'm sorry to have to do this today, but I have to go over there and at least see what, if anything, is going on."

"I understand." Megan leaned over toward Declan and kissed him. "I love you."

"I love you," he replied.

"Get going and hurry back."

"Will do." Declan looked at his watch, and saw that the time was 4:13. "I'll be back by quarter to five, at the latest."

———————

Declan arrived outside David Stanton's apartment building at 4:32, and parked 200 feet or so down the street, where he had a clear view of the building and parking lot. He wasn't certain why he'd had to go back to Stanton's apartment, or what exactly he planned to do. Something, intuition or whatever you want to call it, told him that was where he needed to be.

He scanned the parking lot and saw that Stanton's SUV was missing. Declan desperately wanted to do something, to just get out and look around the building, maybe approach the front door and listen for any movement inside or see if he could pick up any strange odors emanating from within, but Kevin Cameron's warning hung in the back of his mind like a wet towel. He sat in the car, keeping his eyes peeled for any movement, of which there was none.

Declan looked at his watch again at 4:48, and sat back in his seat, unsure what, if anything, to do. Finally, he made sure his sidearm was loaded, grabbed a small Maglite out of the glove compartment, and decided to get out of the car and take a quick look around. He stepped out into the cold, bundled his coat collar tight around his neck, and briskly walked across the street toward the apartment building.

There were a few cars in the parking lot, all of which he'd seen previously and run the plates on, so he knew they belonged to some of the building's other residents. The bitter cold surrounded Declan and filled his senses as he walked across the parking lot and approached the building, still uncertain about his objective. He looked up to the second floor, scanning the two windows on the east side of Stanton's apartment, both of which appeared to be open.

A small sidewalk went from the parking lot up to and around the building, leading to each of the entrances to the first floor apartments and the stairwells which climbed up to the second floor apartments. Declan walked slowly along the sidewalk, almost completing the circle, until he finally came to the stairwell which led up to Stanton's apartment. As he stood there for a second, he felt his phone vibrating in his pocket, and took it out. It was Megan. "Hi babe," he answered.

"Is everything okay?"

"Yeah, it's fine. I'm on my way back. Is everyone there?"

"Yep, we're all here. I just wanted to make sure you were alright."

"I'm fine. Sorry, I'm on my way back. Just tell everyone I'll be back in ten minutes or so."

"Was anything going on at the apartment?"

"No, nothing."

"You didn't see Stanton?"

"No, it doesn't look like he's home."

"Then get yourself back here. Everyone wants to see you."

"Sorry, I'm on my way. I'll be back soon."

"Okay," Megan responded, and hung up.

Declan stood looking at the stairwell, then, on an impulse, swiftly headed up the steps to the second floor of the building, where he took a quick left and found himself standing five feet from David Stanton's front door.

Chapter 30
December 24th

David Stanton looked down at his watch, which read 4:53:04. From his parked SUV, he sat watching all the people, dressed up in their Christmas finery making their way across the church parking lot into the sanctuary. Many of them he recognized from his years working as the church janitor, although he was quite certain that not one of them knew him. They all filed in, families, elderly couples, young newlyweds, the inevitable boyfriend trying to make a good impression. To Stanton they just looked like blank faces, nameless, hopeless lemmings, many of whom, he was certain, didn't even believe in the God they were hurrying over themselves to "worship".

The ludicrousness of it all made him sick. They had no idea what true worship consisted of, no acquaintance with genuine sacrifice and obedience. How could people who only bothered to give their God a thought once or twice a year know anything at all about worship? Were it not so vulgar and sickening to him, it would have been laughable. In their designer dresses and suits, in their fashionable coats and shoes, they filed in to do their duty, to see and be seen on one of the two days each year that going to church actually mattered to most of them. They were, for the most part, more concerned with how they looked, and how cute their children looked, than with the Savior whose birth they'd supposedly come to celebrate and worship.

In truth, they had sealed their own fate long ago. It was their total disregard and callousness, their complete absence of genuine heartfelt worship and awe of the God they all supposedly loved and sought, on the outside at least, to emulate, which had brought about their imminent destruction. Abaddon was not the cause of their destruction, he was merely the instrument being employed to carry out a sentence they'd brought upon themselves. The first cleansing in what would ultimately rid the world of hypocrisy and naked self-indulgence.

Declan knocked lightly on David Stanton's front door twice, but, as he'd anticipated, he couldn't hear any movement or sounds of life inside. He placed his hand gently on the doorknob and gave it a slow careful turn. To Declan's surprise, the knob turned smoothly and the door to Stanton's private abode stood opened before him.

Declan instinctively drew his sidearm and slowly stepped across the threshold, into the dark apartment. He was at once struck by the intense cold within, and by a subtle, yet discernable, odor of what could only be described as staleness. Despite all of the shades being drawn and crudely covered with hung dark sheets or blankets, Declan sensed that the various windows were all open.

The entire place was almost as dark as a moonless night, illuminated solely by two dim, yet contrasting, sources of light: the yellowish light from three burning candles on what looked like a bookshelf against the opposite wall and a small amount of white light emanating from a laptop computer sitting on the floor.

As Declan's eyes slowly adjusted to the dim interior, the first thing that caught his visual attention was writing all over the walls. Each wall featured a delicate, painstakingly-handwritten, black calligraphic script and words and phrases began popping out of the mass of print into Declan's consciousness:

They are corrupt, and their ways are vile; there is no one who does good.

Why do you boast of evil, you mighty man? Why do you boast all day long, you who are a disgrace in the eyes of God?

Even on his bed he plots evil, he commits himself to a sinful course and does not reject what is wrong.

The fifth angel sounded his trumpet, and I saw a star

*that had fallen from the sky to earth. The star was given the
key to the shaft of the Abyss. When he opened the Abyss,
smoke rose from it like the smoke from a gigantic furnace.
The sun and sky were darkened by the smoke from the Abyss.*

The words poured into Declan's eyes and senses from
all sides of the room and, despite the eerie awe that had
overcome him, began to realize they were all, each and every
one, passages from the Bible.

"What the…," he whispered to himself, watching his
breath growing deeper and more frequent in the cold air
before him.

As his eyes spun around the room, trying to take in
the fullness and total insanity surrounding him, Declan
caught sight of something hanging from the ceiling in the
center of the room. It was small and difficult to make out in
the sparse light. Declan moved slowly toward it, and caught
sight of another similar object hanging a few feet away. As
he got closer, he could see that it was a ball, about the size of
a decent sized marble, pierced with what appeared to be a
fishing hook, and hanging from the ceiling with some sort of
thin reddish cord or rope.

Something inside him told Declan to look up. As his
eyes followed the cord up to the ceiling, he was met with a
life size Vitruvian Man, again carefully and perfectly drawn
on the white apartment ceiling, almost like a Michelangelo
fresco in the Sistine Chapel.

Declan held his sidearm in his left hand, still ready,
pulled the small flashlight from his pocket with his right
hand, and turned it on. He scanned the Vitruvian Man with
the light beam, taking in the detail and the genuine artwork
involved. It was stunning, even beautiful in a strange way. It
appeared to be a charcoal drawing, perfect in every respect.

A total of four thin reddish cords hung down from the
Vitruvian Man, one from each hand and one from each foot.
Declan shined the beam of light on the cord beginning in the
left hand and slowly followed it down three feet or so until
the light reached the hook and the ball. Declan examined the

ball closely in the light.

"Oh my God," he exclaimed.

Declan's hand began to tremble with a surge of fearful, yet excited, energy. He quickly shined the jittery light on the ends of the other cords and saw that each held a human eyeball.

"I've got you. I've got you, dammit."

In a nervous rush, he reached into his coat pocket, fumbling and dropping the flashlight on the carpeted floor, as he tried to take out his cell phone.

"I've got to call Bleeker or Kevin. I've got this bastard. I've got him. I knew I was right about this guy."

Declan took out his phone, and quickly holstered his weapon so he could dial Kevin Cameron's number. He rushed to type in the seven digits. As he waited for the first ring, Declan walked a few steps toward where his flashlight had fallen, next to the laptop on the floor. The phone rang once, then twice, as he knelt down to pick up his flashlight. As the phone rang a third time, Declan shuttered, again dropping the flashlight, when he saw Megan and his mom walking to their seats on David Stanton's laptop.

"Cameron here."

Declan stood silently, watching the video feed of Megan and his mom, along with hundreds of others in the congregation, take their seats for the Christmas Eve service.

"Declan?"

He hung up the phone and, in a panicked dash, bolted from the darkness of the apartment back out into the cold twilight of the late afternoon.

Chapter 31
December 24th

As he'd done countless times in his mind, David Stanton stepped out of his parked SUV at precisely 5:10, clad in his crisp black suit. A few late arriving congregants were still making their way inside the church, but, for the most part, the parking lot was empty. Stanton took a calm look around, taking the crisp night air deeply into his lungs.

Finally standing at the doorstep of history filled him with exhilaration and a thorough sense of accomplishment and pride. He'd been focused and taken what was once merely an idea, a daydream of sorts, and through imagination, work and perseverance, crafted it into reality. At that moment, nearly alone in the church parking lot, David Stanton was filled to the brim with a feeling that was entirely foreign to him up to that point in his life: pride.

He looked down at his watch and saw that it read 5:11:05, and casually walked to the back of his SUV.

Declan was awash with panic as he weaved left and right, from one lane to the other, hurriedly dodging traffic with one hand on the steering wheel and the other repeatedly dialing Megan and Evan's cell phones while listening to the police scanner in his car.

"C'mon, answer the stupid phone Megan. C'mon and pick up."

Despite his pleas, Megan's phone went to voicemail again. "Megan, I'm on my way back and I'm not sure what's going on. I think Stanton is at the church, so if you get this get mom, Evan and everyone outside right away. I'll be there in a few minutes."

He hung up and tried Evan's phone again, but it went straight to voicemail, so he didn't waste time leaving a message. The clock on Declan's digital dashboard display read 5:18. Just a few minutes away, he thought. Just five more minutes.

"Christmas Eve service is always a bittersweet experience for me," the pastor began. Megan nervously scanned the packed sanctuary for Declan. Not seeing him, she looked again at her watch and grew moderately annoyed at how late he was. The pastor continued, "I say that because, while it brings me great joy to see so many faces, familiar and unfamiliar, here tonight, on this Christmas Eve, to celebrate the birth of our glorious Savior, it also saddens me that we don't get such a large turn out every Sunday, every day for that matter."

"What is it about the Christmas season that makes it so special? People are generally a little kinder, a little more thoughtful, a little more joyful. In short, we're a little less selfish this time of year and a little more focused on Christ. This is the part of Christmas that gives me great joy. However, that joy is tempered with a touch of sadness, because it seems to take this holiday to bring out our more selfless qualities when, in truth, as Christians, as the undeserving recipients of God's grace through the blood of His son, Jesus, whose very name means 'He Saves', shouldn't every day be Christmas? Not in the sense of giving gifts and all that stuff, which is fine, but in the sense of applying the selflessness of Christmas to our daily lives and interactions with those around us. What if, just what if, we treated every day like we treat today and tomorrow? What if we truly loved our neighbors as we love ourselves?"

At 5:20, and right on schedule, Stanton finished locking the main entrance to the church from the outside, leaving no unlocked exit, other than the rarely used back door, for anyone inside the church. As he turned, he saw a young man and woman, likely in their early-twenties, walking up the sidewalk to the front door.

"Hurry," the girl said. "We're really late."

"Okay, okay."

Stanton looked down at his watch, which read 5:20:45.

"Merry Christmas," the girl said as she approached him.

"I'm sorry, but you're too late. We're not letting anyone else in tonight."

"Really? But my family is inside. Can't you just let us in?"

"I'm sorry. I suggest you try the next service."

"This is stupid. C'mon babe, let's just try one of the side doors," the young guy said to his girlfriend. "This guy's just a janitor or something."

"Fine, let's go," she replied.

"Those are locked too," Stanton offered, but the pair ignored him and headed for one of the other locked entrances. David Stanton looked at his watch again, which read 5:21:30, and began to get agitated.

"Here, wait, I'll open this door for you," he called out.

The pair quickly turned around and made their way back through the cold toward the front entrance as Stanton placed his black bags on the concrete and reached inside his coat.

"That's what I thought," the guy snorted.

"Let me just get the keys out," he said as they came close.

"Thank you," the girl said. "I really appreciate it."

"What's with the chain on the doors?"

With his hunting knife drawn, Stanton turned swiftly and plunged the knife deep into the guy's chest, dropping him instantly onto the frigid concrete path. The girl squeaked as Stanton grabbed her by the throat with both hands, stifling her scream in its infancy, and took her violently down to the ground. He kept one hand wrapped tightly around her throat and grabbed her hair with the other and in three quick successions, slammed her head against the pavement until she was no longer conscious.

David Stanton stood back up, looked over the ground at the dead and dying, and looked again at his watch: 5:22:20. Having no time to move or hide his victims, Stanton hurriedly picked up his black bags and ran around the building toward the back entrance.

Chapter 32
December 24th

Declan raced into the parking lot just in time to see Stanton's silhouette rushing away from the front of the church. He slammed the car to a stop, jumped out and sprinted to the front door, where he saw the couple left for dead on the walkway. The girl was still breathing, but only barely, while the guy appeared dead.

He quickly scanned the locked entrance and, making a split-second decision, drew his weapon and ran as fast as he could around the church in the direction he'd seen Stanton go seconds earlier. As Declan neared the turn toward the back entrance of the church, he slowed down and ducked into a dark niche to catch his breath and further assess the situation.

Peering through the growing darkness, he made out Stanton's crouching silhouette about twenty-five feet ahead, near the back door to the church. Stanton appeared to be facing away from Declan, reaching into one of the two large black duffle bags. Declan crept slowly and quietly along the cold stone wall, inching closer to Stanton in the darkness with his weapon ready.

Stanton attached and fastened the chest harness, on which his mobile GoPro camera was mounted, over the tactical vest and turned on the video function. Then Stanton withdrew the first AR-15 from the black bag and smoothly inserted the sixty-round clip into the rifle. He slung it over his left shoulder and looked again at his watch, which read 5:24:01. Reaching into the bag again, he removed the second AR-15, along with the one hundred-round drum magazine and quickly loaded the weapon.

"My time is now," he said aloud into the chilling night air. "The great work of Abaddon shall begin now. Give me strength and focus, great Destroyer, as I fulfill the task I've been charged to undertake."

Stanton looked down at his watch once more: 5:25:03. "I'm ready."

Declan watched Stanton intently as he crept against the wall toward him, closing within fifteen feet or so when he heard Stanton say, "I'm ready," and saw him move to open the back door, with the loaded AR-15 in his left hand. Declan thought of Megan and his family sitting inside the church and, acting on a reckless impulse, jumped forward from the wall with his weapon drawn and aimed directly at David Stanton and yelled, "Don't move, Stanton."

David Stanton shuddered at the unexpected sound of Declan's voice breaking through the still night air and removed his right hand from the door as he turned in Declan's direction.

"I said don't move," Declan yelled again. "Put the rifle on the ground slowly and step back from the door."

Stanton stood staring through the darkness at Declan, barely able to make out his face, but he could see Declan's sidearm pointed at him as Declan moved slowly closer.

"I can't do that. This is my destiny. It's my way back. You're not going to take this from me. I won't let you."

"Put your weapon down, Stanton!"

Suddenly, an explosion jolted the still tension surrounding them, causing Declan to flinch. Stanton moved to raise the AR-15 and Declan instinctively squeezed one round from his 9mm. Two shots rang almost simultaneously through the night, and less than a second later, Declan felt an excruciating searing heat rip though his upper torso, just below his left shoulder, and throw him to the ground with a degree of force and violence he had never before experienced. His weapon fell a few feet away as his body hit the cold pavement with a jolting thud.

Each of Declan's senses were overloaded, blurring everything as he lay on the ground with heavily-labored breathes, feeling the unbearable pain pulsating throughout his body. Declan's thoughts raced uncontrollably toward his own death, then to Megan and his family. David Stanton's image flashed through his mind and he rolled over to try and see the back door, to see if he'd hit Stanton, or if he'd failed everyone inside. Straining to focus, for just a second, immediately before everything went black, Declan clearly saw David Stanton's unmoving body lying about ten feet away, and his lifeless open eyes staring back at him through the night.

Chapter 33
December 24th

"He's dead," said Special Agent Costello as he stood over David Stanton's body.

John Bleeker walked over to the body and peered down at Stanton's still bleeding corpse. He called over to Kevin Cameron, "Cameron, what about Parker?"

Kevin had knelt down close to Declan and was able to make out very faint breathes coming from him. "Declan's still alive, but not by much. We need to get him help, fast."

"Time is short, Cameron. In a few minutes this place is going to be crawling with uniforms and first responders. We don't do anything until I get everything straight," Bleeker said taking out his secure phone.

"Man, the kid is a good shot," Costello said. "Look at that, he hit Stanton right in the jugular. The bullet went clear through. The guy never had a chance."

"Shhh," Bleeker ordered. "It's Juliet Bravo...He's dead....Yes, it's confirmed...an explosion, no casualties...Agreed, I believe it's still useful, particularly with Eve 2 proceeding...Will do."

Bleeker hung up and put his secure phone back into his coat pocket.

Costello asked, "What's the plan, sir?"

Sirens came roaring closer from all sides of the church and people could be heard outside the front of the church, most trying to figure out what was going on. "Eve 2 is already underway, and this one will serve its purpose. Costello, you and I will make certain we maintain possession of Stanton's body and all the evidence back here. Call in backup agents and get our forensics people out here ASAP. This is a federal crime scene and I don't want any of the locals or first responders tracking through."

"Gotcha."

Kevin Cameron looked down at Declan again, and asked Bleeker, "What about Declan?"

"Is he still alive?"

"Yes."

Voices and footsteps could be heard moving quickly toward the back of the building. "We're seconds away from being swamped with uniforms. Get your credentials out. Get Parker an ambulance. It's too late to deal with it any other way. We'll get him to the hospital and, if he survives, I'll address his situation. For now, nothing to the locals or to the press, other than that he's FBI and he's down. No name, no other information of any kind, period. That goes for Stanton too. No names yet. Understood?"

"Loud and clear."

"Here they come," Bleeker said. "We're FBI, don't shoot," he called out in a booming voice to the approaching uniformed police officers.

"Hands up, all of you!"

"Okay, okay. Just keep it calm. I'm Special Agent in Charge, John Bleeker. I have my badge and credentials out for you, and we have an agent down who needs an ambulance right away."

Chaos enveloped the church. First responders and shaken, but uninjured, churchgoers were everywhere, along with the press, which had arrived in droves after they'd made the connection between the explosion and the emails from Stanton they'd been bombarded with earlier.

Stanton's name was out in the press, although details were vague, and Megan was frantic after listening to the various voicemails Declan had left for her on his way back from Stanton's apartment building. Evan and Mrs. Parker tried to calm Megan, although they were both just as worried. They finally left the church around 7:30 and went to Declan's mom's house. Megan had spent over an hour checking her sources at Homeland for any information, when her cell phone rang.

"Hello."

"Megan Neary?"

"Yes, who is this?"

"I work with Declan."

"Is he okay? Do you know where he is?"

"He's at St. Paul's."

"Is he okay? The news is saying an officer or an agent was down. Is it Declan?"

"He's at St. Paul's, Room 445. Get there now and don't leave him alone," the voice said, then hung up.

"Hello. Are you still there? Hello?"

Chapter 34
December 26th

After waiting by his bedside for nearly thirty-six hours, Megan finally saw Declan's eyes open slightly, taking in just a glimpse of the brightly-lit hospital room, then closing again quickly. She squeezed his hand excitedly and, for the first time, he responded with a light squeeze of his own.

"Megan," he whispered.

"I'm right here, babe. I'm right here."

Declan tried to open his eyes once again, but the light in the room was too much of a shock for him and he quickly closed them again. Megan got up and turned off the main room lights while turning on only the light in the bathroom, making the room substantially darker.

"Here babe, maybe that will help," she said softly.

Declan's eyes opened a third time, ever so slightly, but they were finally able to stay open and gradually take in Megan and the hospital room. He asked, "Where am I?"

"You're at St. Paul's. They brought you here on Christmas Eve."

"What day is it?"

"It's the twenty-sixth, the day after Christmas."

"I've been out for two days?"

"Almost. You were shot just below the collarbone, in your shoulder area. You hit your head really hard on the pavement when you went down. The doctors say you're going to be just fine though, with some rest. They got the bullet out."

"What about Stanton?"

"He's dead. He was shot outside the church."

"So he didn't get anyone inside?"

"Nope. You guys apparently got him outside, before he could do any real damage."

"What do you mean by you guys?"

"The FBI, you and the other agents on the scene."

"There were no other agents. It was just me. I shot Stanton and he shot me, just after the explosion."

"That's not what the news reports are saying, Declan. They're saying the FBI had him under investigation and was able to take him out before he could complete it. Bleeker has been interviewed numerous times already. They were able to stop Stanton, but there was another mass shooting down in Alabama on Christmas Eve. He says the FBI is investigating to determine whether there is a connection."

Declan was exhausted and somewhat groggy from the pain medication he'd been put on, but he wrestled to try and sit somewhat upright.

"I don't think you should be sitting up yet," Megan said.

"Will you help put a couple of those pillows under me?"

"Of course."

Once he was better positioned, Declan said, "This doesn't make any sense. Bleeker wasn't there, Megan. There was nobody but me and Stanton. Stanton wasn't even under investigation by anyone but me, and Bleeker called me off of him."

"I know. It sounds to me like he's trying to take the credit to cover himself or something. The whole thing is weird. Even the way I found out about you being here."

"What do you mean?"

"I got a call on my cell from someone who knew my name that night, after everything went down at the church. I was with your mom and Evan and we were all worried because we hadn't heard anything from you. The caller said he worked with you and said you were here and to get down here right away and not to leave you alone."

"Did he say who he was?"

"Nope, he told me to get down here and then hung up."

"Has anyone been in to see me?"

"No, just the doctors and nurses. I've been in touch

with your mom and Evan, but I told them not to come down yet. Something just feels off. Bleeker's been all over the news, but there hasn't been any mention of your name on the news at all. They've just reported that an agent was shot and that he's in critical condition, but no name and no hospital location. There's not even a name on your room outside. If I hadn't gotten that phone call, I wouldn't have had any idea where you were or what had happened to you."

"You're right, something isn't right. You said there was a shooting in Alabama on Christmas Eve?"

"Yes, in Birmingham. The guy down there targeted a Christmas concert. The news is reporting that he shot over 300 people and killed at least 100 or something, at least as of an hour or so ago. The story keeps changing, but Homeland's initial records show 48 confirmed fatalities."

"I wonder if he was connected to Stanton somehow."

"I don't know, but between the Birmingham shooting and Stanton's attempt, it was enough to get a confiscation bill passed through the House and the Senate last night."

"What?"

"Congress passed gun confiscation legislation last night, the Firearms Protection Act, which was signed by the president shortly before midnight. They called a special session on Christmas Day, and rushed it through the House and Senate. It gives all registered and non-registered gun owners ten days to turn in their guns or face criminal prosecution."

"Holy crap, I don't believe it. How'd it pass so quickly?"

"Someone obviously already had a bill drafted and they pushed it through a special session that wasn't fully attended, kind of like when the Federal Reserve law was passed back in 1913."

There was a light knock on the room door, and one of Declan's doctors entered slowly. "Good morning. It looks like our patient is finally awake."

"Hello doctor," Megan replied. "Declan, this is Dr.

Kincaid. He performed your surgery and removed the bullet."

"Hi, doctor."

"Good to see you're awake, but I'm not sure I like you sitting up yet. How do you feel?"

"Tired and a bit groggy."

"That's the pain meds and the lingering impact of the concussion. How's your pain level?"

"Sore all over, like a truck hit me, but otherwise okay, I think."

"Well, I'll keep you at current levels for the time being. You need to make sure to rest and keep your fluid intake up."

"Will do. I'm getting kind of tired again already."

"That's normal," the doctor replied. "Frankly, you're lucky to be alive. The bullet itself wasn't the worst. The impact caused you to hit the ground pretty hard, causing head trauma and a concussion. I'm still concerned about the potential for head related issues, so we're going to be monitoring that for the next few days, but, otherwise, you should be back to about 80% in a couple weeks. It certainly helps that we were able to get that 9mm slug out of you without any additional complications. I'll send one of the nurses in shortly to get your IV changed out and administer your pain meds. I think Nurse Foster is still on duty for another thirty or forty minutes."

"Wait," Declan said. "Did you say it was a 9mm slug?"

"Yep."

"Are you positive about that?"

"Of course. Why do you ask?

Declan looked puzzled and was silent for a few seconds, then replied, "No reason."

"Alright, well then, I'll send Nurse Foster, or whoever's out there, in shortly," Dr. Kincaid replied and left the room.

Megan could see that something wasn't right in

Declan's expression. "What is it?"

"Megan, Stanton had one of his AR-15's in his hand, and it wasn't a 9mm AR. That's what he raised at me right after the explosion, just before I fired my round."

"So…"

"So, if they took out a 9mm slug, it means Stanton didn't shoot me. Someone else did."

Chapter 35
December 26th

Declan woke up from a heavy sleep in the early afternoon. He rubbed his eyes to clear out the sleep and looked groggily over to the fold-out sofa expecting to see Megan, but instead found John Bleeker sitting patiently and quietly across from him.

"Sleep well?"

Taken off guard, Declan merely undertook the painful process of sitting upright.

"Getting plenty of rest is the key to a quick and complete recovery," Bleeker said. "Did your doctor tell you that?"

"A few times."

"How are you feeling?"

"I've been better."

"That's a bit of an understatement. You still don't look at all well, Parker, and that's quite a change for you."

"Thanks, I appreciate your concern."

Bleeker sat silently, looking Declan over then scanning the generally taupe hospital room. "Your girlfriend went down to the cafeteria with Cameron to grab a bite to eat. She looked famished and I thought it would be a good time for her to get out of here for a bit."

"She's been here twenty-four seven since Christmas Eve," Declan replied uneasily, as he tried to gauge Bleeker's purpose in bringing up Megan.

"She's quite dedicated. Of course, in light of the media lockdown I'm still curious as to how she found out you were here."

"I didn't know it was a secret."

"That's one of the funny things about secrets, Parker; we don't always realize we've encountered one until it's too late."

"So my being here was a secret?"

"Not a crucial one."

"I see. So what about me being shot by someone other than David Stanton on Christmas Eve, is that a crucial one?"

"I always liked that you get right down to the point, Parker. It can be disarming to some, but I quite like it. It's clear that the Bureau is in your blood. In response to your rather pointed question, the answer, very simply, is it depends."

"On what?"

"On you of course," Bleeker replied with a broad smile. "See, you stumbled upon a secret or two, extremely crucial secrets to highly-significant people. You failed to heed advice, follow directives, or otherwise be dissuaded, and you put yourself in the dead center, the cross hairs if you will, of those secrets. As we all know from our high school science classes, every action has an equal and opposite reaction. In other words, consequences."

"And my being in this hospital bed is the consequence of getting involved in your secrets?"

"No, you being in here is a consequence of getting in the midst of something you had no business getting into. As is often the case when we make decisions and undertake actions, there are generally numerous consequences, some foreseen and some unforeseen, which tend to vary in degree and intensity. Some consequences are relatively trivial and limited to the individual who acted, while other consequences are more broad, possibly affecting the individual's family and loved ones; more permanent; more painful. The key is to try and limit the consequences to the less painful and less permanent type."

"How does one do that?"

"In the same manner he initiated the consequence in the first place, by making a decision and taking action. Only, when the goal is to limit the adverse consequences of a poor decision, he needs to decide and act wisely."

"I see," Declan replied.

"Do you, Parker? Do you really see?"

"I do. So, what type of decision would eliminate further consequences?"

"That's actually fairly simple. You can decide to be the hero who stopped David Stanton from killing hundreds of innocent people on Christmas Eve."

"I already am the one who stopped Stanton."

"Maybe you are, and maybe you aren't. That's one of the things about the world we live in today. For better or worse, it's all about perception. Lives, careers, you name it, nine times out of ten, they are made or broken in large part on perceptions. As things stand right now, only you, me, and possibly your girlfriend know that you shot David Stanton. However, unfortunately, that story doesn't yet fit into the official narrative, the perception if you will, everyone else has at this point."

"Which is?"

"Which is, through our hard work, data gathering and tireless investigation, the Bureau sniffed out and stopped Stanton's heinous and appalling plan just in the nick of time. So far, it's an intentionally vague narrative, and this is where perception comes into play. You can fit into the narrative as the perceived hero, or, I should correctly say, one of the heroes."

"And if I were to decide not to be the hero, but to..."

Bleeker cut Declan off, "That would be an extremely unwise decision to make, Parker."

"For argument's sake."

"If you're not one of the heroes, you can always be perceived as one of the bad guys. Every good story needs a bad guy or two."

"Meaning?"

"Meaning you were also under investigation with Stanton and were seen on Christmas Eve acting in concert with him. When you refused to surrender and threatened to fire on me, Special Agent Costello took you down and, despite the doctors' best efforts, you died in the hospital of complications relating to your gunshot wound. Or, I suppose a third option, because I'm a big fan of options, could be that you don't fit into the story at all. Your and Ms. Neary's scenes, though well played, just end up on the cutting room floor, victims of the final cut."

"Hmmm," Declan replied. "The hero, the villain, or nothing."

"It's really a no-brainer, Parker. The hero can protect his girlfriend. He can protect his family. The other two options can't protect anyone from the grave. Frankly, if we'd had more time at the church, or if Costello was as good a shot as you are, you'd likely already be dead. Alas, no situation ever plays out perfectly, so here you are with a reprieve."

"You make a compelling argument."

"Like I said, it's a no-brainer," Bleeker said as he stood up. "I'll be back tomorrow. We'll have you familiarize yourself with, and sign off on, your official report, get you very briefly in front of the press, and you can officially join the hero club."

"Great, do I get a green jacket or something?"

"Nice one, Parker. I like the way you think."

"Bleeker, I do have one question I need answered."

"Let me put my extensive Bureau training to the test and take a guess: you want to know why."

"I do."

"Turn on the news and you'll see why. The vast majority of people in the world are lazy, stupid, or worse. They want someone to direct them, to do their thinking for them when it comes to anything more than which crappy fast-food place to grab dinner at. The masses aren't smart enough to know what's good for them and what's not. They need the small percentage of us who are, in a manner of speaking, better equipped, to make the big important decisions about the course of the world for them. That's really what the populace wants. They want to be led and protected and, frankly, they need to be protected from themselves most of the time. This is nothing more than that. The more enlightened among us want guns off the streets and out of the public's hands. We didn't create David Stanton, or that other nut job down in Birmingham, or any of the multiple nut jobs before them. We didn't need to. We simply sat back and let them do their thing, which is to create chaos and fear. Once we have chaos and fear, the people naturally beg for order and protection. They willingly, gratefully even, ask the government to do something to make sure this type of thing never happens again, and the government gives them a solution."

"In other words," Declan replied, "you create a crisis and let the people ask you to find a solution, to do what you wanted to do anyway."

"You catch on quickly. This is merely a means to an end, Parker. It's giving the masses what they didn't realize they needed, for the good of all. An economist would describe it as creating demand. It's an admittedly nasty, but necessary, step toward a better world; a new world which has been a long time coming, but is finally here. Welcome to the new world order, Parker," Bleeker responded as he walked out of the room.

———————————

Kevin Cameron sat across a small table from Megan in the hospital cafeteria, silently watching the steam from their coffee cups swirl and fade into the atmosphere between them. Megan looked nervously at Cameron, who had, at Bleeker's insistence, escorted her from Declan's room to the cafeteria for "a well-deserved break." Cameron's silence and stiff demeanor did nothing to reassure her, but she finally forced herself to ask him, "Are you the one who called me?"

"I am."

"Thank you. I appreciate that."

"Don't thank me," he responded flatly. "I don't deserve any thanks."

The two sat silently again for a minute or so. Megan asked, "Do you think they'll be much longer?"

"Not sure. I'll know when they're ready for you to go back up."

"Okay."

Cameron could see the tension in Megan's face, the uncertainty in her eyes. He felt sorry for her, sorry for Declan and the perilous situation which, at that moment, neither fully understood they were in the midst of. Kevin Cameron reached into his coat pocket and pulled out a pen. He took one of the napkins on the table and wrote down one sentence, then slid the napkin under his hand to Megan.

Megan looked down at Cameron's hand and the white napkin with the blue writing on it which read, "Get him out of here today ASAP and out of the country or you are both dead."

Bleeker met Special Agent Costello in the hall and they made their way toward the elevator. As they stood waiting for the elevator, Costello asked, "Is the kid going to play ball?"

"In Parker's case, there's no ball to play. He's too much of an idealist, or whatever. He's ultimately ill-suited for our purposes."

"So, should I give Foster the go ahead?"

"Yes. Make sure she's back on with this afternoon's shift change. It should merely be a matter of changing out his IV bag, and I don't want Parker to see another sunrise."

"And the girlfriend?"

"Let's wait until she gets back to D.C. With Parker gone, her situation should take care of itself for the time being. It will just look like Parker's suffering from complications stemming from the head trauma. That shouldn't raise any eyebrows and Ms. Neary can find her way into a fatal accident when she gets back home."

"What do you have in mind?"

"Something creative with a subtle touch of tragic

irony. Call Cameron and have him meet us outside, I'm ready to get out of here. I hate hospitals."

"Why's that?"

"Sick people, blood, I don't know. Does anyone really enjoy them?"

Chapter 36
December 26th

With a sharp pain pulsing through his head, Declan reached for the telephone on the end table next to the bed and dialed Evan's cell number.

"Hello."

"Evan, it's Declan"

"Hey, how are you feeling? Megan called earlier and said you'd woken up."

"I've been better, but I'm okay."

"Just take it easy. You need to rest. I'm going to come see you later today, but I won't stay long."

"Good. Can you stop by my apartment first to bring me some things?"

"Sure, what do you need?"

"Just grab some clothes, jeans, a few sweaters, some shoes. I'm sick of this hospital gown and I want to get some air. Also, my toothbrush and other toiletries. I also want you to bring up the Lone Ranger. It's under the left side of my bed, up toward the headboard."

"You need The Lone Ranger?"

"Maybe."

"Is everything alright?"

"I'm not sure."

"Okay, I'll see you soon."

"Don't take too long."

Declan turned on the television to see what Bleeker had meant. He was conflicted and had little intention of sticking to the script Bleeker had laid out for him. What Declan needed was a few days to come up with an alternative plan. He figured playing along with Bleeker would buy him the time he needed.

He flipped from channel to channel until he came across one of the news stations, which was showing video of rocket fire, explosions, and what appeared to be fighter jets streaking through the night sky. He turned up the volume a bit to hear the reporter's voiceover:

"The crisis in the Middle East is escalating as Israel continues to face retaliation on essentially all of its borders. We've received reports that the IDF has been engaged by Palestinian militia groups and ISIS forces on the Israeli – Jordanian border. At this point, the IDF is still going it alone as the United States, along with the rest of the world, has strongly condemned Israel's unilateral action against Iran and its nuclear and military facilities. The hostilities only appear to be gaining momentum, with no immediate end in sight."

"We'll keep you posted on the situation as things develop, but now let's go to Armen Jansen in Memphis, Tennessee, to get an update on the ongoing protests in response to the newly enacted and controversial Firearms Protection Act."

"Thank you, Carolyn. As you can see, police in riot gear are moving into the area. The local police are working in concert with officers from Homeland Security to quell the protests and unrest taking place here in downtown Memphis. The protesters converged on downtown early this morning, shortly after news of the passage of the Firearms Protection Act hit the internet and the airwaves. Many here have dubbed it the 'Infringement Act' and have pledged a fight with the federal authorities before parting with their firearms. Earlier, I was able to speak with many of the protesters, and here's some of what they had to say."

The picture on the television switched from an image of the riot police slowly getting into position to the image of a man who appeared to be in his early-forties talking into the reporter's microphone. The audio picked up with him saying, "The Infringement Act is downright illegal and a clear violation of our constitutional rights. I'm never turning in my guns to the government, ever. They can try to come and take them if they think they can, but they're in for one hell of a fight. Mark my words, one hell of a fight and I'm not the only one."

The camera switched to another protester saying,

"The whole congress and the president should be impeached and arrested. If they want a war, a revolution, that's exactly what they're going to get."

Then again to a third protester saying, "I'm a veteran. I served my country in Iraq and Afghanistan. I fought to protect our constitutional freedoms over there and I'll fight to protect them here in Memphis against any traitorous government bureaucrat who comes and tries to enforce this illegal act by taking my guns."

The reporter appeared on camera for the first time, apparently standing on a rooftop or balcony somewhere over the street where the protesters and riot police were inching closer together in the background. "Obviously, the protesters here in Memphis, of which there are quite a few, as you can see behind me, have no intention of handing over any guns in compliance with what they view to be a constitutionally questionable new law. They are not alone, as similar protests and demonstrations are taking place in cities and towns across the country, with very few exceptions. With riot police, military, and Homeland officers mobilizing here in Memphis and elsewhere, we'll see how much longer the protests last or whether the protestors' anger escalates into violence. The situation is eerily reminiscent of what we saw in Missouri when protestors and police clashed in 2014."

Declan flipped the channel to another news outlet, where the Director of Homeland Security was giving sound bites to a horde of reporters, "The Firearms Protection Act in no way violates our Constitution or the Second Amendment contained therein, which addresses the right of a militia to keep and bear arms. The Second Amendment says nothing about individual private citizens possessing firearms or having a right to do so. This was carefully crafted legislation, with a specific and, quite frankly, crucial public policy and safety goal, which is to eliminate, once and for all, the random mass shootings which have plagued our nation for far too long. We understood going into this that we'd get some pushback from the more radical-right fringe groups, the survivalists, the religious-right, and other dangerous domestic extremists out there and, as I believe you'll see very soon, we're prepared to effectively and efficiently deal with that pushback. Honestly, I find it sad and ridiculous that so many are protesting and threatening violence and civil insurrection over a constitutionally consistent and valid law that was put into place to protect all Americans from future senseless shootings like we suffered through on Christmas Eve and like those we've suffered through as a nation all too often in our recent history. As the president said earlier today, 'Enough is enough. It's time to get to the root of the problem, and the root of the problem is the proliferation of firearms in our society.' The proliferation of firearms amongst individual citizens in this country is a relic of a bygone era, and there's no place for such a barbaric and dangerous relic in the new world order, of which we are all a part."

Declan turned the TV off and closed his eyes, searching for something that made sense. "God, at this point I honestly have no idea if you're there, but there's a part of me that wants to believe in you again. I want not to hate you for taking my dad. I want to believe that what I'm seeing is all because you have some perfect plan, like Evan and mom keep saying, and that my dad's death somehow fit into that plan. I really want to believe all this has a purpose, that life has a purpose. If you're really there, if this is really all part of some prophecy or something, if your Son really is the only way to be saved and is coming back here someday, please, open my eyes and help me to see it. Help me to believe."

Chapter 37
December 26th

Before going back to Declan's room, Megan found an unoccupied hospital room and quickly called her father at home. "Dad, it's me."

"Hi, Pumpkin. Is everything okay down there? Your mom and I saw what happened on the news. That wasn't Declan's church, was it?"

"It was, but I'm fine, Daddy. Declan was injured though, and I need your help."

"What do you need?"

"I need the plane, and I need it right away."

"Why? Are you in trouble?"

"No, not exactly, but Declan is and I need to get him out of here as quickly as I can."

"I'll call Tom right now and have him out as soon as possible. It will probably take about three hours from takeoff to landing from Boston."

"That's fine."

"What's the itinerary?"

"First to D.C. for a quick stop, then to Uncle Ignacio."

"All the way down there?"

"Yep."

"No problem, Pumpkin. I'll make the arrangements and tell Tom to give you whatever you need. Is there anything else you need?"

"We could use a car in D.C. and some cash too."

"A car will be waiting at the airfield and there'll be plenty of cash for you on the plane."

"Thank you. I love you, Daddy."

"I love you too. Be careful, whatever's going on. Things are starting to get crazy out there."

"Will do. I've got to go, but I'll call again from the plane."

She immediately picked up the phone again and

dialed the number for a cell phone in Chicago.

"This is Louis."

"Louis, it's Megan."

"Hey there. What's happening, Neary?"

"I have a scoop for you on the David Stanton story."

"No kidding? What kind of scoop?"

"The big and unbelievable kind, but don't worry, I'll have evidence to corroborate it. Things are not what they seem."

"They rarely are nowadays."

"I'll meet you at Potomac Airfield tonight at eight. If I'm not right on time, just wait and I'll be there. We'll have plenty of time to talk on the plane."

"I'll be there."

"Don't be late or I'll leave without you. I'm on a tight timetable."

"I'll be there at eight sharp, Neary."

Megan hung up the phone and thought for minute, trying to formulate a plan. She needed two things. First, she had to get clean alias passports for the two of them. That could be accomplished easily enough from her office at Homeland, which necessitated the stopover in D.C. The second, and more pressing issue, was how to get Declan out of the hospital without being seen. She recalled seeing an elevator down the hall from Declan's room, in the opposite direction from the nurses' station and thought maybe she could use that elevator.

Megan rushed out of the empty room and took the main elevator back up to Declan's floor. She walked past the nurses' station, saying hello to Nurse Sanchez and Nurse McDonald, both of whom she'd spoken to before, and headed down the hall past Declan's room toward what appeared to be a service elevator. She pressed the down button, but the elevator required a security badge to operate it, so nothing happened.

"Damn," she said to herself. "I'll have to think of something else." Trying to come up with an alternative plan, she walked down the hall again and past the nurses' station to the main elevators, intending to check out the floor just beneath Declan's. The elevator dinged, the door slowly opened, and Megan saw Evan inside the elevator about to make his way out.

Instinctively, she hurried in and stopped Evan from exiting. The door closed behind them.

"Megan, what are you doing?"

"You have patients here, right?"

"Yes."

"So you have a security badge that will access the service elevators?"

"You mean the elevators we use for transporting patients and stuff?"

"Yes."

"Of course. Why? What's going on?"

"Does anyone know Declan is your brother?"

"I don't think so. I haven't spoken to anyone about him."

"Good."

"What's going on? Is he in some kind of trouble?"

"Yes, and I need you to help me get him out of this hospital and to the airport right away."

Chapter 38
December 26th

Evan handed his security card and car keys to Megan. "Remember, you can't remove his IV, or you'll set off an alarm and prompt one of the nurses to come in to replace it. Just hang it on the back of the wheelchair."

"Got it," Megan responded.

"Also, remember his hospital bracelet has a GPS chip in it, which will alarm if he gets beyond the secured areas of the building. Here is the key to remove it, but once you take it off you've got to reconnect it within a few seconds or it will trip the system. Take it off once you get out to the east patio, reconnect it and toss it into the trash can near the doors. Don't take it with you or you'll set it off."

"Okay."

"I'll wait a few minutes after you go in and then I'll do my best to distract whoever's at the nurses' station. You'll want to get him in the chair and have him ready, then go out and hit the elevator button because it could take a few minutes. Here, put these scrubs on when you get into the room and just hang this badge backwards on your waist, so that the picture isn't showing. It's one of my old ones. That should be enough not to attract anyone's attention when you get down to the main floor."

"Alright, thanks."

"Wheel him casually out the east entrance; that's the one to your left when you come off the elevator. If anyone asks, which they likely won't, just say you're taking him out to the east patio for some fresh air. Make sure not to rush or appear hurried, just take your time. When you get outside, wheel him down the sidewalk past the east patio and into the doctor's parking garage. My car is parked in the second space across from the walkway, No. 183. I'll meet you at the car, but if I'm not there for some reason, don't wait. Get Declan into the car and go. There are security cameras all over the parking garage, and the entire building for that matter, so you'll be picked up on at least one of them somewhere."

"That means they'll likely know which car we're in."

"Most likely. That's why I want to drive you, so you don't have to leave my car at the airport. But, again, if I'm late, don't wait for me."

Megan took a long deep breath and said, "Okay, I can do this."

"Don't worry. The difficult part will be getting him out of the room and onto the patient elevator without one of his nurses noticing. After that, it should be relatively smooth sailing. Like I said, I'll try and keep whoever is there distracted."

"This is going to work, right?"

"It'll work, but let's both keep praying just to be sure."

"I've never been really good at praying, Evan."

"Well, now would be a good time to get some practice in," Evan replied with a reassuring smile.

Megan stuffed the light-blue hospital scrub into a small cafeteria take-out bag and said, "We'll see you at the car."

"Yes you will."

A few minutes later, Megan quietly rolled an empty wheelchair from the hall into Declan's room. She looked over to the bed and saw Declan sleeping and, wanting to take no chances, rolled the wheelchair into the bathroom, then closed the bathroom door so she could put the scrubs on over her clothes.

Once dressed, Megan came out of the bathroom and brought the wheelchair next to Declan's bed. Noticing Declan's hospital chart on his bed, she took it and slid it into the back of her jeans, under the loose fitting scrubs. She leaned over and gently kissed him on the forehead. "Declan, babe, wake up," he whispered.

Declan slowly opened his eyes and smiled softly. "What time is it?"

"It's a little after four."

"Where've you been?"

"Just taking care of a few things so I could give you a chance to rest."

"You know Bleeker came to see me?"

"I know," she replied, while at the same time motioning for him to be quiet and not say anything further.

Still holding her index finger to her lips, Megan drew Declan's attention to the wheelchair. He looked back at her with a puzzled expression, still silent.

She asked, "How are you feeling?"

"Okay, I suppose."

Megan handed Declan a piece of paper with the words "We have to leave NOW" written on it. He read the words and looked up at her, still unsure as to what was happening.

Evan exited the main elevator and approached the nurses' station, where he saw two nurses sitting. One was on the phone and the other appeared to be doing something on the computer. "Good afternoon," he said as he reached the desk.

"Hello, Doctor. What can we do for you?"

"Well, I'm hoping you can give me the status on the patient in 422."

"Oh, do you mean Mr. Peterson or Ms. Kiser?"

"Sorry, I didn't realize it was a double," Evan replied as he looked past the nurses' station to see Megan quickly pop out of Declan's room and go toward the patient elevator. "Um, Mr. Peterson. He's the one in recovery from CABG this morning, right?"

"That's right, Doctor."

"Good. And, can you tell me how he's doing?"

"Of course, Doctor. Let me just pull him up here real quick."

Evan saw Megan hurry back into Declan's room, while the nurse looked intently at the computer screen. The other nurse hung up the phone and said to the nurse on the computer, "I'm heading down to 440. It's time for Ms. Costa's pain meds."

"Okay," the other nurse replied.

Just then, Evan saw Declan's room door open and Megan quickly wheel him out into the hall. Trying to think of some way to keep the other nurse from turning around, he quickly said, "I don't believe we've met. I'm Evan."

"Um, I'm Alisa Foster."

"It's nice to meet you Nurse Foster. How long have you been here at the hospital?"

Megan had Declan sitting in the chair at the elevator, waiting for it to open. Evan had to keep Nurse Foster distracted until they were on the elevator.

"Not long," she replied. "I'll be back in a few minutes, Carol."

"Okay. Here, Doctor. I have Mr. Peterson's records up. Do you want to take a look?"

"C'mon, c'mon," Megan whispered nervously, looking at the elevator door and then over to Evan, whom she could see talking to the nurses. "C'mon dammit…open."

Declan sat motionless in the wheelchair, feeling the soreness from his bullet wound and the throbbing in his head. Megan kept her eyes on the nurses' station, praying silently that neither of the nurses looked down the hall toward them. "C'mon."

Evan could see Megan and Declan were still sitting in front of the elevator and quickly stammered, "Where were you before?"

"I'm sorry," Nurse Foster replied, turning toward Evan again.

"Where did you work before coming here?"

"Nowhere. I mean, this I my first hospital job. I graduated from nursing school a few months ago."

"Which school?"

"State," she replied impatiently.

The patient elevator finally dinged and the door began to open slowly, too slowly.

"That's a good program, don't you think?"

"It was fine."

The elevator doors opened completely and Evan watched Megan quickly wheel Declan inside, and heard the doors begin to close.

The nurse on the computer asked, "Was that the patient elevator I just heard?"

"Yes," Evan replied right away. "It looks like they had the wrong floor. I just saw a head pop out, and back in, then the doors closed again."

"I hate that. I really don't see how it's that difficult to pick the right floor."

"It was nice meeting you, Doctor," Nurse Foster said. "I've got to get down to Room 440 now."

"Of course. Nice meeting you too."

"Doctor, do you want to see Mr. Peterson's records?"

"Absolutely."

Evan leaned over, pretending to review the patient records on the computer, but really watching Nurse Foster walk down the hall toward Room 440, only she didn't make it to Room 440. Instead, she stopped in front of Declan's room, and began to open the door.

"Thank you, it looks like his recovery is going well," Evan said and walked briskly down the hall after her. The phone rang and the other nurse picked it up, no longer paying attention to Evan, who hurried into Declan's room after Nurse Foster.

When Evan entered the room, he saw Nurse Foster picking up the telephone on the table next to Declan's bed. Without thinking, Evan rushed toward her, shoving her with all of his force. Nurse Foster's body jerked violently backward. The phone fell from her hand, and her body crashed into a heap onto the hard white floor. Her head snapped back against the unforgiving floor then bounced up slightly and fell against it again.

Evan stood over Nurse Foster's unconscious body, immediately stricken with a pang of remorse and hoping he hadn't accidentally killed her. "What have I done?" He quickly kneeled down next to her and felt her pulse. She was still alive.

Evan hung the phone up and lifted Nurse Foster gently onto Declan's bed. He placed her head softly onto the pillow, turned her so that she was facing away from the door, and pulled the sheet and blanket up so that it covered everything but her head.

"I'm sorry," he whispered. "I'm truly, truly sorry."

Megan looked back at Declan, who was lying in the backseat of Evan's car, then looked nervously at her watch, and, finally, turned the ignition and began to back the car out of the parking space.

"Megan, wait," Evan called hurrying into the passenger seat.

"What took you so long?"

"I had to get extra medications for Declan to take with him. Let's go, we've got to hurry."

Megan slammed the car into drive and screamed out of the hospital parking garage. A few minutes later, they were on the highway headed toward the airport, and soon thereafter they were within a few exits of the airport. The drive both flew by and dragged on, as though the airport was hours away.

Evan saw an exit with a truck stop. "Get off here for a minute."

"Why? We don't have time for a stop, Evan," Megan responded.

"Just exit here and go to the truck stop."

Declan asked weakly from the backseat, "What do you have in mind?"

The car pulled into the busy truck stop and parked outside. "I'll be right back," Evan said, and he hurried into the truck stop. About a moment later he got back into the car with a roll of duct tape.

"What's that for?"

"Here, give me your phones."

Megan handed her smart phone and Declan's smart phone to Evan. "What are you going to do?"

"I'm going to send these, and their GPS chips, on a little trip."

"That's brilliant."

"Okay, pick me up over by the gas pumps in a minute."

Evan got out of the car and walked quickly toward where a large number of semi's were parked. When he found one that looked like it was getting ready to leave, he walked around to the back, ducked underneath and taped the iPhones to the bottom of the trailer.

When Evan got back into the car he said, "I'm not sure where that truck is headed, but as long as it doesn't end up at an airport in D.C. in the next few hours, that should keep anyone who figures out you're gone busy for a bit."

"Let's go," Megan responded, and they were off to the airport.

Chapter 39
December 26th

The plane landed without incident at Potomac Airfield shortly after 7:00 p.m. Megan left Declan sleeping safely on the plane with her father's longtime pilot and trusted friend, Tom Langham, and drove into D.C., to Homeland Security Headquarters. She passed numerous fast moving emergency and military vehicles on the way into the city, a combination of police, various fire departments, Army, and Homeland Security personnel presumably responding to the protests which had been sparked by the passage of the Firearms Protection Act.

Once Megan had finally made it to Homeland headquarters, she cleared the outer security perimeter, parked in a spot somewhat away from the building, and made her way inside. For the first time, she was struck by the realization that the use of her security card would create a record of her location which could surely be found by anyone who'd be looking for them.

Unable to turn back, Megan swiped her security card and peered into the retinal scanners. The security doors opened, and she was back inside Homeland, for what would very likely be the last time, she thought. As she entered the elevator and pressed the button for her floor, she calculated that it should take roughly ten minutes to boot up the system, access photos of her and Declan from the database, and create two alias passports. If she could keep her total time in the building under fifteen minutes, everything would likely go as planned.

Alisa Foster groggily came to with a splitting headache in the pitch black hospital room. It took her a moment to get her bearings and realize she was lying in a bed. Slowly, and with considerable effort, Foster sat up and the throbbing in her temples increased to an almost unbearable degree. She tried to steady herself, then stepped clumsily onto the floor, and reached over to turn on the bedside lamp. The sudden light initially blinded her, shooting a feeling akin to a puncture wound through her head. When the pain finally subsided somewhat, Foster picked up the in room phone.

A voice answered, "Costello."

"He's gone," she stated flatly. "Parker and the girl are gone."

"When?"

"I'm not sure. It could have been hours ago."

"Where were you?"

"Incapacitated."

"Come again?"

"I was incapacitated. I got hit by a doctor, or someone saying he was a doctor, and woke up just now in Parker's bed."

"Alright, I've got to make a call. You find out who the doctor, or whoever, was that took you out."

"I've got an idea."

"Well, figure it out and be ready to give me a name. I'll get back to you on your cell shortly."

"Okay."

"Michelle, it's me," Evan said trying to disguise the panic in his voice.

"Where are you?"

"I'm at the office. Listen, I don't want to alarm you and I don't have time to go into detail, but something happened today and you need to take the kids and my mom up to the lake house, right away."

"Why? What's the matter?"

"Declan was in major trouble and I helped get him out of the hospital and out of town. There could be repercussions and I don't want to take any chances with you and the kids. Don't panic, just pack some things, pick up mom, and drive everyone up there tonight. Mom already knows you're coming and she'll be ready to go."

"Are you in trouble, Evan?"

"No, I don't think so. It's too early to tell, but I don't want you guys at home if anyone comes looking for me. Plus, things are getting a bit nuts out there right now with the protests and everything. I'll feel better knowing you all are safely out of town and away from all the chaos."

"This is crazy. It feels like everything is falling apart all of a sudden."

"Things are a bit crazy, but just stay calm, pray, and get up to the lake house."

"When will you be up there?"

"Hopefully late tonight, tomorrow at the latest. Don't worry, everything will be fine and I'll explain more when I see you."

"Okay, I'll get things together and get going."

"Good. Go as quickly as you can and I'll see you all soon. I love you."

"I love you too. Be careful."

"I will. Like I said, don't worry. It will all work out. Just move quickly, don't panic, and avoid downtown at all costs. That's where the bulk of the protests are and I've heard the riot police and Homeland forces are moving in to put them down. Take all the cash we have in the drawer and any cash you have. Grab our passports too, and the kids' passports. They have some, right?"

"Yes, we got them before going on that cruise with your mom last year, but why do we need our passports?"

"Just in case. Please, just take them with you and have my mom bring hers too. I'd also take some food and water, enough to last for two or three weeks, just in case. The lake house is pretty well stocked and mom will have some stuff too, so have her bring whatever you can pack, and plenty of blankets for the cold. Also, leave your phones behind. Don't take them or you could be tracked to the lake house. "

"If I don't have my phone how will I know what's going on or be able to reach you. I don't like that, Evan."

"I understand, but you have to leave them behind. With the GPS in the phones, it's just too easy to locate them. Trust me, I'll get there as soon as possible. As soon as I think it's safe."

"Okay, but I don't like this."

"Neither do I, but it's necessary. I've got to go, but I'll see you soon. I love you," he said again and hung up the phone.

Declan woke up and saw Tom Langham rustling through some papers in one of the seats across from his makeshift bed, while kind of half-watching the muted flat screen TV that was mounted on the cabin wall in front of them. He asked, "Where's Megan?"

"She had an errand in D.C. She said she'd be back in an hour or so."

"When did she leave?"

"About forty-five minutes ago, so she should be back soon. How are you feeling?"

"Decent. I'm Declan Parker."

"Tom Langham. I'm Megan's dad's personal pilot, and a good friend of her family."

"It's nice to meet you."

"You too, son," Tom replied getting up. "We should be taking off once Megan gets back."

"Captain Langham, where are headed anyway?"

"Please, call me Tom, and we're heading down to Peru. Flying into Cusco specifically."

"What are your thoughts on the chances of me getting my gun through customs down there?"

"I'd say about zero."

"Is there someplace here on the plane you could stash it for me, so I can get it back later? It was my dad's and I'd prefer not to lose it."

"Sure, I have a tucked away place for sensitive type items. I'd be happy to keep it onboard for you. I'll put it with the Remington Model 700 I keep aboard. "

Declan pulled the 9 mm Glock 19, the Lone Ranger, out of his backpack along with three full clips, and handed them to Tom. "Thanks, I really do appreciate it."

"No problem. Just try and make yourself comfortable. I expect Megan will be back soon."

"Will do." Declan looked around the luxe, well equipped cabin. "That shouldn't be too difficult," he said to himself. He rummaged through the remaining contents of his backpack, and found some of his clothes, a pair of running shoes and his Bible.

Declan looked up at the TV and took in the silent images of the riots which had broken out around the country. Fully armed American police, soldiers and Homeland Security troopers clashed with American citizens in scenes even the most pessimistic could not have imagined would ever take place in the United States. Declan watched the blood and carnage fill the HD screen, looked down to the Bible on his lap, and opened randomly to the Gospel of Luke, Chapter 21. He read the words: "[28]When these things begin to take place, stand up and lift your heads, because your redemption is drawing near."

The words sat in front of Declan, sinking slowly into his understanding and he thought back to the signs Evan and his mom had talked about so many times: the wars and rumors of wars; the earthquakes; nations rising against nations and brothers against brothers; and the persecution of those who follow and believe in Jesus. "Maybe," he whispered to himself. "Just maybe."

At that moment, Megan stepped back onto the plane with a guy Declan had never seen before.

"Hey, you're up," she said. "How do you feel?"

"I'm getting better. Who's this?"

"Declan Parker, meet Louis Martino."

"It's a pleasure," Louis offered as Declan nodded.

"Louis writes for the online 'Free Voice'. I've given him some background info and he's going to tell your side of the story. By the way, Louis, here's Declan's medical charts, which will show that he wasn't shot by an AR-15, but by a 9mm. I'll have some more information on the Stanton case for you as well, I just need to go through the files first."

Declan asked, "Where did you get Stanton files?"

"I downloaded Homeland's files on the incident. I just haven't had a chance to see what's there yet."

"Oh, I've gotta get a look at those, Neary," replied Louis.

"I'll have a flash drive for you before you get off the plane. Now, babe, are you up for talking?"

"Sure."

"Good. I'll tell Tom we're ready to roll and let you two get started. Louis, we can drop you in Miami or Dallas. What's your preference?"

"Let's go with Dallas. I'm actually going to catch a flight out to Israel sometime tomorrow, but I want to get a line on what's happening with the gun protests first. Things are heating up here and really getting crazy in the Middle East quickly too. It's almost like there's just too much to cover."

"If anyone can, it's you. Dallas it is then," Megan said as she headed for the cockpit.

"So, Declan," Louis asked, "Where should we begin?"

Declan sat up a bit more and thought for a second. "Hmm…Where do I start?"

PART II

"I make known the end from the beginning, from ancient times, what is still to come. I say, 'My purpose will stand and I will do all that I please. From the east I summon a bird of prey; from a far-off land, a man to fulfill my purpose. What I have said, that I will bring about; what I have planned, that I will do."

Isaiah 46:10-11

Chapter 40

Kevin Cameron sat impatiently in his vehicle, the heater blasting a nearly tropical warmth all around him, watching the house. The lights were on in all but two rooms and he could occasionally see the silhouetted movement of a person, likely a woman, inside. To lessen the monotony, he had the radio on, listening to the news reports about the various protests which had devolved into small scale riots and clashes between citizens and militarized law enforcement units in most of the larger cities around the country.

The silhouette's movement on the first floor caught his attention again, then, for the first time, the front door opened and Kevin watched Michelle Parker walk outside into the cold carrying two small travel bags, one hot pink and the other red and navy blue. She loaded the travel bags into the back of a large silver Denali SUV parked in the driveway, and headed back inside, only to return a few minutes later with two black rolling suitcases, which she also loaded with some difficulty into the rear of the SUV.

"Looks like someone's taking a trip," he said to himself.

A few moments later, Michelle came out of the house again carrying three large reusable shopping bags, and again with three more and, finally, with what appeared to be a pile of blankets or bed sheets, as Kevin watched her from his car.

A voice came across his radio, "Cameron, give me an update."

Kevin slowly picked up the radio from the passenger seat as the impatient voice spoke again, "Cameron, where are you? What's happening there?"

"Calm down, Costello. I'm right here."

"What's the story? Any movement?"

"No, nothing yet. I'll let you know if anything changes."

"Alright."

Michelle moved frantically through the house, unable to focus her attention on any one thing for more than a minute or two. A purple reusable Whole Foods shopping bag rustled back and forth in her nervous shaking hands as she began throwing in anything that looked like it might be beneficial to have at the lake house.

A flashlight in the kitchen drawer, AAA batteries, C batteries, boxes of mac and cheese for the kids, a half full jar of creamy peanut butter, what was left of the bread. She began to fill up the bag with whatever random provisions her scattered mind could focus on. Band-Aids, she thought suddenly, and rushed from the kitchen to the upstairs master bathroom. As she searched for Band-Aids, she found and threw a bar of soap into the bag, then the kids' toothbrushes, then sunscreen, and, finally, the box of Band-Aids which had brought her to the master bathroom in the first place.

As she turned from the bathroom closet, Michelle caught a glimpse of herself in the mirror and stopped in her tracks, trying to recognize the pale, harried, panicked eyes looking back at her. Suddenly, she broke down and fell to the floor in tears, unsure exactly why, except for an unshakable foreboding about what lay ahead.

"A margarita, rocks with salt, please," Louis Martino said to the waitress in the airport lounge. "And is it too late to get something from the kitchen?"

"No, what would you like?"

"How about a burger and fries, well done."

"No problem."

Louis took his notes out of his bag and looked them over for the third time since getting through security at Dallas - Fort Worth International Airport. His eyes rolled with excited ease through Declan's entire story, a story which, in all fairness, would practically write itself. The angle was clear, and entirely in opposition to what the mainstream media had been reporting about David Stanton.

"Here's your rita," the waitress said. "The food should be out in a few minutes."

"Thank you."

After taking a sip of his drink, Louis pulled out his iPhone and checked his texts to find one from his co-editor, Alyssa Chambers, which read, "Where R U?" Louis quickly texted back, "DFW, on my way to Jerusalem. Flight leaves in 2 hours," and hit send. He took another sip of his margarita, savoring the salty sour flavor, and thought about how best to open the article on Declan and, more importantly, when to break it.

A text came back from Alyssa, "Riots in DC, downtown Dallas too, and lots of other places."

Louis replied simply, "Riots? Seriously?"

Less than thirty seconds later, "Seriously. Homeland & police moving in with military gear. Looks like Ferguson. Clashes with citizens. Reports of gunfire. Can you get downtown to cover? I'm covering DC."

"Yep," Louis texted.

He turned his tablet on and hit his Twitter app. Quickly looking to see what was trending, he saw 1.1 million tweets about the trend, #infringement. Louis took two big swigs from his drink and picked up his bag. "Excuse me, ma'am. I've got to go. Can I pay the tab and get the burger to go?"

The front door opened again and Kevin watched as Michelle came outside carrying a young child wrapped in a navy-blue or black blanket, who appeared to be sleeping on her shoulder. She placed the child into a car seat in the back of the Denali and ran quickly back inside, appearing less than a minute later with another young child, wrapped in a pink blanket, whom she placed into the opposite side of the SUV. With both children safely in the car, Michelle locked the front door of the house, got into the driver's seat, turned on the ignition, and backed gently out of the driveway.

"Alright, let's see where you're going," Kevin said as he turned on the headlights and pulled out slowly behind her, careful not to get too close.

Chapter 41

"This is as close as I can get you, pal," the cab driver said to Louis. "It's twenty-eight bucks for the fare."

"Here's forty. Just keep the change."

"Thanks."

"No problem. Tell me, how difficult will it be to get a cab back here in, say, two hours?"

"I can put in the order for you. A pickup at the corner of North Lamar and Ross at 1:30 in the morning, right?"

"Perfect. I'll be here. Thanks again."

"Hey, what's the name?"

"Sorry, Louis Martino."

Louis began making his way on foot toward the Earle Cabell Federal Building, which was five or six blocks away and where the protests had initially been centered. After walking only a block, he could hear shouting, sirens and shots ringing through the cool night air, and nervously picked up his pace, unsure what he'd find.

At the next block, Louis encountered a barricade manned by Homeland troops. He got his credentials ready and approached cautiously.

"This is a secure area! Don't come any closer," a voice bellowed.

"It's okay, I have press credentials. Here, I'll…"

"I don't care if you've got a key to the city. I said back off!" The trooper raised his rifle and Louis looked down to find a red laser point bouncing around his chest.

"Okay, okay," he replied. "Don't get excited. I'll stop here, but I'm a reporter, and I need to get down to the federal courthouse to cover the riots."

"Nobody gets in."

"Not even press?"

"Are you deaf? I said nobody gets in. This is a secure perimeter and only authorized personnel are allowed past this point."

"Aren't press authorized?"

"Listen, I already said I don't care who you are. You're not getting past this barricade, and if you keep bugging me, I'm going to shoot you in the chest like the rioter you are. So, back off!"

"But, I'm not a rioter, I'm a reporter," Louis replied.

"Volquez," the trooper said to one of his two partners, "What is this guy?"

"Looks like a rioter to me," Volquez responded flatly while raising his weapon in Louis' direction.

"That's what I thought," the trooper stated, his rifle's red laser mark still dancing on Louis' chest.

Louis stood frozen, unsure what to do, not wanting to make the wrong move.

"See, idiot, this is the part where you run," the trooper yelled, then quickly raised his weapon and fired one round into the air above Louis' head. Louis flinched at the sound, then turned and sprinted as fast as he could back in the direction he'd come, hearing the three Homeland troopers laughter echoing through the street behind him.

Evan parked his car in one of the packed long term parking lots at the airport, and took out the handful of cash, about $320.00, he had taken from the petty cash drawer at his office. He didn't want to use his credit card or debit card for anything, as any such purchases would be easily traced by anyone who might be looking for him.

The main terminal of the airport was open all night and Evan figured he could blend in with the remaining holiday traffic, try to get a few hours' sleep without looking too conspicuous, then head up to the lake house around dawn. He stepped out into the frosty cold, locked the car and pulled the collar of his wool overcoat tightly around him.

The wind had picked up considerably, making the clear night air bitingly cold. He plunged his hands deep into his pockets and trudged past the various parked cars, walking slowly against the gusting wind toward the airport terminal.

Evan looked up to see a pair of headlights coming slowly down the parking lot aisle, seemingly looking for a parking space. The icy wind raged and sliced through him, sending chills up and down the length of his body. He looked down into the collar of his overcoat again, in an effort to duck the cold.

The headlights crept closer and closer, causing Evan to move from the center of the aisle to one side, in order to allow the car to pass. He looked up again briefly and noticed an open parking space to his left a few feet ahead, and took one hand out of the warmth of his coat pocket to motion to the car, which was almost upon him. Evan pointed quickly to the open parking space. The driver noticed and waved back, then slowly pulled past the quickly freezing Evan.

Not giving the car any further thought, but only able to focus on the bitter cold around him, Evan continued ahead. A few seconds later, he heard faint footsteps behind him, and turned around, to be met with the solid thrust of a wooden police baton into his gut. The blow knocked the air out of Evan and dropped him instantly onto the frozen asphalt, where he struggled to breathe. Another hard painful blow came down on his shoulder, then another on his arm. Pain shot throughout his body, as a third blow from the baton landed squarely on his back. He looked up just for a second to see the blinding headlights of a car in front of him, felt the baton land for a final time on the back of his skull, and everything went black.

Out of breath, Louis Martino finally stopped running a few blocks from the barricade and threw himself down onto the curb to catch his breath. "Holy crap," he said to himself, gasping. "Damn, I'm out of shape."

Sweat poured out of him uncontrollably, like his heart rate, and he finally just laid flat on his back on the sidewalk. Louis tried to focus on the point where the building towering above him met the faint twinkling sky. After a few minutes on his back, he was able to regain some control over his breathing and stopped panting. His pulse subsided somewhat and his hands stopped shaking.

With a bit of effort, Louis pulled himself up off the sidewalk and took a look around. Suddenly, just as all seemed calm, he heard the unmistakable sound of gun fire, followed by shouts. Both sounded very close, too close. The shouts moved toward him quickly, frantically, until their source, three young men and a young woman, finally came around the corner of the building he was standing in front of.

"Hurry, c'mon," a man yelled. "They're right behind us."

Another called out, "Did they get anyone?"

"I don't think so," the girl said. "C'mon, let's go."

Louis stood staring at the group as they ran toward him. The girl looked up, caught sight of him, and froze in her tracks.

"It's okay," Louis said quickly. "I'm only a reporter."

A second later, two figures came running around the corner behind the group. "Shit, run," one of the young men screamed.

"Rat- tat, rat-tat" rang out and Louis watched as one of the three young men fell face first to the ground, his head smashing against the concrete sidewalk. The others scattered and kept running and Louis, afraid he wouldn't have time to explain his press status to the shooters, dashed after the girl. Three more shots darted through the air, followed by a man's voice screaming, "I'm hit. I'm hit."

Louis and the girl sprinted toward the end of the block and around the corner of the building. They kept running as fast as they could away from the gunfire, neither slowing to look behind them. They ran to the end of the next block, and turned another corner. Louis realized that they had to get off the street and tried to take in his surroundings to see if there was an open building or somewhere they could hide.

He spotted a parking garage and called to the girl, "Hey, in there."

She slowed her pace, gasping for breath, and looked toward the parking garage.

"We can hide in there," Louis said, panting. "Get off the street."

"Okay," she replied.

The two headed quickly into the parking garage and made their way up the staircase. Louis' quads and lungs burned in a way he'd never thought possible. He felt like he was going to vomit and wanted to stop, but the girl kept running up the stairs. Not wanting to lose her, Louis tried his best to keep up, until they finally reached the open air top level of the garage.

The girl stopped running and ducked down in a dark shadowed spot next to one of the walls. Louis fell down onto the ground next to her, again unable to catch his breath and feeling his heart practically beat out of his body. They were both quiet for a few minutes, listening for any sound of footsteps.

After getting his breath back, Louis asked, "What are you, a marathon runner or something?"

The girl smiled slightly and, despite the circumstances, Louis was unable to stop himself from noticing how beautiful she was. "I wish," she replied.

"My name's Louis Martino."

"Jessica Ehlers."

"Nice to meet you, Jessica."

"Do you think we're safe here?"

"I think so. I don't think anyone saw us run in here. Besides, I think there were only two of them."

"Back there, you said you were a reporter?"

"Yeah, I'm co-editor for The Free Voice. It's an online indie news publication."

The sound of more gun shots echoed through the streets below them. Jessica froze, then looked toward the staircase.

"I don't think those were nearby," Louis said. "They sounded like they were more from a distance."

"I think two of the guys I was with got shot."

"I think so too. Were they friends?"

"Not really. They knew someone in the group I went to the protests with tonight. We were hanging together down there until the Homeland riot police started moving in. I didn't even know their names. Everyone just scrambled when they started shooting tear gas canisters off and then they started shooting people."

"What were the protestors doing? Was it provoked?"

"No, they demanded that everyone break up and leave. When nobody did, the riot cops began with the tear gas, then shots started going off. I don't know if it was protestors or cops at first, but then the police started shooting into the crowd and everyone scattered. I was down there with my brother. I lost him in the crowd when the shooting started."

"How many protestors were there?"

"I don't know. At least three or four thousand. Maybe more," Jessica said as she stood up.

"Where are you going?"

"I've got to try and find my brother."

"You can't go back out there now, it's not safe."

"I'm not headed back to the federal building. Aiden, that's my brother, and I came up with a meeting place in case we got separated. It's only a couple blocks from here. I've got to get over there so he doesn't think something happened to me and goes back to look for me."

"I'll come with you."

"It's okay. I'll be fine. It's better on my own. If I run into any police, I can just say that I'm just getting off work down here or something."

"I don't know."

"I'll be fine," Jessica replied. She put out her hand to shake Louis' hand.

"It was nice meeting you."

"You too," she said, and took off toward the stairwell.

"Stay safe," he called after her.

Jessica turned around and replied, "You do the same," then headed briskly down the stairs.

Michelle pulled off the county road and onto a gravel road leading up to the lake house. The kids were asleep in the backseat and Evan's mom had begun to doze off in the passenger seat. Michelle yawned as she tried to keep her own eyes open and focused on the road in front of her.

The SUV jostled over the bumpy gravel road, further into the dark forest, until it finally pulled into a clearing and onto a small circular gravel driveway. Michelle stopped the car in front of the house, turned off the ignition, and walked briskly through the darkness to open the front door. A second later, the lights inside the house flipped on.

The lights from the lake house popped in and out of Kevin Cameron's view through the trees. He walked slowly in the dark along the gravel road, until he was able to see the Denali parked outside the illuminated lake house and Michelle's silhouetted figure unloading the various supplies she'd packed.

"Not a bad little hideout," he said to himself. A moment or two later, he turned and began the walk back up the road to his parked car. As he walked along the dark road, Kevin's phone vibrated on his belt.

"Cameron," he answered.

"We've got Parker's brother," Bleeker said. Where are you?"

"There was nothing going at the house, so I headed out. I think the wife and kids must have already left. No movement. Where'd you take Parker's brother?"

"We're at Zulu 12 Charlie."

"Do you need me there tonight?"

"No, we've got it under control. Find out what you can about the rest of the family. I want them all. The president is going to declare martial law at some point tomorrow. All field offices have been instructed to gear up for the apprehension and detainment of regional threats."

"Got it. I'll do what I can to track down the wife and kids and touch base again in the morning."

"Meet us here at 06 hundred."

"Will do."

Chapter 42

Estimating it would take about ten minutes on foot to get back to the intersection of North Lamar and Ross to meet his taxi, Louis left his hiding spot at the top of the parking garage at 1:15 a.m. Louis was operating almost solely on adrenaline as he made his way down the stairs and back out onto the street. Once again on the street, he pulled out his iPhone and tapped on the "Maps" app. Within a few seconds, a little blue dot appeared where he stood, just about four blocks from where he was supposed to meet the cab.

The streets were eerily still as he made his way up to Ross. The pops of tear gas canisters and gunfire could be heard in the distance, in the direction of the federal building, but Louis didn't encounter anyone until he turned onto Ross, where he practically walked right into the blasting headlights of a pair of parked Homeland cruisers.

"Hands above your head," a voice called out from behind the blinding lights. Louis slowly placed his hands on top of his head and stood still.

"I'm press," he called back.

"Just stand still, hands on your head. I'll come to you."

A military looking figure, weapon raised, emerged from behind one of the cruisers and into the glare of the headlights. Louis couldn't make out any features until the trooper was within five or six feet of him. "Do you have credentials?"

"I do. Can I show them to you?"

"Do it slowly. I'd prefer not to shoot you."

"That makes two of us. I've got them on a lanyard, tucked into my shirt. I'm just going to take my left hand and raise them out."

"Slowly," the trooper advised again.

Louis slowly pulled on the lanyard and took it off altogether so the trooper could examine his press card. "Here's my card. I'm Louis Martino, with The Free Voice."

"Hold the card up in the light facing me."

"Here you go."

The trooper, with his weapon still raised, carefully examined the name and photo on Louis' press card, then looked up at Louis to compare the photo with the face. "It's okay," he yelled out, lowering his rifle, "He's just a reporter."

"Can I take my hands off my head now?"

"Yeah, you're good. Where are you headed? You know the perimeter surrounding the federal building is a restricted area, right? Off limits even to press."

Louis replied, "I'm just headed to meet my taxi at Lamar and Ross, a couple blocks up I think."

"Actually, you're only a block and half away from Lamar. There's nothing going on in that direction, so you should be fine."

"Thanks."

"I'll walk with you to the end of the block," the trooper said. "You know, I read The Free Voice sometimes. I've read some of your articles."

"Really? That's always nice to hear. How have things been down here tonight?"

"Our unit was assigned to the outer perimeter. We've kept busy, but it looks like everything has pretty much calmed down out here, at least for tonight."

"Do you have any idea what happened outside the federal building earlier?"

"I wasn't there, but my understanding is that a group of armed rioters opened fire on our guys when they were ordered to vacate."

As the two walked next to the parked cruisers and finally out of the headlights' blinding glare, Louis looked toward the cars and saw another Homeland trooper in the passenger seat, with Jessica sitting handcuffed in the back. She appeared to have dried blood from a wound on her forehead. The other cruiser held two men in the backseat, whom Louis hadn't seen before. They were both handcuffed and also looked like they'd been roughed up. Jessica stared through the glass window and gave Louis a slight smile, which struck him as both beautiful and completely out of context in light of her circumstances.

"Looks like you've got some full cruisers," Louis said to the trooper.

"Yeah, just some rioters we picked up a bit ago."

Louis stopped and looked back at Jessica in the car. "You know, the girl in there, I know her. She helped me out of a tight spot with some rioters earlier tonight. She's not a rioter, but I think she works down here cleaning offices in one of the high rises or something."

"That's what she told us, but her story didn't entirely wash after we ran her through our system."

"How'd she get roughed up?"

"She fell while running from us. Accidents happen."

"If it helps, I can vouch for her. I saw her coming out of one of the buildings with a co-worker earlier."

"Sorry, I can't let her go."

"But, I know she didn't do anything tonight. She wasn't one of the protestors."

"Look," the trooper responded impatiently, "I'd like to help, but there's nothing I can do. Lamar is just ahead, the next intersection. You'd better get going."

"But,…"

The trooper cut him off, "I'm a fan of your work, but, like I said, there's nothing I can do. Unless you want to join her, I suggest you get moving."

Louis saw his cab pull up at the intersection ahead, and looked back at the cruiser for a second, somewhat conflicted. "Okay, okay. Can you tell me one thing though?"

"Maybe?"

"Where will she be taken?"

"I'm not at liberty to say, officially, but if I had to guess, I'd say she'll be processed through the detention facility in Fort Worth. That's where some of the other rioters who've been picked up tonight were taken. After that, who knows?"

"Fort Worth?"

"That'd be my unofficial bet."

"Alright, thanks. I appreciate it." Louis said, and headed quickly toward the taxi.

"No problem. I'd like to be more helpful. I even sympathize with some of the protestors, but there's nothing I can do to release her."

A scream pierced the late night silence of the lake house, causing Mrs. Parker to shoot up out of bed and rush, in a panic, to the other bedroom. Her grandchildren, Will and Charlotte, were alone, sleeping soundly beneath the warm down blankets. She turned and hurried into the living room, where Michelle sat breathless and stricken on the sofa.

"Are you okay? I heard a scream."

"I'm okay," Michelle whispered, still trying to catch her breath. "It was just a dream."

"I'll sit with you."

"Thanks. I had a dream about Evan. We were walking together with the babies. Out of nowhere, and for no reason, someone shot him in the head and he died right there. His blood was all over me."

"It was only a dream, my dear. I'm sure Evan is just fine. He'll be here in the morning."

"I hope so, but something just doesn't feel right."

Jessica's head kept falling forward slightly as she tried to keep her eyes open. The Homeland cruiser sped along the highway in the direction of Fort Worth. Her head hurt and her lower lip had begun to swell painfully. The adrenaline that had sustained her for much of the night had finally worn off and it took every ounce of energy she had just to keep her eyes open. She thought of her bed at home and wanted nothing more than to fall into it and sleep for days, or better yet, weeks.

The Homeland troopers had put her brother, Aiden, into the other cruiser with another protestor they'd picked up. She had no idea if they'd end up in the same facility or what to expect, but she was desperate to sleep and, finally, stopped fighting the ever-strengthening sense of fatigue and closed her eyes.

Jessica's thoughts wandered off, far away from the backseat of the Homeland cruiser to the warmth of the sun beating down on her skin and the subtle rhythm of waves flirting with the seashore. The ocean water enveloped her sandy toes then receded again, and the pattern repeated itself as she sat looking out over the ocean to the blue horizon.

"Hey, wake up," a faint voice said. "Hey, I said wake up."

Jessica pulled her heavy head up from the car seat. It took her a second to adjust to reality again, but when the grogginess from her all too brief sleep had been shaken off, she looked around and realized the cruiser had stopped again. The Homeland trooper was sitting in the backseat, next to Jessica, his thigh touching hers.

She asked the trooper, "Where are we?"

"Arlington, near Cowboy Stadium."

"Why are we here?"

"You said that you were only working downtown tonight and weren't part of the riots."

"That's the truth."

"Well, I'm not sure I believe you, but, you're a damn pretty girl, so I figured I'd stop here for some privacy and give you a chance to earn your freedom."

Chapter 43

The minty aroma of eucalyptus wafted lightly through the open window with the rays of warm morning sun. The heat of the sun felt refreshing on Declan's cheek and he opened his eyes after one of the deepest sleeps he could remember. He sat up slightly and breathed in the eucalyptus-tinged Andean air. Megan's side of the bed was empty and he could hear movement and rustling in the house.

With a bit of effort and soreness, Declan sat completely upright and, leaning against the window sill, pulled himself up to see what was outside. A moist breeze enveloped him and his eyes immediately feasted upon the serene idyllic beauty of the Urubamba Valley, or as it was called by the Incans who lived there centuries earlier, the Sacred Valley.

His window opened onto a lush well-kept garden, overflowing with color and vibrancy. Declan watched for a few minutes as a hummingbird hovered and flittered just above a collection of bright-red zinnias a few feet from him. The garden sat overlooking the green fertile Sacred Valley, with the snaking Urubamba River below and countless ancient Inca terraces neatly climbing the mountainsides. The whole scene struck Declan as paradise and he stood silently trying to take it all in, trying to fill each of his senses with the beauty that surrounded him.

"Hey, you're up," he heard Megan say behind him.

Declan turned around and smiled at her, asking, "Where are we?"

Megan set down a steaming tea cup she'd brought in and walked over to Declan at the window. "It doesn't suck does it?"

"Far from it," he replied. "I thought I may have actually died overnight and this was heaven."

"No such luck, Declan Parker," she said and kissed him. "If that was the case, I'm not so sure I'd be here."

"Seriously, is this your uncle's house?"

"No, my uncle's house is the bigger one a little further up the mountainside. This is one of the guest houses. My mom's family has owned this hacienda going back to the early-1700's."

"It's absolutely gorgeous."

"I know."

"How long are we going to be here?"

"Who knows? Forever maybe."

"Sounds good to me," Declan replied as he looked back out over the garden. "Forever sounds good to me."

"Here, drink this," Megan said picking up the tea cup.

"What is it?"

"It's coca tea. It's good for you. Andeans swear by it and it'll help your head and the healing process."

Declan took a sip. "It's good, kinda like a green tea."

"Sort of. Are you hungry?"

"Starving."

"Good, I'll bring breakfast in. Atau made scrambled eggs, Andean potatoes and quinoa pancakes."

"What kind of pancakes?"

"Don't worry about it, you'll like them."

"Can we eat in the garden?"

"Do you think you're up to it?"

"Absolutely. I can't think of anything that would make me feel better than being out there, with you, in all that beauty."

"Okay, the garden it is then. It's a rare sunny day during the rainy season. We may as well take advantage of it. I'll ask Atau to get a table set."

Chapter 44

Evan sat, handcuffed to a steel chair, in the center of a non-descript windowless room. He was unbearably sore from head to toe. The handcuffs seemed to him practically unnecessary as he suspected he couldn't lift either of his arms anyway. Pain throbbed throughout his bruised and beaten body.

"The Lord is my light," he whispered slowly to himself, "and my salvation. Whom shall I fear? The Lord is the stronghold of my life. Of whom should I be afraid? When evil men advance against me to devour my flesh, when my enemies and my foes attack me, they will stumble and fall. Though an army besiege me, my heart will not fear. Though war break out against me, even then will I be confident."

A door opposite Evan opened and John Bleeker entered, along with two other men who took up positions against the wall on either side of Bleeker. Evan looked up to see Bleeker approaching him and whispered again, "The Lord is my light and my salvation. Whom shall I fear?"

Picking up on what seemed to him as Evan's mumbling, Bleeker asked, "What was that?"

Evan looked up at him and mustered an intentionally ironic smile, but said nothing.

"I see, still not going to say anything. That's okay, you will in time, and I've got all the time in the world."

"I've already told you, I'm not talking to anyone until I'm allowed to see my attorney," Evan responded softly, the pain and soreness in his jaw preventing him from speaking with any level of forcefulness.

"I thought we covered this last night. You're being held as a suspected domestic terrorist, Dr. Parker."

"Suspected of what?"

"Oh, I don't know, attempting to blow up the White House maybe. Who cares? It really doesn't matter because I've got you pursuant to the NDAA, and under the NDAA you don't get counsel, nor do you get to go until I say you do. You've got a better chance of talking to Abe Lincoln than you do of talking to your attorney. It's not going to happen. So, you can tell me where your brother and the girlfriend went or we can go another round with my friends here. Your choice."

Evan sat silently, looking straight ahead at Bleeker.

"Fine, have it your way. He's all yours gentlemen," Bleeker said, as he turned and left the room with a dismissive wave. Feigning no attempt to hide his eagerness, the agent on the left reached down into a blue plastic bucket filled with water and pulled a wet faceless hood out. He approached Evan, who merely closed his eyes and tried to ready himself for what he knew would come, and placed the hood over Evan's head and face. A few seconds later, Evan felt his head being jerked backwards and the rush of water pouring onto his face and mouth. His body jerked uncontrollably as he struggled to breathe and to fight the painful panicked sensation that he was drowning.

After cleaning up and getting a few hours' sleep, Louis Martino took a shuttle back to DFW International Airport, rebooked himself on a flight into David Ben-Gurion Airport leaving later that evening and rented a car for the day. He left the airport and headed to the relatively obscure federal detention facility in Fort Worth, where he hoped to find out something about Jessica Ehlers.

About an hour later, after getting lost a few times, Louis arrived at the inward facing barbwire fences surrounding the modestly marked facility. He could see Homeland personnel trucks moving about, and with some straining, was able to make out the Homeland Security and Federal Emergency Management Agency logos on many of the trucks and vans inside the facility. After a few minutes, Louis approached what appeared to be a main entrance, which was manned by what appeared to be armed, plain-clothes, private security personnel. As his rental car approached, one of them waved Louis to a stop.

"This is a restricted area, sir."

"I understand. I'm trying to locate a woman who was mistakenly arrested with protestors in downtown Dallas last night. One of the Homeland troopers told me she'd likely be processed here."

"I'm sorry, but I'm not aware of any such processing."

"Were any of the protestors brought here last night or this morning? Is this a federal prison?"

"I'm not at liberty to discuss the nature of the facility, sir, other than to inform you that it is a restricted area and you'll need to leave."

"I can't go in and ask about the woman I'm looking for?"

"No, I'm sorry, but you can't."

"I have press credentials. Does that help?"

"No, sir, it doesn't. I'm sorry, but I'll have to ask you to turn around and leave the area."

"But I haven't actually gotten into the area yet," Louis replied. "I'm still on the street."

"Sir, you're going to have to leave the area. Please turn your vehicle around and go back the way you came. This is a…"

"I know," Louis cut him off, "it's a restricted area. I got it."

"Have a good day, sir."

Louis rolled up his window, turned the rental car around, and began driving back in the direction he'd come from. As he looked back at the security personnel at the check point in his rear view mirror, he saw a silver unmarked sedan exit the facility and proceed to follow his car. From what he could tell, there were two men in the sedan, which followed him until he'd left the area completely and got on the highway headed back toward Dallas.

Chapter 45

Despite the nearly constant drizzle, Declan spent as much time as he could in the garden overlooking the Urubamba Valley below. He spent hours counting the visible Incan terraces and tracing them up the mountainsides and along the river banks, trying to imagine what the area must have looked like hundreds of years earlier when the Incas populated the region.

The climate, cuisine and sheer beauty of the Peruvian Andes agreed with Declan. He'd never seen such an awesome and stunning place before, so different in every respect than anything he'd known in the United States. His energy and strength increased steadily, as did his appetite, both physically and spiritually.

Atau, the young man of Quechua descent who cooked the meals and was responsible for overseeing the care of the guest house in which Declan and Megan were staying, had set up a comfortable chaise lounge and small table under a canopy in the garden for Declan. Noticing Declan's interest in the Incan terraces and the Sacred Valley more generally, Atau had brought out a few books written in English about the Incas and Peru. Declan spent most of the day reading about the Incas and the Andes. He also began delving more and more deeply into his Bible.

He wasn't quite sure why exactly, but something about reading his Bible in that setting, amidst the seemingly endless beauty surrounding him, brought the pages to life for Declan. He read about Adam and Eve and the Garden of Eden in Genesis 2 and tried to imagine a setting more scenic, more perfect than the one he was in. It wasn't that Declan fully believed yet, or at least he hadn't yet acknowledged a renewed belief in God. However, something was undeniably drawing him, pulling on him, calling him if you will, and for the first time since his dad had passed away, Declan wasn't inclined to fight it. Whatever, or whoever, it was.

British Airways Flight 167 touched down at David Ben-Gurion International Airport. After collecting his bag and clearing customs and immigration, Louis Martino caught a cab for the relatively short drive to Jerusalem.

The taxi driver asked in English, "Where are you headed?"

"To the King David Hotel."

"You'll like the King David very much. In my opinion, the top hotel in Jerusalem."

"Oh, I'm not staying there. I wish I were. I'm staying at the Crowne Plaza, but I'm a journalist, so I'm headed to the King David first for the press conference with the Foreign Minister and to see what kind of newsworthy gossip I can pick up. Do you live in Jerusalem?"

"Yes."

"How have things been? It seems pretty quiet at the moment."

"It's the calm before the storm so to speak, I fear. Jerusalem has been relatively safe. Tel Aviv, as you probably know, was hit. The rocket fire has been almost constant near the borders. The airport, Tel Aviv and Jerusalem are very well protected, relatively quiet the last couple days, but most think that's going to change soon as the IDF response accelerates."

"What do you think?"

"I think we're about to find ourselves engaged in an all-out war very soon. Maybe hours, maybe days. But, we're ready. The IDF, our leaders and our people are well prepared. We'll come out of it stronger than before. 'Never again' we say, 'never again.' If you've come for news, you'll have no trouble. It will find you soon enough."

Having heard nothing from Evan, Michelle left the

children in the care of her mother-in-law and drove back into the city to try and find him or find out what had happened to him. With the ongoing protests and riots, conditions in the city had devolved into something just shy of chaos.

Already concerned foreign markets had significantly tapered their purchase of U.S. treasury bonds, which had sparked a minor sell off. The interest rate on 10 year treasury bonds had shot up over 200% and the U.S. dollar's continued reign as the world reserve currency was in doubt as governments and institutional investors around the world, fearing a potential civil war in the United States, had begun calling for the United Nations and the IMF to institute a new reserve currency to replace the dollar. The foreign market for U.S. treasuries had all but dried up.

The immediate results could be seen and felt in every city and town in the United States. As she headed toward Evan's office, Michelle passed gas stations advertising gas at $8.17 a gallon with lines of cars stretching blocks waiting to fill up. The grocery stores appeared almost under siege, with people rushing to buy whatever food was still on the shelves and the lines at the banks and ATM machines, for those that were still operating, were at least two hour waits to get cash. A general sense of panic filled the air all around town.

Michelle finally reached Evan's office and parked outside. She rushed inside to find the receptionist sitting at her place at the front desk. "Hi, Mrs. Parker," the receptionist greeted.

"Have you seen Dr. Parker today?"

"No, he hasn't been in for the past few days and nobody has heard anything from him. Is everything okay?"

"He hasn't contacted any of his partners or been in to see patients?"

"No, I've had to cancel all his appointments. We've tried to call his cell and the home phone, but only got his voicemail. Is he okay?"

"I don't think so. Thank you, I've got to go," Michelle replied as she rushed back outside with tears beginning to pour out of her. She had no idea where Evan could be or what to do next, where to go.

Michelle hurried back to her SUV, but as she was about to get back in, a man came up quickly behind her and shoved her to the ground. Not knowing what had happened, Michelle looked up to see the man in her face, yelling "Give me the keys!"

"What?"

"Give me the damn keys," he yelled again as he knelt down and began patting her coat pockets. Michelle screamed and the man, getting more and more frustrated, backhanded her across the mouth, busting her bottom lip open.

Suddenly, another man violently pulled Michelle's assailant off of her and threw him against the SUV. The would-be-car-thief slammed into the side of the silver Denali and bounced off, landing hard on the ground. Michelle scrambled to get up off the cold pavement as the second man pulled a handgun from inside his coat and pistol whipped the assailant in the street.

Finished, he turned to Michelle and asked, "Are you okay?"

She stood trembling uncontrollably, still trying to comprehend what had happened and unable to say anything. The second man took hold of her hands gently and looked her in the eyes. "Try and calm down," he said. "It's okay. I'm Kevin Cameron, Declan's friend from the Bureau. You're alright, but you need to get out of here and get back to the house you're at out by the lake."

"How'd you…"

"Look, I want to help you. Get out of town. Don't stop anywhere for anything. Go back to the lake house and I'll get in touch with you in the next day or so."

"But, I'm looking for my husband."

"I know, and I know where he is. You have to trust me and you have to go right now."

"You know…"

"I know where he is," Kevin said again as he gently

forced Michelle back into the SUV. "I'll contact you at the lake house in the next few days and explain everything, but don't, under any circumstances, leave the house or come back to the city. It's not safe. Now go and don't stop for anything or anyone."

Chapter 46

Tear gas canisters exploded on all sides of Jessica and the white smoke began to fizz and sizzle into the night air. Jessica was jostled by bodies running chaotically in all directions around her. She stood still for a moment, her mouth and nose covered by a bandana tied around her face, trying to regain her composure and figure out the best way to safety. Gun shots whipped loudly to her left in succession and as she turned in that direction, she watched as another female protester was thrown backwards through the air before landing lifelessly a few feet away.

Jessica's pulse quickened and her body began to shake uncontrollably. Rage and panic overtook her as she looked through the white gas into the open lifeless eyes of the dead woman. In a dash, she ran in the opposite direction, trying to escape the tear gas and gunfire, trying to find some sort of shelter from the storm, a place to hide from the screams and pain-filled shouts that permeated the air around her.

The scene was complete chaos. Death littered the streets. Jessica hurried away from the stinging gas into a small open area featuring a series of park benches set around a circular concrete fountain. It was an idyllic setting in other, normal, circumstances. More gunshots raced past her, seemingly targeted at her. Jessica threw herself down onto the pavement behind the small fountain wall and laid there almost prostrate with her face pressing hard into the cold concrete. She could hear gunfire and footsteps running around the little park, but refused to raise her head or eyes to look. Then, more gunfire and a scream, followed by more shots and the heavy lumbering sound of boots running on the pavement right past her.

The rush of noise and violence finally carried past her and, for a second, there was only her heavy breath against the cold silence. As she lifted her head, she could hear a faint voice on the other side of the fountain saying, "Come in, come in."

Jessica pulled herself slowly up onto the fountain and, peering over, spotted a Homeland trooper lying in a small pool of blood on the other side. He appeared to be talking into a radio in his helmet, saying "Come in, I'm hit. Come in." From what Jessica could tell, he had no idea she was behind him. The trooper was wearing the same uniform as the Homeland trooper who had, nights earlier, forced Jessica "to earn her freedom". The pain and anger of that all too recent violation suddenly flooded her senses. She simultaneously wanted to kill someone, anyone, and to crawl up into a small ball and die herself. Her eyes burned into the back of the trooper's helmet. Whoever he was, she wished he was dead. Tears of rage and humiliation burst from her eyes.

As she stood sobbing, Jessica saw the trooper's weapon on the ground a few feet away from him, just out of his reach. Without thinking, she ran across the fountain and jumped down on the other side, swiftly picking up the rifle. The trooper saw her and tried to pull himself up, but was unable. Jessica, who had never before held a gun, turned and aimed the weapon at the injured trooper. He looked no older than twenty, maybe even younger and she could see the fear of death in his eyes.

"Please," he quivered. "Please, I don't want to die."

All Jessica could see was that uniform, that logo on the sleeve and those thick black combat pants tucked into his stupid black boots. A hatred she had never known before seethed within and her mind, unwillingly, took her again to the backseat of the Homeland cruiser. Tears continued to stream down her cheeks as the weapon trembled in her shaking hands.

"Please," he pleaded again. "Please, God, don't kill me."

Jessica heard nothing but the heavy breathing of the trooper above her in the backseat of the cruiser. She saw nothing but the small erratic lines in the black interior ceiling of the cruiser, she'd focused on so intently in order to avoid looking at her rapist. Her hands squeezed the rifle as though she sought to crush it. She fired off two rounds from the automatic weapon, both of which found the lower torso of the already badly wounded Homeland trooper. The trooper let out a labored howl and writhed on the ground in his own blood.

Jessica dropped the weapon on the pavement and ran in the opposite direction away from the ironic serenity of the fountain and back out into the chaos of the surrounding streets. As she reached the next intersection, a concussion grenade exploded nearby and Jessica was thrown against the wall of a building, where she collapsed, unconscious on the sidewalk.

Chapter 47

Bleeker and Kevin Cameron entered the small dark holding cell where Evan lay in a crumpled ball on the floor.

"Lights," Bleeker called out. "And let's get two chairs in here as well."

A few seconds later, a dull, yellowish, artificial light partially illuminated the cell. Evan's eyes closed, then flickered a few times in an effort to adjust to the dull light. A guard brought two brown metal folding chairs into the cell and set them up opposite one another, then stepped back outside, the cell door closing securely behind him.

"Cameron, pick him up and set him as upright in the chair as you can," Bleeker ordered. Trying to handle the battered Evan as gently as possible, without looking like he was attempting to be gentle, Kevin slowly lifted him from the floor and propped Evan up in the metal chair opposite Bleeker.

"He's burning up," Kevin said.

"What, does he have a fever?"

"It feels like it to me. His body feels like it's on fire."

Bleeker looked Evan over and said, "You do look like crap, my friend."

Evan's head hung low as he sat slumped over, looking as though he might fall forward. Whether it was the light or the upright position, a disoriented nausea overtook Evan and he suddenly vomited what little food he'd been given on the floor next to the chair. Kevin, who had been standing behind the chair, reached over and caught Evan as he was about to fall back down to the floor.

Bleeker quickly pushed himself back in his own chair, away from the vomit. "Let's make this quick," he said. "I'm due in D.C. tomorrow and I'm gonna be pissed if this guy gets me sick."

"Agreed," Cameron replied.

"So, Dr. Parker, you're relative usefulness to me has run its course and you've run out of time. I'm on my way to

D.C. tomorrow, where I'll be taking up a special advisory role on the president's national security staff. Part of my new duties will be devoted to the recently implemented martial law and quelling the various civil insurrections that have broken out. The other part will focus on more targeted, sensitive matters. I know, your heartfelt congratulations aside, none of this really means anything to you. However, my first act in connection with the more targeted sensitive matters I spoke of should interest you. It's been decided to go public with the story about how your brother, and possibly even you, were working with David Stanton on his failed plan."

Evan raised his head slightly, looking at Bleeker the best he could," What?"

"Ah, it speaks," Bleeker responded with a laugh. "I see that got your attention. Good. Yes, it seems your brother was working with Stanton. It's believed that Special Agent Parker used his position in the Bureau to falsify documents and expunge data relating to David Stanton in an effort to conceal his demented agenda. Obviously, his efforts were in vain, thanks mainly to me. Nonetheless, he's still a criminal and a wanted man."

"That's a lie."

"You know, the funny thing about truth and, conversely, lies, is really just the simple matter of perception and who's telling them. Tomorrow, all the major news outlets will begin running this story and to millions and millions of people around the country and the world, it will therefore become the truth. Regardless, let's circle back to how all this impacts you. I no longer really care where your brother is. As of tomorrow, he'll have no credibility and the array of problems he presented are, for all intents and purposes, solved. So, that leaves me with the question of what to do with you."

Evan stared at Bleeker, unsure as to what would come next and, at least for that moment, less sure that he cared. "Whatever, you have no power over me," he said softly.

"Come again."

"You have no power over me, so do what you will."

"Of course, because you're a Christian and all that. Daniel and the lion's den and all that stuff. No mere human being can touch you because you belong to God or Jesus or whomever, right?"

"Basically."

"Right. That seems to be working out swimmingly for you so far, I'll admit. Well, power or no power, I've been given the discretion to do with you whatever I see fit, although I haven't quite decided what that will be. I came in here to maybe give you some say in the matter. To beg for clemency and the chance to maybe see your lovely wife and beautiful children again, provided of course they're still alive. But, since…"

"What did you say about my family?"

"Nothing. I have no power over you, remember," Bleeker said as he stood up. "I'll just have to come to my own, admittedly fallible, decision regarding you and your family. Of course, your Jesus could clearly veto whatever decision I reach. Open 3!"

Clearly agitated, Evan asked, "What do you know about my family?"

The cell door opened and Bleeker and Kevin Cameron stepped out without another word to Evan.

"Where's my family!"

The guard came back in, shoved Evan off the folding chair back onto the floor, folded up both chairs and left. The cell door slammed shut behind him. Evan lay near death, disillusioned and sobbing, praying that his family was still alive somewhere.

As they stepped outside the building, Bleeker scrolled through emails on his smart phone. Kevin asked, "What should I do with him?"

Not looking up from his phone, Bleeker responded dismissively, "Just kill him."

"What if we were to keep him alive?"

"Why would we bother to do that, Cameron? He's going to die anyway, did you see the guy?"

"I did, and he may. But, if we keep him alive and put him in a detention center, maybe it will lure Parker back."

"Parker's irrelevant now. He'll be a fugitive and have zero credibility in the morning."

"True, but collaring, or even killing Parker would bolster a resume."

"Mine or yours?"

"Both."

"Fine, move Dr. Parker to a detention center; but, not one nearby. Send him off somewhere to one of the centers in another state. I don't want any chance of his family trying to find him or, more importantly, for him to have any hope of ever finding them again. Understood?"

"Clearly."

"And if Parker is stupid enough to come back for him, the collar, the kill, whatever, is fifty-fifty, capische?"

"Absolutely."

"I'm in D.C. for the next few days, then I'll be back here. In the unlikely event something comes of this while I'm gone, I want to be notified before anything goes down."

"You'll be the first."

"I've got to go. I'll leave the good doctor's final destination to you."

As Bleeker headed to his car, Kevin went back inside trying to decide on the best location for Evan. None were ideal, but he knew of a facility in North Texas that, while meeting Bleeker's other-state criteria, was not unreasonably far away. Kevin flagged the desk guard and said, "Alright, we're transferring Dr. Parker to the federal detention center in Fort Worth, Texas within the next couple days. I don't want him to die in the meantime, so get him out of that holding cell to one with a bed and heat. Clean him up, get him food and water, and let's get one of the medics in here to take a look at him. This is a detainee who has a certain level of strategic value, not some street rabble, and I want him treated as such moving forward. Understood?"

Chapter 48

Watching the sun rise over the Sacred Valley each morning had become almost ritual for Declan. On the odd morning when there was no rain, the pink, orange and yellow of the sunrise danced about with the greens and blues present in the Urubamba River and the fertile lands and mountainsides bordering it. Yet, even in the drizzly rain, the valley was majestic. Each morning, sitting under the canopy, Declan would read from his Bible. It began with a verse or two, then a chapter or two, until he found himself spending a good portion of the morning before breakfast coming to know the Bible, and consequently, God as he had when he was a young boy.

Declan said a short prayer, opened his Bible, and began reading Ephesians, "[1]Paul, an apostle of Christ Jesus by the will of God, to God's holy people in Ephesus, the faithful in Christ Jesus. [2]Grace and peace to you from God our Father and the Lord Jesus Christ." Declan took a quick look up, through the new morning light in the garden and out onto the winding river below.

"[3]Praise be to the God and Father of our Lord Jesus Christ, who has blessed us in the heavenly realms with every spiritual blessing in Christ. [4]For he chose us in him before the creation of the world to be holy and blameless in his sight. In love [5]he predestined us for adoption to sonship through Jesus Christ, in accordance with his pleasure and will – [6]to the praise of his glorious grace, which he has freely given us in the One he loves. [7]In him we have redemption through his blood, the forgiveness of sins, in accordance with the riches of God's grace that he lavished on us."

Declan stopped reading again and tried to let the meaning of the words, the implication of the passage, sink in fully. "A God who would give His only son for all of us," he thought to himself. It was a difficult concept to fathom. Declan understood sacrifice for one's own family, but he didn't think he'd be capable of sacrificing himself, much less a son or daughter, if he'd had one, for a bunch of people he didn't know.

As he read on, Declan came to Verse 13, which read, "And you also were included in Christ when you heard the message of truth, the gospel of your salvation. When you believed, you were marked in him with a seal, the promised Holy Spirit…"

"Hey, good morning," Megan said coming up behind him.

"Good morning. How'd you sleep?"

"Great. I don't know if it's the air here or what, but I always sleep like a rock. You looked like you were deep in thought."

"I was just reading this passage and it reminded me of my dad. Actually, it was more than a reminder. I could see him reading it to me and Evan when we were kids. I hadn't thought about it in forever, but reading it just now, I saw it like I was there again."

"You've been reading the Bible quite a bit since we got here."

"Everyday. It's hard to explain because, since my dad died, I couldn't care less about God. I didn't really think there was a God, most days anyway. But since we've been here, I can't really explain why, but I feel like I have to read it. Almost like I'm being compelled, or called, to read it."

"Did you believe in God when you were younger, before you lost your dad?"

"I think so. Our parents did a really good job with teaching us about God and Jesus. It was a consistent focus in our home, but, when dad died, I don't know, something in me just changed."

"And you stopped believing?"

"Yeah, at least that's what I used to think until these past few days. Now I'm not so sure I stopped believing as much as I just…I just…"

"You what?"

"I hated God. I hated Him for taking my dad from

me, for stealing him from me," Declan responded as water began to well up in his eyes. "I think what I really did was take away my love for God, my acknowledgement of His existence, in order to try and punish Him for what I felt he'd done to me."

"That's an understandable response."

"I suppose. It's at least a human response, but I'm beginning to think it was the wrong response and definitely not what my dad would have wanted for me."

"That's probably true, based on what I know of your dad."

"Anyway, the passage I just read, from Ephesians, the one that brought dad to mind, was basically about how you're sealed with the Holy Spirit from the first second you believe. It made me begin to think, if that's true, then all this time, through all my anger and hatred toward God, if I really did believe in His son, His spirit would have still been in me."

"Sounds like it."

"It's just hard to fathom, that's all. It's hard to grasp a God who still loves us when we hate Him or refuse to acknowledge Him altogether."

"That's what I've always been told He does though, amazing as it seems."

"It really is amazing. What do you think of all this?"

"What do you mean?"

"About God and the Bible and everything. Do you believe it?"

"Yeah, I believe it. Things were always pretty simple with my family. We went to church, we said prayers, mostly at meals and when things didn't go well, and we quietly believed in Jesus as the only way to heaven. The basic run of the mill Christian life, I suppose."

"Have you read the Bible?"

"Never from cover to cover and probably not in ages, but I still believe it. It's just something that's in me I suppose."

"Do you remember when you were saved?"

"I sure do. It was at our church when I was eighteen. Our pastor had just finished his sermon, which was on the parable of the mustard seed, and I think, for the first time, I really understood what it was all about, why I needed to be saved and why that could only happen through Jesus. So, I said the prayer we had been taught in Sunday school, you know, admitting my sins, telling Jesus I believed in him and loved him, and asking him to save me. I remember it like it was yesterday. I was super-excited and wanted to do all these things, to go out and volunteer in church stuff, feed the poor, all that stuff. The enthusiasm lasted for three or four months, then wore off as I got into college and the various demands and distractions of campus life. Sometimes I feel like I should be doing something more, but for the most part, I'm happy and I know I'm going to heaven. I guess I don't need much more than that."

"You know, it's funny, but I think in all the time we've known each other, all the time we've been together, this is the first time we've ever talked about this."

"I think you're right. We must be growing up, Declan Parker," Megan said with a smile and kissed Declan on the lips.

"We must be."

"Oh, I almost forgot why I came out here in the first place. In light of Dr. Mendoza's report on your progress, I thought we could go up to Cusco for lunch and a very low key look around town in the next couple days. As gorgeous as it is here, I think a change of scenery would do both of us some good."

"Sounds like a plan."

"Excellent. I'll make the arrangements."

Chapter 49

Louis flipped through his outline one final time to verify each point he'd wanted to make had been included in his article. After a final read through, Louis was satisfied that he'd carefully and convincingly laid out all the salient points and facts with respect to Declan's innocence in the David Stanton affair, which conflict with the story being carried by all the mainstream media outlets. He read over the closing lines for the tenth time,

"As evidenced by the classified Homeland Security documents I've obtained, if just one thing from the David Stanton debacle is clear, it is Special Agent Declan Parker's innocence. In trying to do what we, the taxpayers, pay him to do, Special Agent Parker stumbled into a web of federal government corruption and manipulation targeted, like so many others we've seen these past years, at the systemic and total elimination of our civil rights. For the crime of doing his job and fulfilling his duty, Declan Parker was the victim of two attempted murders and now, slander of the worst variety. Don't be fooled, this government and its media stooges are lying to you, each and every day. Investigate every word that spills from their mouths, because THINGS ARE NOT WHAT THEY SEEM."

Louis converted the Word document for web release and uploaded the article, along with copies of the relevant internal Homeland documents and hospital records Megan had given him. He published the article on The Free Voice website, along with a link to the documents.

"Well done you," Louis said to himself. "And just in time."

He grabbed his desert-beige military surplus backpack, stuffed in his laptop, along with the clothes and other items already inside, and headed out of his hotel room to the lobby, where he found an IDF Samal, or Sergeant, Ariel Ya'alon waiting.

"Sergeant Ya'alon?"

"Yes, Mr. Martino?"

"Yes. It's a pleasure to meet you."

"Likewise. Do you have your paperwork?"

"I do," Louis replied, pulling out the letter of introduction provided to him by his friend, Adam Benjamin, a former college roommate who was on the Prime Minister's staff."

Sgt. Ya'alon read over the letter carefully. "So, you're to be imbedded with my unit for the next five days."

"That's correct."

"Well, it looks like everything is in order. Are you ready?"

"Absolutely. Thank you again for picking me up."

"Not a problem, Mr. Martino. I'll take you to meet up with the rest of the unit and we'll head out."

"To the Golan Heights, correct?"

"That's correct."

Evan sat up in the cot, which in spite of its Spartan comfort was worlds beyond the hard cold floor in his prior holding cell, as he saw Kevin Cameron stepping in.

"How do you like the new accommodations, Dr. Parker?"

"A definite improvement," Evan replied.

"Good. You're looking a bit better."

"A case of looks being deceptive, I'm afraid."

"Well, regardless, we'll be transferring you to another facility shortly."

"Am I being charged with anything?"

"I believe Special Agent Bleeker already explained your circumstances and the authority under which you're being held."

"Of course, the NDAA."

"Don't be a smartass," Kevin suddenly said raising his voice. He rushed toward Evan and shoved him back down into the cot, with his forearm against Evan's chest. Getting his face as close to Evan's as possible, almost uncomfortably so, Kevin leaned over him and whispered, "Your family is okay," then Kevin put his index finger up to his mouth to say, "Shhh." Evan looked up at him somewhat stunned, but remained silent.

Kevin quickly whispered again, "I know where they are and they're safe. I can't say more now, but you'll have to trust me."

Evan whispered, "Who are you?"

"A friend," Kevin replied softly, then jerked Evan up from the cot and said threateningly, "I don't like smartasses, understood. Any more comments like that and you'll be back where you started. Open 8!"

Chapter 50

Declan couldn't pull his eyes from the quaint, narrow, colonial streets of old town Cusco. It was a town unlike anything he'd ever seen, something akin to living, breathing history.

"This is amazing," he said to Megan.

"I know. There's nothing like this in the States. Do you see the stone work on the base of the buildings?"

"Yeah."

"That's Incan. When the Spanish came, they essentially built on top of the Incan foundations. They built right over important Incan religious and government buildings. The Church of Santo Domingo is literally built on top of Qorikancha, the Inca Temple of the Sun."

"It's all incredible."

"Wait until you see where we're having lunch."

The ride lasted a few more minutes as the car bobbled and jostled up the ancient, narrow stone streets, until it came to a stop in a small square surrounded by Spanish hacienda-style buildings, all built on top of superbly crafted Inca stone-worked foundations.

A young Peruvian man in a dark suit came out to open the car door, umbrella in hand, "Buenos Dias. Welcome to the Monasterio."

"Gracias," Megan replied. She and Declan walked inside the warm and ornate Hotel Monasterio. "This place was an old Spanish monastery. It was originally built in the 1500's or something and then rebuilt again after an earthquake in the mid-1600's."

"It's beautiful."

They walked slowly through the baroque-inspired lobby to the restaurant. One of the hosts approached and led them to a table looking out onto the drizzly serene courtyard in the center of the hotel. Declan sat down and stared up at a huge tree standing in the midst of the courtyard.

"That's the only remaining Andean Cedar tree in

Cusco," Megan said to him.

"Seriously?"

"Yep. They were all over this area, but when the Spanish came, they cut them down for building. That's the last one and it's over 300 years old. The Andean Cedar was a sacred tree to the Incas. The locals say this one keeps the memory of those times alive with its scent."

"It's beautiful. I can only imagine what this place looked like when they were everywhere. It must have been stunning."

"That's what I've always been told. After lunch we'll walk over to the little chapel, San Antonio Abad. It's just right over there, across the courtyard. It's a really impressive Cusco Baroque chapel."

"Sounds good to me."

"How are you feeling? This isn't too much too soon is it?"

"No, not at all. I actually feel pretty good. It's nice to get a little change of scenery and get out with you. We haven't done anything like this in a while."

"It is nice."

The waiter brought two bottled waters and two cups of coca tea to the table, along with a three or four page printout of various news articles from the United States. "I'll be right back with your salads."

"Gracias," Declan responded.

Megan looked over the news articles. "Oh my God, they've declared martial law in the States."

"What?"

"That's what this says. The initial protests have turned into all out riots and the government implemented martial law trying to keep the peace."

"I don't believe it. That's insane."

"This says they've established nationwide curfews. There's widespread looting. The stock market dropped by nearly 20% in the past two days and there are all kinds of food and fuel shortages across the country."

Declan sat in silent shock as Megan continued reading, thinking about all the times he'd heard his mom and Evan talk about the degenerating freedoms in the U.S. and how martial law would probably be put into place someday. Megan continued, "This says the dollar appears to be falling and prices on everything are skyrocketing, to the extent basic necessities are even available."

"This is crazy," Declan replied soberly. "This kind of stuff happens in other countries, but not in the U.S. It's a total disaster."

"I agree. It's surreal."

"I mean, why do we even bother to have a constitution if the government isn't going to follow it?"

"Some would say we stopped following the constitution a long time ago."

Declan's eyes began to well up at the thought of riots and martial law back home. It had just never seemed possible. "Can I see that?"

Megan handed him the paper and Declan read over the entire article, still unable to believe the scenes described. Nearly sick to his stomach, he tossed the paper back down onto the table in disgust and said, "The government is killing and imprisoning its own citizens for expressing their constitutional rights. We're done. We may as well be the Soviet Union or Nazi Germany."

"I just hope everyone back home is okay," Megan responded.

"Have you heard anything from anyone back home? I hope my mom, Evan, Michelle and the kids are all alright. I've had this sinking feeling lately that something is wrong."

"I haven't heard anything, but I'll ask Uncle Ignacio if my mom has called him when we get back. Truthfully, I have a Homeland program on my personal laptop that should allow me to check email without anyone being able to trace my location. It's a pretty sophisticated scrambler, but I've been reluctant to try it yet. I suppose I should check to see. I had no idea things were that out of control."

"Neither did I."

Megan turned the page and came face to face with a small photo of Declan's Academy graduation photo on the next page, which didn't much resemble his worn, unshaven, scraggy post-shooting look. "Umm…"

"What's wrong now?"

"Look at this."

Declan took the paper and saw his photo, then read the article below. The soberness and sadness in his eyes turned to outright shock and anger. "They're saying I was helping Stanton, that I deleted investigative records and records of his ammunition purchases. This says I manipulated Bureau and Homeland data files to try and keep his activities under the radar and was at the church on Christmas Eve to set off more explosive charges and, likely, fire on any first responders. I'm wanted in the States."

"We'd better go. I don't want to take a chance with someone recognizing you."

Declan stared at the photo of himself, the bright eyed and optimistic new FBI Agent. The image of himself on the paper looked nothing like he felt. "Sadly, this picture doesn't look much like me anymore, even though it was only a year or so ago."

"I don't care. Go back out to the car and take that with you. I'll pay the bill."

"Do you think Louis' story has run yet? Maybe that will offset this somewhat."

"I'm not sure, but I'll get on The Free Voice when we get home and check. Even if it has, I doubt it will matter much. These days, perception is reality and most people's perception is supplied by the big media outlets. We'll see."

Chapter 51

Kevin waited until it had been dark for an hour or so, then slowly approached the lake house, careful to continually check behind him to make sure no one had followed him. As he walked around a small bend in the frozen gravel road, the lights in the lake house windows finally came into view.

Kevin took his time and tried to make some noise as he walked along the gravel in the hope that Michelle or someone inside would hear him and he wouldn't catch them completely off guard. As he neared the front porch, he could hear movement inside and the sound of a woman trying to "shhh" small children. Not wanting to scare Michelle, he called out from the porch, "Mrs. Parker, it's Kevin Cameron, Declan's friend."

A few seconds passed and the front door opened ever so slightly. Then, after having recognized Kevin, Michelle opened the door and said, "Please, come in."

Evan's mom came into the small living room from the kitchen, where Kevin could hear the children. "This is my mother-in-law," Michelle explained.

"Thank you. I won't stay long."

"No, please, stay as long as you like," Michelle replied as her eyes began to well up with tears. "You said you knew something about Evan and we haven't heard from or spoken to anyone in a long time. Is Evan okay?"

"He's alive and he's getting better."

"Better? What happened to him?"

"Please, just calm down and I'll explain. At the moment, your husband is okay. He's in federal custody…"

"What? Why?"

A frantic look came across Michelle's face and Mrs. Parker walked over and put her hand on Michelle's trembling shoulder.

"He was picked up for helping Declan escape from the hospital. I don't know if you've heard yet, but Declan's wanted in connection with the David Stanton case."

"That's all a lie," Declan's mom replied sharply. "He had nothing to do with that."

"I know that. It's a sham story manufactured to discredit him because he's one of the few who knows the truth. The real reason Dr. Parker was picked up, and is being held, is because the powers that be were hoping he had information about where Declan is hiding out. That's why I was assigned to watch you."

"How'd you know we were here?"

"I followed you from your house the night you left town. The night your husband helped get Declan and Megan Neary out of the hospital."

Declan's mom asked, "So Declan and Megan are together?"

"I believe so."

"Are they safe?"

"I have no idea, but I suspect they are. Obviously, you haven't heard from them?"

"Not a word. We haven't heard anything from anyone since Evan called that night. We don't have any phones, computers, or any way to communicate with anyone up here. All we have is a radio, which gives us news about all the craziness going on out there."

"That's a good thing," Kevin replied. "It's probably the only reason you're still safe up here."

"What should we do? Can I see Evan?"

"No, not yet. I'm trying to come up with a way to get him out and get him, and all of you, safely out of the country. I'd better go, but I'll be back in touch. Stay here and don't venture out unless you absolutely need to. Martial law has been declared and there are curfews. How are you on food and water?"

"We're good for another two weeks or so."

"Good," Kevin replied as he moved toward the door to leave. "I know it's hard, but just sit tight and I'll be back when it's safe and I know more. I'll do what I can until I can come up with a plan that will work."

Mrs. Parker reached out and touched him lightly on the shoulder. Kevin turned toward her and she asked, "Why are you doing this? Why are you trying to help us?"

Kevin hesitated a moment and replied, "Your late husband, ma'am."

"Ronald?"

"Yes, ma'am. He was the special agent in charge when I started with the Bureau many many years ago. I got off to a bit of a rough start, but he took me under his wing and treated me like a son. I owe him."

"Have you ever told Declan this?"

"Only once, but I didn't go into a whole lot of detail. When Declan first started, I asked him about his dad's coding system. Declan was surprised that I knew anything about it. I told him that I'd worked for your husband briefly and he'd shown it to me once, when we were killing time on a stakeout. I tried to mentor Declan and look after him the best I could. I tried to keep him from getting tangled up in all the Stanton mess, but, in the end I failed."

"How'd you get involved in the Stanton case?"

"I don't know. Duty initially. I suppose selfishness and stupidity, ultimately. I've been a good and dedicated agent for most of my career. I've been passed over for promotion who knows how many times. At first I saw it as a way to finally move up, make a name for myself. They promised me Special Agent in Charge. It's not a good reason and it doesn't make what I almost let happen right, but I'm trying to make amends. Your son's a good agent, a good man, like his dad was."

"God bless you, Mr. Cameron. God bless you."

"I don't deserve any blessings, ma'am, but hopefully I will someday."

"None of us do, Mr. Cameron, but we receive them nonetheless. God doesn't bless us because of who we are, but because of who He is."

Bleeker sat at his new desk in his very-tiny White House office, reading Louis Martino's piece for the fourth time.

"John, have you seen this online article, in The Free Voice?"

"I have, sir," Bleeker responded, turning around.

"This Louis Martino evidently has, and published online, confidential Homeland documents."

"I know, sir."

"How do you think he obtained them?"

"My primary guess would be Megan Neary. She checked into Homeland HQ the night she and Declan Parker absconded."

"What are your thoughts on how to deal with it? Anything relating to the Stanton affair is your ballpark."

"I'm already on top of it. Louis Martino is presently in Israel. We're now monitoring his email and all traffic on The Free Voice website. He'll be picked up at the airport when he returns to the States."

Chapter 52

The pungency of stale body odor was the first thing to strike Evan about his new surroundings. Whereas his previous holding cell had been completely isolated, his new "home", a rough taupe cot, sat in the midst of hundreds of others in a general population mass-detention facility. The facility itself appeared to Evan to have either once been a manufacturing warehouse of some type, or was designed in a warehouse vein. Either way, the area was large, open, and relatively warm compared to where he'd been previously. It was also packed to the gills with inhabitants, male and female, of seemingly all ages and backgrounds.

No one had told Evan where he was being transferred. He had flown on some sort of government transport plane for approximately two hours, then been transferred to a windowless van for the ride to the detention center. Based on the slightly warmer temperature, Evan guessed he had been taken south.

After processing, two guards had escorted him, as he was barely able to limp along, to Cot No. G87 and left him there. Evan wasn't sure if it was due to his still bruised and sickly appearance, but with the exception of a couple nods in his direction, the bulk of the other detainees had stayed clear of him. As Evan was completely exhausted and still running a low fever, being left alone didn't bother him in the least. He laid down on Cot G87, pulled the rough army-green blanket over himself and fell asleep, thinking that either the Lord would protect him or he'd never wake up again. Either way, as he was unable to keep his eyes open, the situation seemed out of his control.

"Stay down, Mr. Martino," Sgt. Ya'alon advised.

Rapid gunfire raced above Louis and the IDF troops in the unit, as they hunkered low behind their vehicles. Even without Sgt. Ya'alon's advice, Louis had no intention of raising any part of his body, which was pressed against the side of an armored transport. He heard the thud and clank of bullets against the metal armor on the other side.

"They're really shooting at us," he yelled out.

"Yes, they are," Sgt. Ya'alon responded calmly. "Just keep your head down and stay right next to me. Air support should be arriving any moment now."

"Not a problem."

The unit continued to exchange fire with the group on the other side of the Israeli/Syrian border for about ninety seconds more, then the deafening whoosh of two Israeli Air Force F-15 Eagles shot overhead and Louis heard the heavy gunfire and two large explosions. The gunfire quickly died down and, within another minute, all was quiet except for Sgt. Ya'alon on his radio, "Yes, sir, we'll move forward immediately and secure the area. Understood, sir."

Louis asked, "What's going on?"

"We're taking up a position across the border. We're under attack on various fronts, here along the Golan, as well as Gaza, Lebanon, the West Bank, and the Sinai."

"Sounds like it's coming from all sides."

"It is. We have new reports of skirmishes with ISIS units along the southern-Syrian and Jordanian borders. Also, Hamas fighters crossing over from Gaza and Hezbollah engaging our troops just over the Lebanese border. Lots of heavy rocket fire, with casualties. It's begun."

Adrenaline was still pulsing through Louis as he tried to quickly scribble down Sgt. Ya'alon's report.

Sgt. Ya'alon called out, "Alright, let's load up. We're moving to take up positions across the border! Let's go!"

"I checked our personal emails with the scrambler activated and there's nothing," Megan told Declan. "I'm sure both accounts are being constantly monitored, so it's probably a good thing nobody's sent anything to them."

"What about The Free Voice? Does Louis have an article up yet?"

"He sure does and, not surprisingly, it's outstanding. I printed it for you," she said, handing it to him. "He uses the information we gave him to poke holes in every charge being leveled against you. He even published the classified documents and medical records I gave him. We'll see if it helps at all."

"I'm beginning to get worried about my mom and the family. Evan would have told them everything a long time ago. It just seems like if everything was okay, they'd have at least emailed a short note or something."

"Maybe they're afraid to email, thinking it could be tracked to you."

"Maybe, but it just seems strange. With everything going on up there, my mom would at least want to get me a note saying she's okay."

"Read Louis' article. I'm going up to Uncle Ignacio's house to see if he's spoken with my mom recently and see if he has any news."

"Alright."

"I'll be back. I love you."

"I love you too."

Chapter 53

Evan woke up to the surprisingly refreshing feeling of a cold cloth on his forehead. As his eyes adjusted to the light, the strikingly angelic face of a young woman sitting next to him on the floor came into focus.

"You're awake," she said to him.

"I think so."

"You were running a fever, but I think it finally broke an hour or so ago."

"How long was I out?"

"Over twenty-four hours that I know of. One of your cot neighbors, Mr. Sippel, asked me to take a look at you and see what I could do. I'm Jessica Ehlers."

"Nice to meet you, Ms. Ehlers, and, thank you."

"Jessica is fine. You're welcome, mister?"

"Parker, Evan Parker."

"Nice to meet you too."

"You're pretty good at this."

"I hope so. I'm in my last year of nursing school, at least I was."

"So, what is this place?" Evan asked as he slowly sat up in his cot.

"It's the federal detention center in Fort Worth."

"Texas?"

"Yes. You didn't know where you were?"

"No, I was transferred down here blindly."

"What did you do?"

"Well, to my knowledge I've never been charged with anything, so that's kind of unclear at this point. I helped my younger brother get out of the hospital and may have hurt a nurse in the process, but they've only told me I'm being held as a suspected domestic terrorist under the NDAA. What about you?"

"I was in the protests in downtown Dallas. Most here were, although more and more are coming in who were brought in for refusing to comply with the gun confiscation or breaking martial law somehow."

"Have you been charged yet?"

"Not that I know of. It's the same deal as you, held under the NDAA or whatever."

"Well, as much as I hate to say it, this place actually seems like an improvement over where I was. You're the first non-police type person I've talked to in a week or more."

"It's not horrible, but it's hardly ideal considering none of us actually did anything but exercise our rights."

"It seems kind of calm, relatively speaking."

"A good case of looks being deceiving. Things are intentionally being kept in check at the moment, but there's a definite undercurrent among most of the people here."

"What kind of undercurrent?"

"Let's just say, for many, the fight's not over with quite yet."

"Got it. Anything I need to know?"

"Not yet. I'd just lay low and try to fit in. I'll keep an eye out for you and give you a heads up when you need one. You seem nice enough."

"Another case of looks being deceiving I'm afraid."

Jessica laughed a bit. "Somehow I doubt that."

"I didn't even believe it when I said it," Evan answered. "So, do you get any news in here?"

"The guards don't really interact with us, but we get some, mostly from the new arrivals. That is the new arrivals other than you," Jessica answered with a smile.

"Yeah, I'm afraid I'm not much help in that department. What have you heard though? How are things out there?"

"It seems like the protests in the urban areas have all essentially been put down or are being put down. There's a heavy military presence in most of the larger cities. The fight now seems to be moving out into the country and rural areas. That's where the hardcore holdouts have made their stands."

"That makes sense."

"The feds have declared martial law and put a sunset to sunrise curfew in place across the country. A woman I talked to yesterday was put in here on a curfew violation. A few days ago I heard that the feds have started door to door confiscations of all guns and ammo. They seem to be starting with all the registered owners. We've started seeing some of those who refused to cooperate, and weren't killed, flowing in here. A lot of them are in pretty bad shape. One of the new guys said the prices of everything have shot through the roof and they've implemented withdrawal limits to avoid bank runs."

"It sounds like a mess."

"Yeah, and I think it's going to be for a long time to come. They may be putting down the protests in the cities, but at least from what I see in here, that hasn't done anything to calm down the protesters. I think it's only upset them more. It sounds like a lot of people outside are mainly going into survival mode in the short term, hoping to ride out the worst of it. I guess the people who don't care, or who support the government, are just hoping things get under control and back to normal."

"I'm sure the feds will get everything back under control, regardless of what it takes. That's been the agenda all along. As for back to normal, I wouldn't hold my breath. I think normal is out the window."

"You're probably right. I just want to get out of here and get home."

"Do you have family?"

"My parents are in Denton, just north of Dallas. I haven't seen or talked to them in ten days. My brother was with me in the protests, but I have no idea what happened to him. I've looked all over for him since I got here, but he's not here. I just hope he's home and safe," Jessica said and began crying.

"I'm sure he's fine. He's probably with your parents and I'm sure they are all worried sick about you. Nobody here has let you call home?"

"No, nothing. No communication outside at all."

"That's ridiculous."

"What about you? Do you have family?"

"A wife and two babies, a boy who's 6 and girl who's 3. I just pray that I'll see them again. I pray for that every single day."

"You will."

Evan looked up at Jessica. Tears were in both their eyes. He smiled at her and she gave him a little smile back. "No," he said. "We will. We'll both see our families again."

"I hope you're right."

Evan made the sign of the cross and kissed the bend in his curled right index finger three times. "I know I am. I trust God alone, and He hasn't ever let me down."

Chapter 54

While reading Louis Martino's article on The Free Voice, something clicked in Kevin's mind. He quickly scrolled to the bottom of the article and clicked on the hyperlink for Louis' name, which took him to Louis' bio and email address at The Free Voice. Kevin clicked on the email address and, from his personal Hushmail account, typed: "Louis Martino, I need to get a message to Declan about his family. Please reply. S.A. Cameron."

After engaging in numerous fire fights throughout the day, Louis moved with the Palchod Company, the unit of the 932nd Granite Battalion he had been imbedded with, back across the Israeli border to an IDF post in Mount Bental, near the town of Kibutz Merom Golan, roughly forty miles from Damascus. The company had bedded down to try and get a few hours' sleep. Unable to sleep, Louis decided to take advantage of being somewhere with WiFi, and logged onto the The Free Voice website to upload his relatively short update on the day's events.

Israel was increasingly under fire from all fronts and from just about every bordering enemy. Rockets and missiles were being launched from Gaza, Lebanon, the West Bank, and from ISIS fighters operating in Jordan and Syria and renegade Muslim Brotherhood groups in the Sinai Peninsula. Tensions and fears were mounting among the IDF soldiers, and Israeli civilians Louis had encountered, that Israel could be overrun, as many parts of Syria, Jordan and northern Iraq had been. Stories of the atrocities committed in ISIS captured and held areas ran rampant and rumors were circulating among the population that Israel's last-ditch defense, the "Samson Option", which to that point had mainly served as a strong deterrent, could finally be in play.

Periodic explosions rocked in the distance as Louis

typed furiously, his fingers rhythmically tapping key after key, updating and putting the finishing touches on his piece. Not knowing when he'd next have WiFi access, and a relatively peaceful time to work, he quickly uploaded the article and checked the site for news about what had been happening back in the States. Finally, Louis went through his emails, and found Kevin's message.

He paused for a few minutes trying to figure out who S.A. Cameron could be. The name sounded so familiar. After a few minutes, he finally recalled Megan telling him that Declan's friend at the Bureau, Kevin Cameron, had given her the warning about getting him out of the hospital. Special Agent Kevin Cameron, S.A. Cameron. Louis quickly typed back, "I have an email address I can try. What's the message?"

Within five minutes, Louis received a new email alert. The email was from Kevin, "Dr. Evan was picked. All others are near, hid. All okay. I'm keeping eyes on children, mom. Will use secure mail. Lines knocked out and maybe off electric turns. Back on next week."

Louis replied, "Don't entirely understand, but will pass along. Could be a few days before I respond, but I will." Louis then forwarded the email chain with Kevin to the Hushmail account Megan had given him in case he needed to reach them, turned off his laptop, and closed his eyes, the rhythmic sound of rockets and gunfire serving as an ironic lullaby of sorts.

Atau walked up the garden path toward the house, carrying some type of vegetable as Declan sat in a misty rain looking over the Sacred Valley below. Declan and Atau made eye contact with one another, and Atau said to him, "Something very good for dinner."

Declan stood up and smiled, "Atau, can I ask you a question?"

"Of course."

"It's a personal question."

"Personal?"

"Something about yourself."

"That's fine."

"Are you religious?"

"Religious?"

"Do you believe in God?"

"Oh yes, of course." Atau looked over the garden vista out toward the valley and said, "How could I not. God is all around us. None of this was made by accident. Don't you agree?"

"Yes, yes I do."

"See you inside."

"Thank you, Atau."

Declan looked through the misty rain at the mountains surrounding him. The light water dropping on his face was refreshing, almost purifying, and he thought of the last months he'd spent with his dad so many years earlier.

His dad had done everything he could to downplay, or ignore entirely, his depleting energy and rapidly decaying body, but being only ten years old at the time, Declan had a difficult time understanding what was happening. All he wanted to do was play with him, to have as much of his father's attention as he'd always received. Declan remembered times when his dad just couldn't do it, couldn't get out of bed, and how Declan had been less than gracious when he didn't get what he'd wanted. He thought of how the disappointment, so evident in his young eyes and childish attitude, must have torn his father apart.

Declan wished with all his heart that he could go back, take back the selfishness he'd exhibited throughout his life. He wanted to could go back and, just one more time, tell his dad how much he loved him and how much he'd miss him. Both seemed like such understatements given the influence his father had played, before and after his death, in Declan's formation and development.

Through it all, his father tried his best to make each moment count. He had tried to give Evan and Declan memories, lots and lots of memories, which could never be taken from them, no matter what. Declan's last memory, his clearest, were his dad's last words, which began to make sense to Declan for the first time. They were, simply, "Trust God. In all things, trust God."

Those words lingered between his ears, "Trust God. In all things, trust God." For the first time since his father had passed away, Declan felt himself beginning to do just that.

Chapter 55

All Louis heard was the whistling of streaking missile fire and explosions on every side of him. His ears rang from the constant barrage they'd been under since early morning. The Iron Dome batteries fired constantly, trying in vain to intercept the innumerable missiles being fired from across the Syrian border. IDF personnel ran about the small outpost, IAF fighter jets shot through the early evening sky overhead, but the barrage continued almost unabated for what seemed to Louis like days.

A natural reporter, Louis lived on the adrenaline that coursed through every inch of his body, which was caked in dust, sweat and days old body odor. He observed, and tried to scribble down notes on, everything around him: Sgt. Ya'alon and the other IDF soldiers shouting to another in Hebrew and, sometimes, English; the lingering odor of gunpowder; and the constant fire of automatic weapons mixed with the artillery booms. As much as he hated to admit it, Louis found it all to be a rush.

Sgt. Ya'alon led Louis into a small room in the outpost and closed the door so he could hear the officer on the other end of his state of the art Elad Yarok mobile communicator. "Please, shhh," he advised Louis.

Louis stood still, taking in what little there was to look at in the tiny, windowless, bare room as Sgt. Ya'alon was talking. Suddenly, Louis heard a loud piercing whistle in the air right above the outpost. Then, out of nowhere, an explosion and the entire building rocked, knocking Sgt. Ya'alon and Louis to the ground. Sgt. Ya'alon moved quickly toward a stunned Louis and lifted him up off the floor.

"C'mon, Mr. Martino. We're pulling back right now."

"What's happening?"

"We're sustaining a prolonged attack on all fronts. The Iron Dome can't keep all the missile and rocket fire out.

It's coming from all sides. There's been a confirmed biological attack in Ramat HaSharon, apparently V-X gas from near Damascus. Israelis are dying. All civilians, troops and personnel still on the border are being pulled back to a safe distance immediately. The decision has been made."

"What decision?"

"A targeted nuclear response on Damascus and the surrounding area," Ya'alon responded as they came out of the room. "Right now we're too close. We need to fall back at least another 60 km and have very little time to do so. Stay right next to me, understand?"

"Wow," Louis said stunned.

"Do you understand?"

"Absolutely."

"Good. The IDF has been ordered to initiate a complete evacuation from Golan. We're escorting civilian transports to Nazareth, which is about 130 kilos from Damascus."

Ya'alon hurried back to his unit and quickly gave the orders. Other units had already begun the pull back, loading into armed personnel carriers, Humvees and trucks. Louis followed Ya'alon outside and directly into a Humvee.

Explosions continued to rock in and around the outpost, as the IDF troops began the fall back. Ya'alon drove the Humvee, leading three other Humvees from enough distance so as not to form a cluster of targets. The three vehicles drove quickly through town to the staging area where another IDF unit was helping load civilians onto a number of buses. Ya'alon got out and spoke with one of the other soldiers, then came back to the Humvee.

"We've got the first three," he advised everyone. "They're almost finished loading the final bus now. When it's ready, we'll alternate: our Humvee in lead, then bus, then Humvee, and so on. Keep the required distance as we don't want to create a target cluster. Clear?"

The final bus finished loading and the caravan moved out. As the vehicles rolled at high speeds south along

Highway 98, a Squadron of IAF F-15 Eagles soared past
them heading in the direction of the border. A few seconds
later, as the F-15's reached the border, they could be heard
unloading their bomb payloads and laying ground fire all
across the border area, essentially obliterating anything and
anyone in the vicinity.

Louis looked at Ya'alon and asked, "Is it just
Damascus?"

"As far as a nuclear response goes, yes. Whether it
came from Assad or ISIS, Syria is responsible for the V-X
attack. The other trouble areas, Gaza, the West Bank,
Lebanon and the borders are all too close to home. They're
getting what we just heard behind us: prolonged, widespread,
heavy damage inflicting air strikes and artillery fire."

"What about the civilian populations?"

"At this point, the only issue is Israel's survival.
Unfortunately, we've reached a level in the conflict where
non Israeli civilian populations cannot be a consideration any
longer."

Chapter 56

As Declan closed his eyes, he heard the careless joyful sounds of children playing in the distance. When the light returned, he found himself standing on a playground surrounded by snow-capped peaks. It was warm and sunny out and Declan looked across the playground to spot his niece and nephew, amid a slew of other children, running after one another toward the steps leading up to the top of a twisty spirally slide. Sitting on a bench, watching the kids play, were Evan, Michelle, Declan's mom and Megan.

Megan made eye contact with him and a sparkle lit up her already beautiful emerald eyes. At first Declan couldn't place why, but Megan looked different to him. Her face was a bit more round, her eyes a bit more radiant than he'd ever seen them. Declan marveled at her, awash in the afternoon sun, as he walked toward them.

"You finally made it," Megan said as she hugged him. Declan caught sight of the subtle glint of a wedding ring on her left hand, and looked at his own hand to find a silver band.

"I did. You look wonderful," he replied.

He greeted and hugged his mom, Evan, and Michelle, then took a seat next to Megan on the bench. The kids were running and sliding and swinging and laughing along with the other kids on the playground. Declan sat back on the bench and let the warm breeze whisk across his sunlit face. For that moment, everything was as it should be. He was completely happy.

"Uncle Declan, Uncle Declan, come play with us," Will and Charlotte shouted as they came over to him. "You can be the monster and chase us."

"Okay, I'm in," he responded, quickly jumping to his feet and chasing after them. The kids instinctively split up, Charlotte climbing the steps to the top of the spirally ladder and Will running in the direction of the swings. Declan made a decision and chased Charlotte up the steps. She laughed out loud and let out a little scream as she ran across the play structure toward the slide. Declan had nearly caught her when she slid down the slide to safety at the bottom.

"Haha, I escaped," she called back to him.

"Not for long. Here I come."

As Declan knelt down onto the slide, his ears were suddenly filled with a near-deafening shout which echoed throughout the playground to the mountain peaks towering in the distance. Everyone shuddered at the sound and stopped in their tracks. The voice sounded like a man, but there was a quality to the voice, a tone and tenor, that was otherworldly and unlike anything Declan had ever heard before. He stood back up, scanning the area to see if he could locate the source.

Almost immediately after the shout ceased, Declan heard what sounded to him like a trumpet blast. It was all-encompassing, yet not loud. It was piercing, but not in any way unpleasant. It was continual. The sound seemed to him, celestial.

Still standing atop the play station, Declan continued to scan the area in search of the source of the voice and the trumpet blast, but saw nothing. He looked down to Evan and the others on the ground to find them doing the same. Everyone at the playground had stopped whatever they were doing and were looking around quizzically. It was clear they'd all heard the same sounds.

After a few seconds, Declan's eyes turned back to Evan, who was looking straight up toward the blue sky with a captivated expression of sheer awe on his face and tears streaming down his cheeks. Declan looked up too and, when he finally laid his eyes upon His face, radiating brighter than the sun ever had, he was immediately overcome with a rush of pure, undiluted serenity. As promised, there in the sky amongst the dull clouds which seemed so much whiter only moments earlier, He'd finally appeared.

Like all the others, Declan stood motionless, looking up at the face of Jesus Christ in the sky, the face of the one man who had lived a blameless life on the Earth and who had promised to return "soon".

Then, as quickly as He'd appeared, He was gone and the trumpet blast ceased. A stifling silence filled the area. Declan tore his gaze from the sky above and looked around the playground, but saw no children. He looked to the bench where his family had been, and found it empty. No Evan, or Michelle, or his mom, or Megan. They had all disappeared in a flash, along with His face and the trumpet blast. Panicked, Declan turned to where Will had last been running, but as with all the other children, there was no sign of him. Charlotte, who, seconds earlier, had been at the bottom of the slide, was gone as well. Every child, and many of the adults, had simply vanished.

As the others who had been left behind with Declan on the playground began to realize their children, spouses, or friends had disappeared, the sounds of childish laughter and play that had filled the playground less than a minute earlier were replaced by sobbing and the screams of terror and panic. When he fully understood and recognized the magnitude of what had just happened, Declan let out no sound at all, but simply slumped down at the top of the slide looking down at the gray perforated-metal floor. He knew what had just taken place and, he knew, without any doubt, that he'd missed it. He'd been left behind, and tears of sorrow and remorse began to flow from his eyes because he understood where Megan and the others had gone and what was yet to come for him and those who, like him, had remained.

Chapter 57

"Please, wait here, Mr. Martino," Sgt. Ya'alon requested as he and Louis exited the Humvee. Louis raised his camera and began taking shots of the throngs of Israeli civilians, many of whom wore gas masks, as they were escorted off the busses and into a large school nearby. As they were substantially farther from the border, the sounds of rocket and missile fire had died down. Louis was dirty, hungry and exhausted, but still running on a healthy dose of adrenaline. He found a small energy bar in his backpack and took a large bite, trying to get something into his stomach.

A few minutes later, Sgt. Ya'alon returned and said, "We've been ordered to stay here in Nazareth."

"How are things in the other cities?"

"There's been a substantial amount of damage to Jerusalem and the outlying areas, and they're still coming under fire, although to a lesser degree of late. Much the same for the other major cities. With the bio attack, Ramat HaSharon is hurting the worst. The casualties there are high."

"So what are we supposed to do here?"

"We've been ordered to secure the school and maintain the safety of the civilians inside."

"Are we at a safe distance here?"

"Yes, we're a sufficient distance from the blast radius, although we'll still probably be able to see it from here."

"See the cloud?"

"Yes, it should be visible to some degree."

"When's the strike coming?"

"Anytime time now."

"Seriously?"

"Yes, so we should get you inside. I need to go up on the roof, get a view of the perimeter and get some men stationed up there."

"I'd like to come with you."

"I'm not sure it's safe, Mr. Martino. I think you'd be better off inside."

"Come on, I won't be able to see anything from inside. I'm a journalist, remember? And this is history in the making."

"Almost 3,000 years in the making," Sgt. Ya'alon replied. "So be it. Let's go."

Ya'alon, Louis and ten other soldiers from the unit headed inside the school, to a stairwell leading to the roof. "Sgt., "Louis asked as they climbed the steps, "back there you said 3,000 years in the making. What did you mean?"

"The destruction of Damascus was foretold by the Jewish prophet Isaiah many thousand years ago. It appears we're about to witness the fulfillment of that prophecy."

"You believe in that stuff?"

"Absolutely," Ya'alon replied as they climbed the stairs.

"Really. I've never put much stock in that kind of stuff."

"I suspect tonight your perspective may change."

They reached the top of the stairs and Ya'alon opened the door leading out onto the roof. Dusk had finally given way to night and a cool breeze swept across the rooftop. There was no rocket or gunfire in the area. The atmosphere on the rooftop seemed almost serene. Ya'alon motioned for the soldiers to take up positions at each corner of the building and at various points along a short wall running along the rooftop.

He and Louis walked toward the northeast facing side of the building. Sirens could be heard running to and fro, but, for the most part, the city seemed almost empty from their vantage point.

"It seems somewhat surreal," Louis said. "Almost too quiet."

"Shh," Ya'alon advised, while pushing his headset tighter to his ear. A few seconds later, he looked over at Louis and said, "It's coming."

Louis looked out over Nazareth toward the northeastern horizon. He was awash with anticipation, his hands trembling at his sides. He whispered to Ya'alon, "We're safe here, right," but Ya'alon didn't respond. Both stood motionless and quiet, looking out over the darkened night sky toward the horizon.

To Louis, it seemed like he'd been standing there forever, just waiting for he knew not what. He was at once excited and ashamed to be excited, but he couldn't take his eyes off the horizon or shake the odd eagerness he felt to see what was coming next. As his thoughts raced about, a flash of light, like lightning, but brighter than anything he'd ever seen, lit up the far horizon for just a second, and the mushroom cloud followed, rising ominously against the darkening night sky in the distance.

Louis stood speechless, unable to formulate any words worthy of the moment. He looked to find Sgt. Ya'alon on his knees, praying aloud in Hebrew, and he was, for a reason unknown to him, overcome with emotion. The enormity of what had just taken place in that ever so brief flash of light struck Louis across the face and he began to cry. The emotions were raw, the thought of so many people, people he'd never known or met, literally gone in seconds overcame him. Louis was filled with shame, shame for so badly having wanted to witness such destruction first hand, shame for actually having looked forward to seeing it, and finally, shame for simply being human and all that being human entailed. He slunk down against the wall, next to Sgt. Ya'alon, and wept, not knowing what else he could do.

Chapter 58

Aside from some general soreness, fatigue, and occasional flaring pain from his bruised ribs, Evan felt a world better. He had a healthy appetite again and felt like getting outside into the bright sunlight and temperate breeze during recreation hours. His older cot neighbor, James Sippel, elected to join Evan for a slow walk around the yard.

"So are you from the Dallas area?"

"Not, originally," Mr. Sippel answered, zipping his coat up a little higher. "I grew up in Lubbock, but work brought me to Dallas thirty-five or so years ago."

"What kind of work?"

"I'm a retired civil engineer."

As the two continued their oddly leisurely walk, Jessica hurried up behind them and said excitedly, "It's starting."

"What's starting?"

"The undercurrents I told you about are coming to the surface, now."

Almost instantaneously, an explosion rocked the east building of the compound about forty yards behind them. The three instinctively crouched down. Evan turned back to see fires raging on the lower level of the building, smoke and flames emanating from the shattered, but still barred, windows. Without warning, a second explosion roared forth in the adjacent building, which was one of the main holding areas. The ground shook slightly under their feet as detainees and guards alike began running around the yard in all directions. Rapid gunshots could be heard coming from inside both buildings.

"C'mon, follow me," Jessica said getting upright again. "There's going to be a rush for the fence over there. We need to get over there or we'll miss our chance. C'mon!"

"I'll take my chances here," Mr. Sippel advised. "You go. Go on!"

Jessica reached out for Evan's hand. Reluctantly, he

gave it to her and they ran hand in hand toward the east fence. Evan could see a mass of detainees rushing from the two bombed buildings out onto the yard and toward the confused guards stationed at the fence. Some of the detainees had rifles they'd apparently taken from guards inside, and a firefight ensued. More guards rushed from the opposite side of the yard, firing their automatic weapons into the mass of detainees pushing through the fence.

The scene was total chaos. For Jessica, it was an eerie parallel to the protests. "Hurry," she yelled. "We need to get through the fence before the guards get control again and close it off!"

Evan kept his eyes forward as they ran. His lungs heaved in a way they hadn't in years. He felt as if he might vomit, but, despite the pain coursing throughout his body, he kept pushing forward, pulling slightly ahead of Jessica. There were easily over seven hundred detainees who had pushed through the east fence. Too many people to count were falling to the ground, both detainees and guards. It appeared to Evan that the detainees with rifles or makeshift weapons of varying types were trying to fend off the oncoming rush of guards while the hundreds of others pushed past the fallen barbed-wire fence to the freedom of the outside. Evan and Jessica finally rushed into the fray.

"Don't let go of my hand," he called over to her. "If we get separated, I'll never find you again in this mess."

The mass of humanity closed in around them on all sides, enveloping them in a moving, breathing wall of sweat, blood and flesh. Evan kept his head low and his eyes forward, gripping Jessica's hand like a like a vice. A man fell in front of him, but before Evan could even think to try and help him up, he'd been trampled by the mass pushing forward. Guards fired relentlessly into the crowd from behind and above. Men and women fell constantly on all sides, but Evan and Jessica could do nothing other than move forward, feeling the fallen under their feet as they were pressed ahead. The pressure from behind them was impossible to resist. They were cattle in the midst of a stampede.

At a seemingly arbitrary point just past the opening in the fence, the bottleneck of humanity cleared and the detainees splintered into a million different directions. When the mass of people in front of them had thinned some, all Evan and Jessica could see was a hundred yards of open ground, covered by unkempt brush and weeds. They ran as fast as they could forward, zigzagging in order to avoid the barrage of bullets streaking through the air around them.

When they were enough out of the way of the running masses, Evan drug them down onto the ground where they lay with their faces in the dirt. "We need a plan," he yelled.

"There's a railroad track about another fifty yards diagonally to our right. The track is on a rise. If we can get to the other side we'll have some cover."

"Fine, let's go!"

They both shot up and ran toward the rise. Shots continued to ring out behind them and the screams and groans of those being shot down on either side and behind them filled their ears, prompting them to sprint with every ounce of speed they possessed. Evan looked to his left and saw troop transports moving quickly along the road bordering the field.

"C'mon," he called out. "We've got to get somewhere out of sight!"

Jessica, who had also caught sight of the armored trucks, nodded and they raced the last 10 yards up and over the train tracks, nearly tumbling down the slope on the other side. The land on the other side of the train tracks was wooded, providing better cover in the trees and undergrowth. They dashed into the trees and ducked down behind a set of thick full bushes, both desperately trying to catch their breath.

Evan asked, "What now?"

"I don't know. I think there's a neighborhood somewhere on the other side of these woods."

"How far?"

"I'm not sure."

Detainees from the camp continued to stream through the woods as Evan and Jessica crouched down, trying to catch their breath and come up with a plan. Desperate for more time to gather their breath and thoughts, they heard the sound of heavy brakes stopping back toward the road, followed by the thud of boots hitting the pavement.

"We've gotta go," Evan said. "They're right behind us."

"Okay, let's run toward where I think the houses are and see if we can't find cover there."

They got up to run again. Out of the corner of his eye, Evan caught sight of what appeared to be an open drain pipe protruding from a small hill about twenty feet to their right. "Wait, over there," he said pointing.

Jessica caught sight of it too and said, "Let's try it, but we have to hurry."

They ran to the pipe, which was about two feet in diameter and partially buried by packed dirt and mud, and overgrown with weeds of all varieties. Evan quickly peeked inside, "It's big enough, but we need to crawl back well out of sight."

"Let's go."

They rushed into the pipe, Jessica first, then Evan. Once inside, Evan worked to camouflage the partially visible opening with the overgrowth and they both hurried deep inside the tunnel, well away from the light of day. As they crawled further along, unable to see anything in front of them, they came to a point where the pipe turned to its left.

"Here," Jessica said. "Take the turn, that way we'll be completely out of sight."

"Shhh," Evan whispered and both were silent and still. Evan pushed Jessica forward into the turn, and she slid as quietly as possible ahead, leaving room for him behind her.

"It's a pipe, sir," they both heard a male voice yell

from outside.

"Shoot into it dammit!"

"Yes, sir!"

Evan hurried into the turn as a flurry of bullets rattled through the pipe just behind him.

"If anybody was in there, they're dead now," the guard's voice could be heard saying.

The two sat balled up in the metal pipe, silently for some time, listening to the shouts, screams and gunfire in the woods outside. Finally, Jessica whispered, "Are you okay?"

"Yeah, I'm fine. You?"

"I'm okay. What should we do?"

"Stay here until things out there calm down and then, I guess, try and get you home. Is that realistic, to get to Denton?"

"Yeah. It may not be easy, but it's realistic. What will you do after that?"

"Try and get back up to my family. Let's wait here until it gets dark and then we'll try and get to the neighborhood you said was up ahead. We can figure out what to do from there."

"Sounds good to me."

Chapter 59

Louis sat up through the night, trying to find the words to describe what he'd witnessed. Every inch of his body ached. His heavy eyes desperately wanted to close, but were unable to. He was physically exhausted and mentally drained, yet incapable of sleep. While he had only seen the event from a safe distance, his imagination ran rampant with images of what it must be like at ground zero and within the very real and very messy confines of the blast radius.

His trembling fingers remained at the ready position just above the keys; however, the page remained blank. Louis envisioned people, men, women and children, indiscriminately vaporized within seconds of the blast. Those, he thought, were the fortunate ones. The less fortunate, further out from the center, were likely incinerated and burned alive. The least fortunate, those even further out in the blast radius, had either died slowly or were still in the process of dying from radiation poisoning. By the time the sun rose again, Louis knew the entire city of Damascus and its outlying areas would be nothing but an empty uninhabitable heap of rubble, corpses and waste.

Declan found Atau standing in front of the small television in the kitchen. Opening the refrigerator to grab a bottled water, Declan asked, "So, what's on the menu for tonight?"

Atau remained silent, completely engrossed in the images on the television screen. Noticing Atau's singular focus on the TV, Declan peered around him and, for the first time, saw the images of the nuclear blast being replayed as the backdrop for the Spanish news commentary.

"Where is that?"

"Damascus," Atau answered.

"Did you say Damascus?"

a strong feeling you're not even close to finished yet."

Chapter 60

Evan peeked ahead to the opening in the metal pipe, but could see nothing other than the blackness of the night. The sounds of gunfire and conflict had died off hours earlier. The silence of night filled the little forest outside the drain pipe. Darkness had brought with it cold and, with their already insufficient clothes dampened, Evan and Jessica shivered through and through as they crawled out into the frigid night air.

"At least it was warmer in there," Jessica chattered. "I'm freezing."

"Me too. We won't be able to stay out here very long without getting hypothermic. We'd better head toward the neighborhood and see if we can find a shed or an empty house or something to stay in."

As carefully and quietly as possible, the two made their way through the woods, toward the dim lights of the houses beyond. "Careful," Evan whispered. "There's a log or something here. I nearly tripped over it."

Jessica peered down through the darkness as she carefully placed her foot and saw the blood-caked corpse of a woman on the ground in front of her. "It wasn't a log, it was a body," she said.

Evan looked back and saw the woman's still open eyes dimly reflecting the scant moonlight. He and Jessica stopped and scanned the area in front of them. They were able to make out the outlines of six or seven other corpses littering the forest floor.

"They didn't even bother to pick them up for a proper burial," Evan said. "They just left them lying here to rot and be picked over by whatever animals or insects come along. I've never seen anything so inhumane."

"Let's just take our time," Jessica said.

After about ten minutes of carefully maneuvering around bodies and brush, Evan and Jessica finally reached the edge of the woods. They crouched down, shivering, yet well hidden in the brush, and looked and listened for any signs of life or activity.

"It's quiet," Evan whispered.

"Everyone's inside because of the curfew."

"Let's wait here a minute and see if it stays quiet."

"Okay, but I'm freezing. We've got to get somewhere warm, or get some dry clothes. Do you see any houses that look like they might be empty?"

"Not yet, but I'm looking," Evan answered, scanning the street in front of him. "What time do you think it is?"

"I have no idea. The curfew is sunset and I think that's around six or so now. Maybe, seven or eight."

"I see a house up there with no lights on. If it's only seven or eight, I'd guess it's too early for them to be in bed. What do you think?"

"Let's check it out."

The two crept out from the secrecy of the brush, jetted across the open street and cut quickly through a neighboring yard. They rushed up to the unlit side of the dark house and paused for a second in the shadows. Evan moved forward slowly, trying his best to stay in the shadows. Jessica followed closely behind.

"Let's go around to the back," Evan whispered. He tried to open the door of the wooden privacy fence as quietly as possible, but it creaked the entire way. Evan slid through to the backyard first, hoping not to encounter a dog. When it looked okay, Jessica went in behind him.

The back yard was dark, lit only by a sliver of moonlight, and relatively empty except for a barbeque grill and a couple of plastic lawn chairs on a flat concrete patio. As Evan peered through the sliding glass door, Jessica opened the lid on the barbeque grill to see if there was any warmth, but only found a set of barbeque thongs and a small two-pronged barbeque fork. She stuck the metal barbeque fork into her back pocket, underneath her damp, tattered sweater.

"It looks empty," Evan said. "But I don't see any

way in other than to break the glass."

"That won't work. It'll just make a bunch of noise and get all the neighbors out to see what's going on. Wasn't there a garage around front?"

"I think so."

"Maybe there's a garage door or window that's open."

"It's worth a try."

They headed around to the opposite side of the house and through another gate leading back to the front yard. A few feet past the gate, they found a side door accessing the garage. Evan tried to open it.

"It's locked, but maybe I can try and jimmy it," he whispered.

Jessica looked around nervously, while Evan tried to work the lock. A pair of headlights advancing deliberately down the street caught her attention.

"A car's coming."

"Hurry, let's get back to the backyard," Evan replied.

They rushed back through the fence, shivering in the cold, as a Homeland cruiser passed slowly down the street, shining its spotlight on the houses across the street.

"They're doing patrols. They'll probably come back through to scan this side too."

"Let's try the door again real quick. I think I can get it."

As they came back through the gate to the side of the house, they heard another voice, "Psst. Psst," and both froze. "It's okay," the voice whispered. "I'm a friend."

The voice came from an open, but dark, window of the neighboring house. "I can help you. My front door is unlocked. Hurry and come inside before they come back."

Evan and Jessica looked at each other uneasily, uncertain what to do. They could barely see what appeared to be an older man standing in the window. "It's okay," he tried to reassure them again. "I'm on your side."

Jessica peered down the block, watching as the

Homeland cruiser began to circle back for a second pass down the street. "If we're going to do it, we have to do it now, before they turn around," she said.

Fearing they had no other options, they rushed toward the man's front door. Evan turned the knob and went in first, as Jessica quickly closed the door behind them. They stood, panting and shivering, on the small tile foyer.

"I'm Al Rawlins. Here, warm up and make yourselves at home," the man said, motioning toward the warm yellow glow emanating from the living room fireplace.

Evan and Jessica moved cautiously away from the foyer toward the fire, desperate for the heat, but still somewhat leery of Mr. Rawlins. "Thank you," Evan replied. "We won't stay long."

"No trouble. Did ya'll escape from the camp over the way?"

Neither answered.

"Don't worry. I can tell just by lookin' at you. I saw the others running through here all day. They were shootin' 'em in the streets earlier. Not even botherin' to take 'em back alive, even when they'd surrendered."

Rawlins locked the front door and walked toward the fireplace, where Evan and Jessica stood trying to get warm. "Here," he said to Evan, "That fire's getting a bit low. Move over for a sec and let me stoke it and get another log or two on."

Evan moved back a few feet, toward a light-blue upholstered sofa that looked like it had seen better days. Rawlins picked up a metal fireplace poker and leaned over toward the fire. With a surprising burst of quickness and power for a man his age, he turned and swung the heavy metal poker at Evan's head. The heaviest section of the poker, the end, went a few inches past the left side of his head, but the metal pole hit Evan squarely just above the ear. Evan toppled over, hitting a wooden coffee table on the way down, and landing unconsciously on the taupe carpeted floor.

Rawlins turned back to face a stunned Jessica and

said, "Don't you even think about it sweetie. The troopers are givin' five hundred bucks a piece for you jail breakers. I already made a thousand bucks today. I'm gonna make another thousand with you two, but first, we're going to get you out of all those dirty wet clothes. You can make it easy or hard. I'll like it either way."

The initial shock vanished from Jessica's face quickly. Her eyes, locked onto Rawlins, burned with anger; however, her face went stoic, giving an almost resigned appearance.

"Let's just get it over with," she replied flatly.

Rawlins kicked Evan over to make sure he was still out. Satisfied, he looked Jessica over and motioned her toward a matching light-blue loveseat, opposite the sofa. Making sure to keep Rawlins in front of her, Jessica backed toward the loveseat.

"Now, get those pants off."

"Why don't you get them off me," she replied. "Or are you too old to do it yourself?"

"Oh, I'll do it alright," Rawlins said, moving toward her with the metal poker still in hand.

He came face to face with her. Jessica could feel his breath on her face, taking in the medicinal minty scent of mouthwash, as he grabbed the front of her jeans with one hand and pulled her up against him. She looked down as he smiled widely, dropped the fireplace poker and began to unbutton her jeans. The top button undone, Rawlins' eyes betrayed the giddiness of a teenage boy setting his eyes on a naked woman for the first time.

"Oh yea, I'm gonna give it to you good," he blurted.

Jessica looked back up, directly into Rawlins' overeager eyes. Her own eyes were aflame with rage. The wooden handle of the barbeque forked ground into her vice-like grip and, channeling her ferocious venom, she struck. In a split second, before Rawlins could even take his hands off her unbuttoned jeans, she'd buried all three inches of the two-pronged barbeque fork like a viper into the right side of his neck. The idiotic smile fled from his face as his eyes shot wide open, trying to understand what had just happened. Gasping for air and throwing up blood, Rawlins' hands finally pried themselves from Jessica's jeans and vainly attempted to pull the fork from the fatal wound. He staggered backward as he tugged on the barbeque fork and, a few seconds later, the fork still in his neck, Rawlins fell to the floor a few feet from Evan, dead.

Chapter 61

Louis made his way back to Jerusalem with another IDF unit. He'd been unable to sleep and unable to write, and had spent most of the ride back from Nazareth staring off into the diminishing darkness, taking in the odd juxtaposition of a pink and orange sunrise against the still blazing fires, smoke, and damaged buildings visible in many of the Israeli towns along the route. Louis couldn't count the number of sirens he'd heard, or flashing lights he'd seen. Buildings were crumbling and rubble from the blasts filled entire streets. Cars and busses were bombed out and the hospitals were teeming with the injured.

The true toll of war, of large scale violence, stood manifested before him in the waning hours of darkness. Israel may have "won" the conflict, he thought, but she and her people were surely not victors. They'd merely survived.

Evan woke up around midnight to find himself lying under a flannel blanket on the light-blue sofa. He looked to his left and saw Jessica, who had pulled the loveseat over next to him and sat looking blankly into the fire's yellow flames.

"It seems like we're making a habit of this," he said, wincing from the throbbing pain in his head.

"Making a habit of what?"

"Of me waking up from being sick or hurt and you being the first person I see. What happened?"

"Our gracious host knocked you out so he could sell us to the Homeland troopers for five hundred dollars apiece after he'd had a chance to rape me."

Evan shot up from the sofa, "He didn't..."

"No, he didn't," Jessica replied looking over to Evan thoughtfully. "That will never happen to me again. He's over there on the floor."

Evan looked behind him to find Rawlins' body lying on the carpet with a navy blue sheet covering it.

"I'm sorry," Evan replied. "It was a mistake to come in here. Something didn't feel right, but I didn't know what else to do."

"It's just the world we live in. At least now we have a place to stay warm until morning. We have food, dry clothes, jackets, and a truck to get us to Denton as soon as the curfew lifts."

Evan sat upright, gently rubbing the large knot on the side of his head. He asked, "How are you? Are you okay?"

Jessica sat silently, staring into the flames. Her unaffected demeanor finally cracked and tears began to stream from her eyes down onto her cheeks. She turned to Evan and threw herself against him, burying her face in his chest. Evan took the flannel blanket, wrapped it around Jessica, and held her tight in his arms, letting each pain-filled tear roll down her cheeks onto his blood-stained and tattered shirt. Holding her made him long even more desperately for home.

After hearing the initial reports about Damascus on the radio, Michelle and Mrs. Parker had put Will and Charlotte to bed and sat listening for more news, trying to take in the enormity of what had taken place. They sat up late into the night, fully cognizant that they were indirect witnesses to the undeniable fulfillment of God's Word. They cried, and they prayed, for their family, for Israel, for the people of Syria, and for the survivors.

After arriving back in Jerusalem, Louis split from the IDF unit he'd hitched a ride with and ran to his hotel. The hotel had suffered moderate damage, but was still operating, and he was able to change clothes and grab the rest of his belongings. The water was out, so he wasn't able to shower or wash his face, but the fresh clothes provided him with a little boost of energy, as did an application of deodorant and quick spray of cologne.

The Israeli Prime Minister was scheduled to speak from an undisclosed location at 8:30 a.m. No press were allowed to be present, but the speech was to be broadcast live on television, the radio and the internet. Louis, like the vast majority of the foreign press in Jerusalem, made his way to a conference room set up to receive the live feed at the largely unscathed King David Hotel. There were throngs of press present from all over the world. The room was crowded, standing room only, and loud, with often heated debates raging in twenty different languages about the nuclear reprisal against Damascus.

Before leaving for Israel, Louis had contacted his former college roommate, Adam Benjamin, who served as a staff assistant to the Prime Minister. As a favor, Adam had obtained Louis' necessary press credentials and authorizations for Louis to be imbedded with Sgt. Ya'alon's unit on the Golan Heights. Upon arriving at the King David, Louis again sought Adam out.

"Louis, you're back," Adam exclaimed upon seeing his friend. "Knowing where you were, I was a bit worried I wouldn't see you again."

"I was worried about that myself at times."

"Where were you during the blast?"

"Nazareth. We were at a safe distance, but I was on a rooftop with Ya'alon and could see the flash and the mushroom cloud. It was horrifying, knowing what was happening to anyone on the ground in Damascus."

"It was not a decision the Prime Minister had ever hoped to make, I assure you. It literally came down to that, or facing the eradication of Israel."

"I could see that in the damage all over the place on my way back here. It's certainly not a position I'd want to be put in, not a decision I'd want to face. Frankly, I still can't get the images out of my head."

"I imagine that will take some time. It's not the type of thing we're used to seeing back in the States. I'm glad I didn't witness the strike."

"Have you watched any of the coverage?"

"No. Honestly, it's not something I ever want to see. The lives of so many lost so quickly."

"I understand. I spent the entire night awake trying to get the image out of my head."

"Here," Adam said, taking his clearly shaken friend gently by the arm. "There's a reserved row up front, I'll get you a space."

"Thanks," Louis replied as they walked toward the front of the conference room. "What's the word out the Prime Minister's office? Anything you can share?"

"His speech will be brief, to the point. As I said, this was not a decision that was reached lightly, and that point will be made abundantly clear. In truth, he's been under fire from all sides. Off the record, the U.S. and the E.U. have all but abandoned us entirely. The word is they'll be issuing formal condemnations of the action immediately after the speech in rebuttal, and I understand there's a congressional vote scheduled for later today that would immediately halt all financial and military assistance to Israel and potentially implement economic sanctions."

"Given the general animosity coming from Washington since the failed peace plans and the Iran negotiations, that couldn't have been entirely unexpected."

"No, not entirely," Adam answered. "We were prepared for backlash. Russia, China, India, Turkey and the Iranians have been vehement and antagonistic in their condemnation, in a significantly greater degree than the rest of the world. Russia and Turkey have already summoned their diplomats home and closed their embassies in Tel-Aviv, and we expect China and India to follow suit any moment now. Here, here's a seat for you."

"Thank you, Adam. I'm really sorry to see you, to see this country in this position. I saw firsthand the pressure you were coming under on the Golan."

"Sadly, it came down to a matter of survival. Better to have the whole world mad at the State of Israel than to have no State of Israel at all. How much longer are you staying?"

"I'm headed to the airport right after the Prime Minister's address. I need to get home and try to get recharged, let what happened sink in. I hope to be back within a week or so. There's just too much going on here to stay away."

"Well, let me know when you're back and we'll see each other again then. And, Louis, just give it time."

"Thanks, Adam. I'll email when I'm headed back."

"Safe travels, my friend."

Louis took his seat and at exactly 8:30, the enormous video monitor came to life. The noise in the room immediately died to the point where one could hear his or her own breath. The Prime Minister appeared on the screen and began:

"Israelis, friends, it is with a solemn heart that I stand before you this morning. This is a moment, a speech, I'd prayed I'd never need to make. This is, admittedly, a dark moment in not only our history, but the history of humanity as a whole. When we returned to this land, the land of Abraham and Jacob, and were reborn as a nation in 1948, it was with the hope of a peaceful and fruitful future. As we know, while we have been fruitful and prospered greatly in our land, our journey has been anything but peaceful.

At nearly every turn, from our return to our ancestral homeland through today, we have faced aggression and violence. In every instance, we have persevered and prevailed. Conflict, war, violence, these were not our choices, these were not our desires. However, we have not and will not shy away from those who long to destroy us, to remove us from our land, our homes, to wipe us from the face of the earth. Never Again, we say. Never Again.

I will not stand before you and recite the entire history of our struggles or the chain of events leading to the extremely difficult decision that was thrust upon us. I've said, as have my predecessors, that a nuclear Iran is entirely unacceptable. A regime whose stated goal is the destruction of the Jewish State and the eradication of the Jewish people, cannot be allowed to possess a weapon capable of bringing about that heinous objective.

Thus, in the face of opposition to our right to security and appeasement by the various world powers toward the Iranian regime, we, the Israeli people, took the necessary steps to ensure our security. As with any nation, that is our right. We struck the heart of the Iranian nuclear program, disabling the regime's unimpeded run toward nuclear weapons. In reprisal for this action, we were mercilessly attacked on all sides by Iran's proxies and the radical Islamists whose common goal is our eradication. This was not unexpected. What was, however, unexpected, was the unprovoked use of chemical and biological weapons on our people.

Our intelligence, in which I trust completely, pinpointed the source of the chemical and biological attack to Damascus. Whether the attack was initiated by the Assad government, or by The Islamic State which currently controls large portions of Syria, matters not.

We have always stated, unequivocally, that such an attack, an attack which threatens our very existence, would be viewed as a nuclear attack, as an attempt to eradicate the Jewish State, and would be responded to accordingly. Last night, with heavy hearts, we stood firm to our word and retaliated only against source of the heinous attack, Damascus.

Let me be clear, Israel did not start this aggression. Israel did not want this conflict, nor did we want to respond the way we have; however, backed into a corner and with the fate of our nation on the line, with our very existence in the balance, we did what needed to be done.

While I am greatly grieved by the loss of life on both sides of the conflict, I shall not, nor will I ever, apologize for doing my duty and for protecting the State of Israel and ensuring its continued existence.

Not surprisingly, the nations of the world are coming out in strong condemnation of our action. By doing so, the nations of the world, including many of our closest allies up to this point, are condemning, in effect, our right to exist. It has been said by our ancient prophets, that a day will come when Israel will stand alone, that Israel will be shunned and reviled by the nations of the world. If this is that day, so be it. If we must, Israel will stand alone, but, make no mistake, Israel will stand."

Chapter 62

"Declan, wake up," Megan said, nudging him. "Wake up."

"What's going on?"

"I got an email from Louis."

"What did he say?"

"He was passing a message from Kevin Cameron. It says, 'Dr. Evan was picked. All others are near, hid. All okay. I'm keeping eyes on children, mom. Will use secure mail. Lines knocked out and maybe off electric turns. Back on next week.' He wants to know how we want him to respond, but aside from what he says about Evan and the children, I don't even know what it means."

"Can I see it?"

Megan handed her laptop to Declan, who sat up and wiped the sleep from his eyes. "Can you get me a pen and paper, babe?"

"Thanks," Declan responded as she handed them to him. "We'll see if this is really from Kevin."

"How can you tell?"

"If it is, it'll be coded. Kevin started at the Bureau when my dad was still there. My dad had a special coding system which he taught me and Evan when we were kids. He apparently also showed it to Kevin once. If this is from Kevin, it'll utilize my dad's code and we'll get the real message."

Declan began scanning the message and writing down letters as Megan looked over his shoulder nervously. "What does it say?"

"It says, 'Declan, lake house, Cameron.'"

"How'd you get that?"

"If you know the key, it's easy. Start with the first letter in the first two words, D and E."

"Okay."

"Then the next word has three letters, so you look at the third letter in each of the next two words, which are C and L. You skip the next word and go back to the first letter in each of the next two words, which are A and N. Thus, you get, Declan."

"It's a pattern."

"Exactly. It' not complicated. The next word, hid, is three letters long again, so you look to the third letter in the next two words: L and A. Skip the next word and revert back to the first letter in the next two words: K and E. Now you have Lake. The next word, on, only has two letters…"

"So you look to the second letter in the next two words, H and O."

"Precisely. The sequence continues and you come up with Declan, lake house, Cameron."

"What does it mean?"

"In connection with the surface text, I'd guess it means my family is hiding out at our lake house. I also think it means Evan was picked up, based on the first line."

"We've gotta do something to get them out," Megan responded. "If Evan got arrested, it was for helping us, and if your family's in trouble, we can't just leave them there."

"We won't. We have to go back."

Chapter 63

The curfew lifted at sunrise and, contrary to their expectations, Evan and Jessica arrived without incident at her parents' house in Denton a little over an hour later. They parked Al Rawlins' pickup truck in the parking lot of a grocery store about half a mile from the house and walked the remainder of the way. It was the first time Evan had been outside under somewhat normal conditions since Declan and Megan had left the hospital. He breathed in the cool refreshing morning air with an appreciation he'd lacked for many years.

They moved along at a hurried pace set by Jessica, who was eager to see her family again. Aside from the visibly empty stores of all type and a line beginning to form at a gas station they passed, the neighborhood appeared relatively calm, seemingly untouched by the chaos that had been so pervasive throughout the country since the Firearms Protection Act had been rushed through to law.

Finally arriving at the house, Jessica could no longer contain her anticipation and rushed across the small front yard to the front door. As she had no key, she hurriedly rang the bell, and then turned the doorknob, which was unlocked.

With Evan following a couple feet behind in order to give her some space, she raced into the house, calling out, "Mom, dad, I'm home, I'm home." Seeing nobody in the family room or the dining room, she rushed into the kitchen, still calling out, "Mom...dad!"

Evan followed her into the kitchen, and immediately noticed the disarray inside. Two slices of moldy bread were sitting out open on the small breakfast table along with a thoroughly brown banana. The kitchen, the whole house for that matter, smelt of spoiled food or like something had died. The scene seemed to Evan as if something had happened or as if the inhabitants had left unexpectedly, and in a hurry. He looked over to Jessica, who was also taking in the scene, and whose face had begun to change from an expression of excitement and eagerness to fear. Evan saw the panic in her eyes as she continued to scream for her parents, but received no response.

"I'm going to check upstairs," she said, and ran toward the stairwell in the family room.

"I'm coming with you."

They sprinted up the stairs, and Evan followed Jessica into her parents' bedroom. Seeing nothing at first, Jessica scanned the room and suddenly gasped, putting her hand to her mouth as she caught sight of two bare feet on the floor, protruding from behind the bed.

"Oh, God," she screamed.

Evan reached to try and grab her, to hold her back, but Jessica had already rushed toward them. When she saw her parents' bruised lifeless bodies lying next to one another on the blood-soaked carpet next to the bed, she simply broke down, tossing herself onto the floor at their feet, and wailing aloud.

Declan wrote a coded message for Megan to email back that, when decoded, simply read, "Coming." Megan's Uncle Ignacio had called and spoken with her father and asked that the plane be sent back to Cusco to pick them up. Anxious to get the rest of the family out of the rapidly imploding situation in the United States and to the relative calm of the high Andes, Megan's dad made arrangements for everyone to fly to Cusco two days later.

Despite his desire to get back and do what he could to help his family, Declan was happy to have the extra time. He asked Megan to take a walk with him around the mountainside property. They strolled slowly in the misty rain, looking out over the valley below, Declan half-heartedly responding to Megan's discussion of a plan.

"You're really quiet this morning," she said finally.

Declan turned to her and smiled. He looked into her

eyes and loved the fact that he never had to guess what she was thinking. Megan's eyes, her smile, were the most beautiful sights in his world.

"What?" she asked. "Why are you looking at me like that?"

Without saying a word, Declan took her hand and slowly bent down on one knee. Looking up at her he said, "I don't know where all this is going. I don't know where it will all end up or even how much longer we have in this world, and I don't care. What I do know is that I love you. I love you as much as any person can love another person and I want to spend each and every one of my remaining days here, beginning today, however long or short they may be, as your husband. Will you do me the considerable, and completely undeserved, honor of marrying me?"

With joyous tears flowing down her beautiful light pink cheeks, Megan simply responded, "Yes, absolutely."

"I don't have an engagement ring, but I'll buy one for you in Cusco today."

"I don't care," Megan said embracing him. "Ring or no ring, I love you and I want to be your wife. That's all that matters."

Chapter 64

It took a little time, but Louis found an operating taxi and made his way along the damaged, yet quiet, route from Jerusalem to Ben Gurion Airport. For obvious reasons, the airport and skies overhead had been a priority point of protection for the Israelis. The airport had suffered no damage during the fighting, remaining unaffected but for the grounding of all commercial flights

Limited commercial flights had resumed and Louis managed to get a ticket aboard a United Airlines flight bound for his hometown, Chicago. Once off the ground, the steady rhythm of the engines brought Louis a strange sense of ease, and, for the first time in days, he was able to sleep. He slept for all but the last hour of the flight, waking up somewhat refreshed and finally able to clear his head enough to get the beginning of a story about the Israeli conflict and bombing of Damascus down on paper.

When the plane landed in Chicago, Louis grabbed his carry-on, made his way down the jet way to the gate and, finally, to the customs desk.

"Good afternoon. Passport please," the customs officer said.

Louis handed his passport and customs forms to the officer and stood waiting. The customs officer looked up and compared Louis to his passport photo. "You're returning from Israel?"

"That's right."

The customs officer looked down at his computer again and, a few seconds later, picked up his phone. As the phone rang, he looked up to Louis and said, "Just a moment."

After a pause, the officer spoke into the phone, "Louis Martino…Okay."

"Is there a problem?" Louis asked.

"No sir. It'll just be a moment."

A few seconds later, two armed Homeland officers approached. One asked, "Louis Martino?"

"Yes."

"Please come with me, Mr. Martino."

"Why? Is something wrong?"

"Please come with me, Mr. Martino," the officer repeated.

"Why?"

"We need to speak with you about your activities in Israel."

"What activities? I was in Israel covering the conflict over there. I'm a journalist."

The other officer moved toward Louis and put his hand firmly on Louis' shoulder. "It won't take long," he said. "Now please, we don't want to make a scene."

"I'm not concerned about making a scene. I'm concerned about why Homeland Security has questions for me, an American citizen and journalist, about what I was doing in Israel."

Two other armed Homeland officers moved in behind Louis. The crowd of passengers in and around customs had gone silent, each watching the action closely and wondering who Louis was, what he'd done, and what would happen next.

Realizing there was no point in resisting further and that the scene was about to get ugly, he finally conceded, saying, "Fine, I'll come with you, but I want to know what this is about."

"I'll be happy to explain it to you in my office," the officer replied as the four led Louis away and through a door marked "Authorized Personnel Only".

Evan finished shoveling the cold light-brown soil and earth onto the shallow grave he'd prepared in the backyard for Jessica's parents. He felt an overwhelming obligation to shield her as much as possible from the unpleasantness, to allow her to grieve inside quietly. Evan had cleaned and wrapped the bodies in blankets, dug a hole in the backyard large enough for them to lie in side by side, and gently placed Jessica's parents into their final earthly resting place.

After covering the grave, Evan put the shovel back into the tool shed, and prepared two small memorials, to serve as makeshift headstones, out of rocks and small stones he'd found in and around the yard. He piled the stones side by side on the ground above where their heads lay below. When he'd finished, Evan did his best to clean the dirt and dust from the clothes he'd taken from Al Rawlins' house, and went back inside.

"Jessica," he said softly, "I've put your parents to…um…to rest outside. It's not much, but it's something in remembrance. Would you like to come outside and say something?"

Jessica sat staring at the wall in front of her and replied flatly, "I wouldn't really know what to say. I'm not religious like you are…and they were."

"Maybe, if you just said goodbye. It may not feel like it now, but if you don't, I think you'll regret it later."

Jessica turned to Evan slowly, taking in the gentleness and clearly caring tone of his voice and mannerisms. "Okay," she said, getting up. "I'll come out."

The two walked out into the backyard together and slowly over to the stone markers Evan had made.

"Thank you," Jessica said to him. "This is nice. They would have liked being buried together."

She looked up at the blue sky overhead, and then back to the ground. "I don't know what to say," she began. "Other than to say I love you both with all my heart. I'm sorry I wasn't always the best daughter or the best person, but I loved you. I'll miss you both, wherever you are." Her voice was intentionally flat and lifeless as she tried to fight back the tears. Standing over her parents' grave, Jessica felt as if she'd soon have no more tears left to give.

"They were Baptist," she said to Evan. "I'm nothing, but I think they'd appreciate it if something was said, something from the Bible maybe. Would you mind?"

"Of course not," Evan replied. "Mr. & Mrs. Ehlers, I never knew you, but I'm getting to know your daughter and, through her, I can see clearly that you both must have been extraordinary people. Extraordinarily strong, extraordinarily loving, extraordinarily resilient. As believers in the Lord Jesus, as children of the one true King, I know, we know, that you're at home with our Lord now, finally at peace by His side. One day, when the Lord wills, we'll see you in the place He's prepared for us. A place filled with His love and His light, New Jerusalem. Amen."

"Thank you," Jessica said. "They would have appreciated that. I'm not so sure I'll see them again, but thank you for saying it."

"I wondered that myself for a time when my dad passed away."

"How old were you?"

"I was seventeen. My younger brother was only eleven. My dad was strong in his faith, as is my mom. They introduced us to God, to Jesus, at an early age, and I loved Him from the beginning. As I grew older and came to know more of the world, my faith only grew. I never went through a rebellious phase, never questioned God or His love, except once, on the day we buried my dad. As well as I knew God, as well as I knew His Word and His promises, I questioned everything that day. I worried that maybe there was no God, no heaven, and that I'd never see my dad again. I questioned why God would take away such a great guy, take him from his wife and his two boys. I remember thinking how that seemed totally contrary to the God I thought I knew. I stopped trusting Him."

"What happened to change your mind?"

"God happened. I read Jeremiah 29, verses eleven through thirteen, which said, 'For I know the plans I have for you, declares the LORD, plans to prosper you and not to harm you, plans to give you hope and a future. Then you will call on me and come and pray to me, and I will listen to you.

You will seek me and find me when you seek me with all your heart'. I read that and I realized that God knows what He's doing, not me. If we just give ourselves over to Him, give Him our whole hearts, He promises to work all things, good and bad, for His good and ours. God doesn't cause the bad things in life to happen to us. He won't harm us. But, you see, the key is, He knows, not me. It's for me to know Him and, because of who He is, to trust Him with every ounce of my being. He had a plan for my life, and He has a plan for yours too."

"Right now, I seriously doubt that," Jessica replied. "It's a nice thought, but I doubt it."

"So did I once. So did I. Just know, God doesn't cause evil, sadness, or pain, but He's faithful to get us through them and to work bad situations for our good and the good of others in ways we probably can't even see and don't understand. Our job is simply to trust Him, and when we do that we can have joy in all circumstances."

"Well, I suppose we'll see," she responded beginning to walk back toward the house. She stopped, turned around, and asked, "Would you mind…would it be okay if I came with you, you know, when you try and get back home?"

"I wouldn't have it any other way."

"Thank you, Evan. You're a very kind man, and you've been a good friend. The best I've had lately."

"We make a good team."

"I agree. I'm going to try and get some sleep. Why don't we gather up what clothes and supplies we can and leave at sunrise, when the curfew lifts?"

"Okay."

"We can take my dad's car. It should be in the garage. My parents always kept a small stash of cash and some gold and silver coins. They told me where they're hidden. That should help get us there."

"It'll make all the difference. I'll check out the car and start getting some things loaded up."

"Sounds good. The keys should be on a hook next to

the door in the kitchen. The keys to my dad's gun safe should be hanging there too. I'm not sure if they'd still be in there, or if they were confiscated, but it won't hurt to look."

"Get some sleep," Evan replied. "I'll take care of it."

Jessica went up to her old room and lay down on her bed, emotionally drained and exhausted. Evan grabbed the car keys and headed out to the garage. He turned on the engine to make sure the car was working. As he did so, the radio came on, already tuned into a talk radio station. The broadcasters were discussing the strong condemnations and calls for boycotts against Israel coming from the United Nations and the various world governments in the aftermath of the Damascus bombing. Evan sat listening to the news, the overriding theme of which being that Israel was alone in the world.

"Oh God," Evan said aloud, hearing for the first time what had happened and how Isaiah's prophecy concerning Damascus had finally been fulfilled. "Lord, you are true to your Word and you are most certainly on your way soon, even just around the corner. Now, to get home to my beautiful Michelle and my babies, Lord willing."

Chapter 65

Louis was escorted into a small, windowless office, where a man in a pinstripe, heather-gray suit was sitting behind a small nondescript desk. Another man, in a navy-blue suit, stood to his left. The four Homeland officers brought Louis in and stood for a second behind him."

"Please, have a seat, Mr. Martino," the man behind the desk said. Louis took it as more of a command than an invitation, and, feeling resistance would be a waste of time and energy, he sat down with an audible sigh. One of the Homeland officers took Louis' carry-on from him, removed his laptop, and handed it to the man in the navy-blue suit, who took the laptop and stepped outside. He handed Louis' passport to the man behind the desk.

"Hey," Louis protested, "that's my laptop. He can't take that."

"You can wait for us outside," the man behind the desk said to the Homeland officers.

"Yes, sir. We'll be right outside," one responded, and the four filed through the doorway, closing the door behind them.

"So, Mr. Martino, do you know who I am?"

"Should I?"

"Well, as, based upon your recent article, you seem so exceptionally well informed on the David Stanton matter, I thought you may. Regardless, I'm John Bleeker."

"Declan Parker's boss?"

"No, not anymore. I'm now serving as the President's Special Advisor on Domestic Terrorism, and in some related functions in the realm of Homeland Security."

"Impressive," Louis responded. "It seems corruption really does pay."

"If only you knew, Mr. Martino. Do you have any idea as to why I'd be interested in you?"

"I'm guessing it has something to do with my article."

"More specifically, with how you came into

possession of, and subsequently published online, extremely sensitive, highly classified, national security information."

"I'm a real journalist, Mr. Bleeker. Part of my job is getting the information I need to back up a story, as opposed to just manufacturing what the powers that be want the public to see."

"Of course, and now you'll give me the cute, yet totally irrelevant, song and dance about protecting your sources and all that other Woodward and Bernstein type stuff."

"It seems I don't have to."

"No, you don't, because, frankly, I don't care. The rules have changed, Mr. Martino, and not in your favor. Besides, I already know you obtained the documents from Megan Neary."

"Then why ask the question?"

"Because, I want you to know that I know."

"Well, now I know, but I don't see how it changes anything. I also know you took my laptop to copy the hard drive and, yes, to save you some time, you'll find those documents on it, each and every one of them. But, even if you wipe my hard drive afterwards, I still have the documents saved elsewhere. I'll still be able to use them to refute every stupid, transparent lie about Declan Parker being involved with Stanton that you and your mainstream press lackeys publish. So, who cares? Copy what you want. Delete what you want. It won't stop me from writing the truth."

Bleeker sat back in his chair and began a slow rhythmic clap, which lasted for nearly a minute. "Bravo, Mr. Martino. Bravo. There's certainly no silencing the agent of truth, is there. Well, I'll refrain from offering a retort as, clearly, it would fall on deaf ears. As you've so artfully elucidated, one cannot overcome the truth."

Bleeker stood up from behind the desk, and rolled his head a couple of times, first clockwise, then counter clockwise. "One of the Homeland officers will return your laptop shortly, and you'll be on your way back home. We are, however, holding onto your passport for the time being."

"Under what authority?"

"If I have to pick one," he said as he headed toward the door, "you're suspected of aiding a wanted domestic terrorist. The NDAA provides me with all the authority I need. If that doesn't sit well with you, the president's martial law order sets out discretionary travel restrictions that serve the interests of national security. Good day, Mr. Martino. I'll be in touch."

Louis jumped up to protest further, but Bleeker left the room and two Homeland officers came in and forced Louis back into his seat, one of them saying, "You'll get your computer back in a minute. Just sit tight until then and don't give us any trouble."

In another office down the hall, Bleeker picked up his cell phone and dialed a phone number.

A familiar voice on the other end answered, "Costello here."

"Costello, it's Bleeker. It's come to my attention that your interim Special Agent in Charge, Kevin Cameron, has been communicating with Louis Martino, apparently trying to get a message to Parker."

"Do you think he's trying to help Parker?"

"I've yet to fully form an opinion on that one. He could be attempting to bait Parker with news about his brother being arrested. Time will tell, but in the meantime get Cameron under surveillance. Be subtle about it. I want to know everywhere he goes and everyone he talks to. Are we clear?"

"Crystal."

"Keep me up to speed. I want a report by noon each day."

Bleeker hung up the phone and looked at the man in

the navy-blue suit. "I want a visit paid to Louis Martino tonight. Send him my regards, but don't eliminate him. I want a message delivered that will be both memorable and painful. Understood?"

Chapter 66

"Everything is set inside. Are you ready, my dear?" Megan's Uncle Ignacio asked her.

"I'm ready."

Uncle Ignacio held his umbrella out over the car door. Megan stepped from the car onto the stone walkway and hurried quickly into the ancient San Antonio Abad Chapel in Cusco. She wore a simple, elegant white dress, as understated as it was beautiful.

"I wish we could wait for your parents and family to arrive," Uncle Ignacio said as they walked into the Cusco baroque-inspired chapel. "This is a moment that cannot be relived."

"I know, but Declan and I just wanted something simple, under the circumstances. We can all celebrate together after we get Declan's family down here too."

They stepped quietly to the back of the chapel. Megan looked ahead to see Declan standing at the front, with Atau standing next to him and another local man standing off to the side with a small camera.

"Who's that?" she asked.

"He is my friend, Freddie. I've known him for many years. He's a guide and an expert on the Inca. We needed an additional witness and Freddie loves weddings, so I asked him to meet us here. I thought he could take some pictures also."

The priest approached the steps near the lectern and a pianist began playing Pachelbel's Canon in D, to Megan's surprise.

"I didn't think we'd have any music, given the short notice," she said.

"Another friend of mine and my special treat. My niece can't get married without music. I wouldn't allow it."

"Well, aren't you a regular Red Redding."

"Red Redding?"

"A man who knows how to get things."

"This is only the beginning. Wait until you see the suite I booked for you two here at the Monasterio tonight. Complete with a romantic in-room dinner."

"You didn't?"

"I did. You're my only niece and you're going to be married in style, whether you like it or not. Besides, your mother, my sister, would not let me live another day if I'd let it be any other way."

"What if someone recognizes Declan?"

"My darling, there are only three people in all of the Andes who paid any attention to that article, and we're all here. You needn't worry. The manager of the hotel is also a good friend of mine. I assure you that you're in good hands. You stay here tonight, indulge and enjoy. Atau and I will pick you up in the morning."

Megan's eyes began to well up. "Thank you," she replied, and kissed her Uncle Ignacio on the cheek.

"It's my pleasure. Shall we?"

Megan nodded and began her walk down the aisle on her uncle's arm. Declan stood motionless about twenty feet in front of her, watching her with an enormous smile on his face. Despite having only met Declan, Freddie's smile was nearly as wide as he snapped pictures of Megan making her way down the aisle, in time with the music.

"Freddie's taking plenty of pictures," Megan whispered to her uncle as they walked.

"I told you," Uncle Ignacio replied, "He loves weddings, all weddings."

As they ultimately made it down the aisle and to Declan's side, Declan whispered, "You're more stunning than even I'd imagined."

"You don't look so bad yourself."

Freddie stepped quietly to the side and snapped a few photos of the couple together, before the priest began.

"Who presents this woman in marriage?" the priest asked.

"I do," Uncle Ignacio responded and stepped back,

leaving Megan and Declan standing opposite one another before the priest.

The priest began in English, with a heavy Peruvian accent, "Megan Neary and Declan Parker, have you come here freely and without reservation to give yourselves to each other in marriage?"

"Yes," they responded in unison.

"Will you honor each other as man and wife for the rest of your lives?"

"I will," they answered.

"Will you accept children lovingly from God, and bring them up according to the law of Christ and His Church?"

"I will," they replied again.

"As it is your intentions to enter into marriage, join your right hands, and declare your consent before God and His Church."

Declan looked directly into Megan's green eyes and began, "I, Declan Parker, take you, Megan Neary, to be my wife. I promise to be true to you, to love you with everything I have within me, in good times, in bad times, and in all times in between, in sickness and in health. I will love you and honor you all the days of my life, until the very second my last breath leaves my body."

Megan wiped a tear from her cheek, and began, "I, Megan Neary, take you, Declan Parker, to be my husband. I promise with all my heart to love you and to be true to you, in good times and in bad times, in sickness and health, and through whatever lies along our path together, come what may. I will love you and honor you all the days of my life and throughout eternity."

"The rings," the priest said.

Atau handed Declan a simple, white gold, wedding band, which he slid gently on Megan's finger, saying, "With this ring, I thee wed."

Megan took a matching wedding band from Uncle Ignacio, and slid it onto Declan's finger, also saying, "With this ring, I thee wed."

"What God has joined together," the priest declared, "let no one divide. I now pronounce you husband and wife. Please, you may kiss."

With joyful tears in both of their eyes, Megan and Declan joined hands and moved toward one another. They were buried in one another's eyes, for the moment ferried away from the rest of the world, as if God had reached down and enveloped them in His love, temporarily shielding them from the world. Standing there together, nothing existed but each other. It was with such a singular love in their hearts, a love untouched and untarnished by anything the world had or would throw their way, that they kissed for the first time as husband and wife.

Chapter 67

The L train slowed to a stop at the Logan Square station on the Blue Line, finally just three stops removed from the Damen station near Louis' apartment in Bucktown. The brakes screeched and the train came to a halt. Louis spotted a contingent of Homeland Troopers and Chicago PD, fully clad in tactical gear and carrying automatic weapons, uniformly positioned along the station platform.

The doors slid open and a few people from Louis' car disembarked quickly as four Homeland Troopers stepped into the train car. As the doors slid closed again, Louis watched the passengers who had exited at Logan Square being carded and, in many cases, frisked. Not wanting to make eye contact with the Homeland Troopers on the train, he lowered his gaze to his iPhone, pretending to check his email.

"ID," he heard one of the troopers say to a passenger a few seats away.

"Excuse me?"

"ID, show me your ID."

"Okay, just a second," the woman replied.

Louis looked up to watch the woman's trembling hands frantically search her purse. About ten seconds later, her hand emerged with her driver's license. She handed it up to the trooper, who removed it from her shaking hand and scanned the photo and information.

"Where are you heading?" he asked.

"Home," she replied. "Just on my way home."

Without a word, the trooper returned the woman's driver's license and moved toward Louis.

"ID," he said in the same cold tone as before.

"Here," Louis said, handing the trooper his driver's license.

After reviewing the license, the trooper looked down at Louis, who was looking directly into the trooper's eyes, and asked, "Where are you headed?"

"Home."

"Where's your stop?"

"Damen."

"Are you armed?"

"No."

"Stand up and step out into the aisle."

"Why?"

Another trooper approached and Louis slowly stood up from his seat and stepped into the aisle.

"Put your hands on your head and spread your legs."

Louis obliged and the trooper frisked him, slowly and deliberately, from his calves to his upper torso.

"Here," the trooper said handing the driver's license back to Louis. "You're clear."

Louis took his license back and stood for second in the aisle as the trooper made his way to another passenger a few seats behind him. A few minutes later, the train pulled into the California station and came to a stop. The doors again slid open and the Homeland Troopers exited. Looking out the window as the doors closed again, Louis caught sight of a man and woman in their late-twenties or early-thirties being escorted, in handcuffs, along the platform by two Homeland Troopers.

The scene was the same at each of the remaining L stops. At Damen, Louis quickly exited the train, again showed his driver's license to a Chicago Police Officer stationed at the end of the platform and again answered questions about his destination. Finally making it back to his apartment just before the curfew went into effect, Louis was exhausted. He ate some pasta from a box, took a quick shower, and checked his email from his home laptop. Finding Megan's response, Louis forwarded it to Kevin's email and, unable to keep his eyes open any longer, finally went to bed.

Sometime in the middle of the night, Louis awoke to something that sounded like scraping near his front door. He groggily stepped out of bed, picked up a golf club he kept nearby, and walked cautiously into the living room.

The front door burst open and three men, each wearing a ski mask and carrying a police style baton, burst through. Louis startled, then, instinctively, swung the golf club at the closest of the three, hitting him on the arm. Within seconds, Louis felt a streaking pain on his left side, as another of the men delivered a blow with his hard black baton. The blow caused Louis to fold over and he was quickly set upon by all three men, each bringing their batons viciously down on his head and back, until he finally fell to the floor.

Two of the men headed for the front door. The third, still standing over Louis' badly beaten and bleeding body, leaned over and lifted up his head by grabbing a handful of his hair with one hand. Raising Louis off the floor slightly, the man said, "John Bleeker sends his regards." Still holding Louis by the hair, the man reared back and swung the baton in his other hand as hard as he could, striking Louis squarely in the ribs on the left side of his body. His body jerked sideways and he fell again to the floor, desperately straining for a breath.

The man took Louis' passport out of his jacket pocket, dropped it on the floor next to him, and walked out the front door behind the other two assailants, leaving it open.

Evan and Jessica left the house in Denton at sunrise, the trunk of her father's car loaded with clothes, food and water for the drive to the lake house. They drove slowly, cautiously, out of the neighborhood and back out onto the main road, near the grocery store parking lot where they'd left Al Rawlins pickup truck.

"The truck is still there," Jessica said.

"Good. That probably means nobody's thought to see who it belongs to. There's no line at the gas station yet.

Let's stop and fill up. Who knows what we'll find once we get out away from the city. Your dad had a couple five-gallon gas cans in the garage. I'll fill those up too."

"Wow," Jessica responded looking at the gas station billboard. "It's $10.89 a gallon for regular unleaded."

"And that's if we're lucky enough for them to have any to sell."

They pulled into the gas station, where, given the early hour of the day, there were only a few other cars filling up. Jessica gave Evan some of the cash she'd gotten from her parents' house, which was nearly $1,000.00, and Evan went inside to pay.

Jessica sat in the car, looking at everything around her and remembering what it had been like just weeks earlier. She took a few moments to think back on her childhood, growing up in Denton in the very same house where they'd buried her parents the day before. She thought about her brother and hoped with all her heart that he was out there somewhere, still alive. Sitting in the car, while Evan filled up as quickly as he could in order to avoid becoming a tempting robbery target, Jessica realized she'd very likely never see her home again. Everything and everyone she'd ever known, except Evan, she was saying goodbye to. Evan was heading toward his home, toward his family, while Jessica was leaving hers behind, forever. Despite her prior feeling that she was out of tears, the thought of leaving home forever brought more to her eyes.

Evan hopped back into the car and said, "Are we ready?"

Jessica wiped the tears, vowing to herself that it would be the last time she'd ever do so and replied, "Yes, let's get you home."

Chapter 68

Megan's parents, two older brothers, and their families all arrived in Cusco the following morning, along with Tom Langham, her father's pilot. Uncle Ignacio threw a small celebration at the main hacienda. Despite being somewhat disappointed about missing the wedding, Megan's family was thrilled to welcome Declan into their family. Declan made arrangements with Tom to leave the following morning for the States. They were to fly into a tiny, little used, private airstrip a few miles by road from the lake house.

That night, Declan was unable to sleep and sometime around two in the morning, he gently nudged Megan, who because of her own nerves, was only partially asleep herself.

"Babe, are you awake?" Declan asked.

"Yeah, I'm not having much luck sleeping tonight."

"I want you to stay here tomorrow."

Megan sat up and turned on a lamp by the bed. "What do you mean? I have to go."

"No, you don't. I have no idea what I'm getting into. It could be as simple as getting everyone from the lake house to the airstrip, or it could be a lot more complicated and dangerous. I can't put you in the middle of that."

"Declan, you can't go alone. I'm coming."

"No, you're not. The truth is that I know the forest around the lake house like the back of my hand. Evan and I spent tons of time up there, running around and playing in those woods. Please don't take this the wrong way, but if something does go down, if it gets sticky, I'll be faster and better off alone. I've already put you in harm's way once. You've had to bail on your career, your apartment, everything, for me. Now, your whole family is here and you're safe. I'm not going to put you in danger again. I can't take a chance on losing you."

"But, ..."

Declan leaned toward Megan, gently took her face in

his hands, and kissed her. "You're not going to win this argument, counselor."

"I'm beginning to see that. But you can't go alone."

"I'm not. I'll have Tom there with the plane and I have the Lone Ranger."

"The Lone Ranger?"

"My dad's 9mm. I had Tom tuck it away on the plane, along with a couple clips, on the way down here. He still has it."

"God, I pray you won't need it."

"So do I, but I'll have it just in case."

"I have one request," Megan said as her eyes began to tear up.

"As long as it isn't you coming with me, it's yours."

"Come back. Just come back to me. That's all I ask."

Declan took his wife in his arms, feeling her streaming tears against his t-shirt and replied, "I'll be back. I promise."

"I promise, I'll let you know as soon as I hear something," Kevin told Michelle as he left the lake house amid the moonlight of early morning.

After receiving the news about the escape in Ft. Worth, and calling to check on Evan's status, Kevin had picked up some water and extra food and driven up to the lake house to see if Evan was, by some chance, there, or to give Michelle and Mrs. Parker an update in the likely event he wasn't.

"Please," Michelle responded, "Please let me know as soon as you hear something."

"Don't worry, I will. If he somehow makes it up here, just sit tight. Don't try to contact anyone. I'll check back within the next few days."

After watching Michelle go back inside, Kevin

walked along the dirt road about a half mile, got into his car, and began the drive back to the city.

"Bleeker, sorry for the early call. It's Costello."

"What is it?"

"Cameron just met with Evan Parker's wife at a little country house a few hours outside of town."

"How do you know it's Michelle Parker?"

"There's an SUV parked out front. I ran the plates and they came back to Evan Parker."

"Fair enough. Where are you now?"

"At a little service station down the road from the house. What do you want me to do?"

"For the time being, nothing. Get back to the city. Don't let anyone see you out there. I'm in briefings with the White House Chief of Staff throughout the morning, but I'll catch a flight back early in the afternoon."

"Should I assign anyone out here?"

"No, I don't want to spook anyone. If Parker's family has been hiding there this long, and they feel it's safe, they won't be going anywhere. Just keep an eye on Cameron."

Chapter 69

"Are you all set back there?" Tom Langham asked.

"All set," Declan responded.

"Good, we're next in line for takeoff. Relax, make yourself comfortable and we'll be back stateside in about eight hours. We'll land in Oklahoma City to go through customs, then we're off again to our final destination."

"Do you think we'll have any issues with customs?"

"Nope, none at all. I'm longtime friends with most of the people at Oklahoma City, so we'll be just fine. Sit back and enjoy the ride. We'll be up in the air shortly."

After double checking Declan's coded response in the email forwarded by Louis, Kevin Cameron deleted the email and sat back in his chair trying to determine the best way forward. Declan was clearly bound for the lake house. Kevin just had no idea when or by what means. Strangely, the situation was somewhat complicated by Evan's unanticipated freedom and the fact that, due to his escape, Kevin had no idea where Evan was or what had become of him. He could only hope Evan was alive, because if he was, the odds were favorable that Evan would try and make it back to his family at the lake house.

Kevin's phone rang. He looked at the caller id to see it was Bleeker. "This is Cameron," he answered.

"Cameron, any news on the Parker front?"

"Only that Evan Parker escaped from the Ft. Worth detention facility, or at least he's presently unaccounted for."

"I heard about that. Any line on where the rest of his family may be?"

"Still working on that. I may have something."

"Good. What about Parker? A little bird informed me that you've been in contact with Louis Martino."

His voice giving nothing away, Kevin replied, "It

seemed like a good place to start, seeing that Martino clearly has inside info that could only have come from Declan. I figured he might have an idea as to Declan's whereabouts."

"Good instincts. And?"

"Still developing, but I did receive a response from Martino, so it could be promising."

"Excellent. I'll be in town later this afternoon, in a few hours. I'll call when I land, but I want to meet you and Costello for a full briefing. Understood?"

"Of course. I'll clear my afternoon."

"Good. I'll call when I'm on my way."

Kevin hung up the phone and sat back again, rubbing his temples. Clearly Bleeker had been tracking Louis Martino's emails, a risk Cameron had been aware of, but had been willing to take. Knowing Bleeker as he did, Kevin knew it was safest to operate under the assumption that Bleeker was also somehow aware that the rest of the Parker family was at the lake house, otherwise the question would not have been posed.

For Kevin to have any effectiveness, he had to remain on the inside of the operation, and for that to happen, he had to retain Bleeker's trust. Mulling over his options, Kevin knew the only way to do that was to lay everything out for Bleeker in the briefing, including Declan's response. From Bleeker's perspective, Declan's family was only worth keeping alive for as long as they could be used as bait. By telling Bleeker where they were, and that Declan appeared to be coming back for them, Kevin hoped he'd be able to keep everyone alive for at least a couple more days.

"Just another three and a half hours or so," Evan said to Jessica.

"Do we have enough gas to make it without stopping again?"

"Yeah, we should be okay."

"Good. That last stop made me nervous."

"Me too. Lots of desperate people out there. It'll be good to get off the road."

"What do you think we'll find at the lake house?" Jessica asked.

"What do you mean?"

"Do you think the feds or anyone knows your family is up there?"

"I don't think so, but I suppose we'll find out soon enough."

"What's it like?"

"It's gorgeous. It's a small little town. The house is on a medium sized lake, nothing fancy, but it's in the middle of a wilderness area full of rolling, wooded hillsides. My brother and I used to play in the woods all day when we'd go up there."

"What did you play?"

"Mainly cowboys and Indians. The Lone Ranger was our favorite. We would pretend we were the Lone Ranger and Tonto. There's a cave about a few hundred yards from the house, up in the side of one of the rockier hillsides. That was our main hideout, the place we'd meet up in case of trouble, which inevitably came in the form of cattle rustlers or bandits. The cave had two entrances, one on each side of the rise, basically cutting through the hillside."

"Sounds like the kind of place we could use nowadays."

"Absolutely."

"What was on the other side?"

"Back then, nothing but a big clearing and thirty or so acres of farmland. Now, there's a little private airport over there, but it's hardly ever used."

Chapter 70

Bleeker stepped quickly and confidently into the conference room, where Costello and Kevin Cameron sat waiting. "So, hit me. What do we have?"

Costello looked to Cameron, who spoke up, "Well, as you know, I've made contact with Louis Martino, with the hope of getting a message to Parker to the effect that his brother had been picked up and his family needed help. To my knowledge, Martino passed the message to Megan Neary and sent back a response not long ago."

"And, do we have a nibble on our hook?"

"I think we may."

"What about the family, where are they?"

"Parker's mom, sister-in-law, niece and nephew are hiding out at a place a few hours outside the city. It's a small lake house that's still titled to Parker's parents."

"Have you made contact with them?"

"I have. At this point, they believe I'm working to try and get them reunited with Evan and to safety somewhere."

"Any word on Dr. Parker?"

"None. He was sent down to the detention facility in Ft. Worth. There was an inmate uprising a few days ago and he's been unaccounted for ever since. I suspect he's either dead or, like his brother, on his way to the lake house."

"You don't have any surveillance on the lake house though?"

"No. I wanted to keep it to myself, keep it low key. If they suspect me, the game is off. As things stand, with the family supposedly sitting safely at the lake house, they make good bait. A potentially easy grab."

Bleeker sat back in his chair and ran the various scenarios in his head for a few minutes. "You've done good work, Cameron. Does the family have any communications out there?"

"No, nothing. Otherwise, they'd have been a lot easier to track."

"True, but that works to our benefit now that we've found them. Does Parker know they're at the lake house?"

"I believe so."

"But, because they don't have any phones, internet or any other way to communicate, he has to go there himself to find out."

"Agreed."

"So, until he gets there, he has no idea who's at the house."

"True."

"I want Parker to find us at the house, not his family. Get four men together and a van. I want to take the family tonight, get them out of the house and into custody before Parker shows up. We'll take the house, remove the family, and take up positions inside."

"Bleeker," Kevin interrupted, "why don't we just leave them there? They're the perfect bait now."

"They've already served their purpose. As things stand, I have no control out there. I don't have surveillance and I don't have consistent reliable intel. Parker isn't dumb. He'll scan the area for signs of surveillance units before heading for the house itself. If he finds anything outside, anything at all, it's over and he'll never try for the house. We have to be set up inside waiting for him, without any signs of our presence outside. That means we need to take the house ASAP, so we don't risk Parker beating us there. Costello, get the men together. I want to move out within the hour. Cameron, you're with me. Let's go."

———————

Tom Langham landed the plane softly onto the small airstrip about two hours before sunset. One of the two airport attendants came over to the plane, talking to Tom about how long they'd be on the ground and his fuel needs.

Once he'd finished speaking with the attendant, who'd gone around to one of the four hangars on site, Tom stepped back into the cabin. "You all set?"

"I am," Declan replied, tucking the loaded Lone Ranger into his belt.

"Here, take the Remington too," Tom said. "Hopefully there'll be no need for it, but better safe than sorry."

"Thanks, I will." Declan took the rifle and looked it over. Tom handed him a box of rounds.

"And do you have the cell phone I gave you?"

"It's in my backpack, along with the jacket, cash and silver coins. Just in case."

"You can never be too prepared."

"Agreed," Declan said. "Okay, the entrance to the cave is about three quarters of a mile through the forest due east from here. I'll go through and come out on the other side, on a rise above the house and about two hundred yards away. There's a chance we'll come back by car, but if there's no rush I'd prefer to make the trip back by foot, so just keep an eye out and be ready to fire up the plane."

"I'll be ready to roll."

"And, Tom, if for some reason I don't come back with them, stick to the plan and don't wait for me, okay."

"I'm not so sure about that one. Megan made me promise to look after you."

"Tom, I'm serious. This mission is to get my family to safety. That's the priority here and if it doesn't happen, we've failed. If it comes down to it, don't wait for me. If I get left behind, I'll meet you like we discussed."

"Nineteen hundred hours, exactly thirty days from today at Lakefront Airport in New Orleans," Tom responded.

"Got it."

"Okay," Tom answered with reticence. "You have my word. If it comes down to it, I won't wait, but I hope it doesn't."

"Me too."

"Good luck and God speed."

With that, Declan put his small backpack on, looped

the Remington over his left shoulder, and stepped out of the cabin onto the tarmac. He slipped around the plane and darted quickly across the runway, disappearing into the forest.

Chapter 71

Declan found the cave entrance exactly where he remembered it. Aside from the airstrip, nothing had really changed in the area over the years. He flipped on his flashlight and headed into the cave, which essentially cut through the hillside, acting as a tunnel from one side to the other. Aside from a tight, narrow passage of about twenty feet shortly after the opening, the remainder of the path was relatively wide and easily walkable. Numerous smaller tunnels branched off from the main path, but Declan knew each twist, turn, fall and rise along the way.

About fifteen minutes later, he emerged in the late afternoon sunlight on the other side, in the rocky cliffs about sixty feet above, and a few hundred yards away from the lake and lake house below. The sun was just beginning its slow descent as he emerged from the darkness of the cave into the softening light. He flipped off the flashlight and put it back into his jacket pocket, then moved quietly and swiftly along a little switchback trail leading down from the cave entrance. The trail was just one of many which had been made over the years by his family. There were numerous little trails in the woods around the house, which his family had worn out during their time there. After he'd descended about 30 feet, Declan ducked down behind some brush, in an area giving him a relatively clear view of the house and the general surroundings.

He initially scanned the area with his naked eye, easily able to make out the house and Michelle's SUV parked below. Raising the Remington, Declan peered through the scope, which afforded a magnified view of the forest surrounding the house. Everything seemed quiet and peaceful. Seeing and hearing nothing unusual, and sensing nothing out of the ordinary in the surrounding forest, Declan proceeded down the trail, which would ultimately bring him to the back of the house, which overlooked the lake.

As Declan neared the end of the trail, he began to

hear what sounded like tires rolling along the gravel road leading to the house. He stopped for a second to listen closer and was clearly able to make out the sound, which grew louder and more discernible. At that point, Declan pulled the Remington off his shoulder and sprinted down the last twenty feet of the trail to the back side of the house. He heard the tires come to a stop in front of the house, and ran around the side, toward a brushy spot where he'd have a good view and a clear shot if necessary.

Reaching the spot, he dropped to the ground behind the brush and took aim with the Remington. The car had stopped next to Michelle's SUV. Declan listened for the door of the house to open, or for any sound coming from inside the house, but all was silent. He peered through the scope as the car doors opened, first spotting a girl who looked to be in her early-twenties, and, then, Evan.

"Oh, thank God," he said to himself. Unable to control himself, Declan hopped up and called out, "Evan!"

Evan turned and saw his brother, coming out from behind the bushes. "Declan!"

They met outside the house and embraced. "What are you doing here?" Evan asked. "I thought you left the country."

"I did, but Kevin Cameron got word to me that you all were in trouble, so I came back. I'm so happy to see you. I can't tell you how happy I am."

At that moment the front door of the house flew open. Will and Charlotte rushed toward their dad, arms outstretched, with Michelle running behind them, tears flowing from her eyes. Evan turned from his brother and hurried to meet his wife and children. As Will and Charlotte reached him, Evan dropped to his knees and his arms were suddenly, finally, filled with his children again. Michelle also rushed down toward her husband, falling to her knees as well, and the four hugged each other as never before. Evan couldn't contain his happiness, nor did he try. The joyful tears flowed freely from his eyes.

Declan saw his mom standing on the front porch, her watering eyes raised toward the dimming heavens. He hurried to her, more thrilled to see her again than he could have imagined. Aside from Megan, the entire family was again together, despite everything that had been put in their respective paths. Jessica stood by the car, also crying, taking in the family's reunion, and wondering whether she'd ever see her own brother again.

Chapter 72

Following Declan's instructions, the family hurried about the lake house, each gathering a backpack's worth of possessions, making sure to get their passports, any essentials, and anything of value that could be stuffed inside.

Declan had decided it best to take the trail and cave path back to the airstrip, not wanting to run the risk of encountering anyone on the road. He moved Jessica's dad's car around behind the house, where it wouldn't be in plain sight if anyone were to come out there. After that, Declan stood outside on the front porch, as the sun set, nervously scanning the area and listening for any indication of other people.

Evan stepped out onto the porch, approaching his brother. "This is truly a miracle," he said. "All of us together again."

"Absolutely," Declan responded. "Now God just has to get us all on that plane and safely back to Peru."

"You sound like a man who believes God's capable of doing just that."

Declan turned to his brother and smiled, replying, "It took some time, but I am."

"I can't wait till we have time to talk. I want to hear the whole story."

"For now, let's just say my eyes have been opened and I'm confident, for the first time ever, that, someday, I'll finally see dad again. That we all will."

"What a wonderful day that will be."

"I just pray it isn't today."

Evan smiled and nodded in agreement.

"I think everyone's ready," Jessica said, coming out of the house.

"Good," Declan responded. "We'd better get moving. Alright, we're going to take the trail behind the house, as quickly as we can, up to the cave entrance. You remember how to get up there?"

"Are you kidding?" Evan replied.

"Evan, you take the lead, and set the pace. We'll keep Michelle and Will right behind you. Mom and Jessica shouldn't have any trouble. I'll bring up the rear and carry Charlotte, because she's too young to keep up."

"I can carry her," Evan said.

"No, I'm fine. You just set a quick pace and get us up the cliffside."

Kevin stopped the car carrying himself, Costello, Bleeker and a rookie agent named Jurickson at the turnoff from the main road, and killed the headlights. The unmarked van carrying the remaining three agents did the same.

"This is the road leading to the lake house," Kevin said. "The road has a couple gradual turns and the house sits at the end of the road, about a mile down."

"How far up do you think we can drive without being detected?"

"The second turn is about a half mile away. It's a fairly dense forest, so visibility is low, especially with the sun setting. I'd say we can easily get to that spot. From there, with headlights out, we can probably get pretty close before they'll hear anything."

"Okay, we'll leave the van at the second turn. The four of us will continue on, headlights off. If your intel is accurate, we're dealing with two unarmed women and two children. I want Costello and Jurickson to cover the back and Cameron and I will approach the front. Since they're expecting Cameron, I want him to get them to open the door, and we'll take them when they do. Once we have them, Jurickson will radio for the van, we'll load them up, then five of us will stay behind while the other two get the van and Cameron's car out of the area. Clear?"

"Clear."

"Okay, then let's go."

The family went out the back door of the house, Evan in the lead and Declan carrying his niece at the rear. They walked hurriedly, but quietly, as the sun neared the climax of its farewell for the day. The soft orange light fell over the lake and forest as they reached the start of the trail, and began the trek back up to the cave. After a few minutes of brisk walking, Declan stopped, again thinking he heard the sound of tires on gravel. He stood still for a second, listening. Jessica noticed him stop and held up herself.

"What is it?" she whispered.

"I think it's a car. Shh."

Declan listened for a few seconds more and, as before, the sound grew incrementally louder and more clear. Evan had stopped and was walking back toward his brother, hearing it too.

"It's a car," Declan whispered. "You've got to move, now. Here, take the flashlight."

Declan removed the flashlight from his jacket pocket and handed it to Evan. "Here, can you carry Charlotte?" he asked Jessica.

"Of course."

Declan handed his niece to Jessica and said, "Now go, quickly. Get to the cave entrance and hurry as fast as you can to the airstrip. "Do you remember where it is?"

"Yeah," Evan answered. "But, you're coming with us."

"No, I'm gonna stay to see who it is and cover your backs, if necessary. We don't have time to argue. Now go, and don't wait for me more than a few minutes. If I'm not on the plane, Tom'll come back for me. Don't worry about that. Just go. Get everyone out of here."

"Declan..."

"Evan, go. I'll be fine. Hurry."

Evan and the others hurried up the trail. Declan ran

from the trail into the forest, trying to get wide around the house for a better vantage point. The sound of tires grew louder and noticeably picked up speed.

Declan quickly moved higher up the hillside through the trees, trying to get far enough above the house where he could see the car when it finally came into view. He looked back and up through the trees and saw Evan and the others practically running, Will in his dad's arms. By Declan's estimation, they were still minutes away from the cave entrance.

Finally, Declan saw the car coming and immediately recognized it as Kevin Cameron's. He prayed that it was just Kevin, but was then able to make out the silhouettes of four heads in the car. From his hidden spot on the hillside, Declan had a side view of the house below, and could clearly see the front and the back. The sounds of Evan and the others making their way up to the cave could no longer be heard.

Declan tucked down in the brush, hidden, and raised the Remington as the car came to a stop. He remained dead still and silent as the doors opened and two men, who would have been unseen from inside the house, hurried toward the back. Through the scope, Declan easily made out Costello.

Cameron stepped from the car and approached the front door of the house, leaving one man in the front passenger seat. Declan turned the scope toward the car and saw Bleeker.

Chapter 73

Kevin approached the front door and, as he'd done twice before, called out, "Mrs. Parker, it's okay, it's Kevin Cameron."

Declan could hear him and cursed Kevin, beginning to think the message Kevin had sent was intended to be a trap. Kevin called out again, "Mrs. Parker...Mrs. Parker, it's Kevin Cameron," but nothing happened. He could hear or see no movement in the house.

Bleeker stepped from the car and turned his head in a slow scan of the very dimly-lit forest surrounding the house. Bleeker continued scanning the hillside and forest. Despite the creeping darkness, the sun hadn't completely fallen and a small amount of soft orange light still colored the lake and hillside. Declan began to worry that he would spot Evan and the others moving on the cliffside above. He kept an eye on Costello and the other agent, who had found Megan's dad's car and taken up positions at the back of the house, weapons raised.

As Declan turned back to Bleeker, he noticed Bleeker motion for Kevin to be quiet, but couldn't make out what was said, as Kevin walked back toward the car. Declan watched Bleeker's gaze focus on the hillside behind the house, on a rocky, well-wooded spot about forty feet from the cave entrance. Declan turned his attention to that spot as well, trying to make out any movement up there.

For a split second, he spotted something move through the thick evergreens, and immediately turned his eyes back to Bleeker, who then appeared to be talking to Kevin. Declan caught movement in his peripheral and turned back to see Costello and Jurickson entering the lake house from the rear door. About 10 seconds later, Costello appeared on the front porch and Declan heard him yell, "It's empty, but it doesn't look like they've been gone long!"

Upon hearing the house was empty, Bleeker looked squarely at Kevin. His face betrayed no thoughts whatsoever. His eyes still locked in on Kevin, Bleeker spoke calmly into his radio, "They're on foot, headed up the hillside directly behind the house. Crandon, bring the van up immediately. We need you three here. Costello, you and Jurickson head up after them. I spotted movement on the hillside about forty to fifty feet above the house."

"What do you want me to do?" Kevin asked.

Saying nothing, but with his eyes still locked onto Kevin, Bleeker simply raised his side arm and fired two quick rounds. Each hit Kevin squarely in the center of his chest. The bullets ripped through his heart, throwing Kevin onto the gravel.

"You've done enough already."

Declan jerked his eye away from the scope on the Remington as Kevin Cameron fell to the ground, dead. Without time to let the shock of Kevin's execution wash over him, he caught sight of the van's headlights coming down the road through the trees. Out of his peripheral vision, he saw Costello and Jurickson exit the rear door of the house and head toward the hillside.

"Damn," he said to himself. "Bleeker must have seen them up there."

Still standing near Kevin's body, Bleeker had turned to face the oncoming van. Declan's eyes flashed back and forth from Costello to Bleeker. He knew he couldn't let Costello and Jurickson get up into the forest, or he'd have no shot; however, he desperately wanted to take Bleeker first, thereby finally giving Bleeker what he deserved, eliminating command and, hopefully, causing confusion amongst the others.

Seeing Jurickson almost to the forest line,

immediately followed by Costello, he quickly raised the Remington, lined up his shot through the scope, and fired one round, hitting Jurickson just above the right knee, which was precisely where he'd aimed. Jurickson fell screaming to the ground.

On hearing the shot, Costello hit the ground and Bleeker ran for cover behind Kevin's car. Declan quickly found Costello through the scope, lying flat on the ground, but still out in the open, aimed for the side of his exposed right leg, and fired. As with Jurickson, the bullet found its mark, and Costello screamed out that he was hit.

Evan and the others had heard Bleeker's two shots when they were still about twenty feet from the cave entrance. They'd stopped for a second and, unable to see anything, sprinted toward the cave. Evan had gathered everyone inside, when Declan's two shots rang through the forest.

"That was a rifle," Evan said nervously.

"Are you sure?" Michelle replied.

"I'm certain. It's a different sound than a handgun."

No sooner had Evan spoken, when another rifle shot filled the air. "There it is again. That's gotta be Declan. I should help."

"No," Michelle replied. "You have to get us to the plane. We don't know our way through this cave. You're not leaving us. I won't lose you again."

"You're right, my love, you're right," Evan said. "Okay, let's go. Everyone together." He flipped on the flashlight and hurried them along.

With Bleeker still hunkered down behind Kevin's car, Declan fired a round at the side mirror just above his head, taking it out and keeping Bleeker pinned down. Watching the van's headlights growing larger, Declan waited for the van to come into view, then took aim at the front driver's-side tire, squeezing off two rounds. The second round blew out the tire, causing the driver to lose control. The van hurled off the gravel road and smashed sideways into the heavy evergreen trees lining the road about twenty-five feet from Kevin's car.

Declan was unable to get a sight on anyone inside the van. He scanned back to the car to see if Bleeker had popped his head up, but saw nothing. A few seconds later, an agent stumbled out of the van carrying a rifle and, keeping low and zigzagging, tried to make his way to Bleeker. Declan lined up his shot and fired again, hitting the agent just above the knee. The agent fell to the gravel, writhing in pain.

Bleeker took out his phone and dialed 911, "I'm FBI and we're under fire. I'm pinned down and I have men down. I need anyone and everyone you can get out here and I need them now!"

Evan and the family could see the plane on the landing strip just about ten yards away. Evan's mom ran ahead and when Tom Langham saw her emerge from the forest, he fired up the engines. The plane was fueled and cleared for takeoff. After starting her up, Tom came out onto the tarmac and met Mrs. Parker, saying, "Is everyone okay? I could hear gunshots out there."

"We're fine, but Declan isn't with us. We need to wait for him."

"I'll do what I can ma'am, but I gave him my word I'd get you all safely out of here, with or without him. Please climb aboard."

A few seconds later, Jessica, Michelle, Charlotte, Evan and Will arrived. Tom helped them all into the plane.

"We have to wait for Declan," Evan shouted.

"I'll wait for a few minutes, but I've promised to get you all to safety."

"Just wait, he'll be here. We can't leave him, I don't care what you've promised."

"Trust me, I don't want to take off without Declan any more than you do, but the objective of this mission was clear. We'll wait a few more minutes. That's the best I can do."

———————————

Declan continued firing rounds, keeping Bleeker and the agents in the van pinned down. They tried to return fire, but in the darkness, couldn't get a solid location on Declan. Each time he'd fire, he'd zigzag a bit further up the hillside, slowly making his way back toward the cave entrance.

Nearing the edge of his range, Declan heard sirens in the distance and assumed, correctly, that Bleeker had radioed for back up. Finally, he put the Remington on his shoulder and hurried up the hillside toward the cave entrance, at once thankful and annoyed that he hadn't heard or seen the plane takeoff yet.

As he finally reached the cave, red and blue flashing lights could be seen outside the house below. Declan watched for a few seconds, unable to tell whether they were police or Homeland, but he was able to make out three squad cars and an ambulance. More sirens could be heard in the distance, and spotlights had begun scanning the forest and hillsides surrounding the house.

Taking the first step into the dark of the cave, he finally heard the jet overhead and looked up to see its lights flashing as it sped off against the stars in the newly black night sky. Watching Tom's plane bank slightly and begin the journey south, Declan breathed in deeply, relieved beyond measure that his family was onboard and safe.

Looking up to the stars in the sky, too numerous to count, for the first time in years Declan remembered something his dad had told him as a boy when visiting the lake house in summers gone by. Quoting Psalm 147, Verse 4, his Dad had said of God, "He determines the number of stars in the sky and calls them each by name."

Standing between the red and blue lights flashing below and the innumerable stars glistening above, the true number and names of which were known only to the God who had created them, Declan was at peace, for he knew with absolute certainty that he was anything but alone. The Lord was with him, and would deliver him safely back to Megan and the rest of his family. He didn't know how, or when, but just as his dad had done before taking his final breath, Declan kissed his closed hand three times, made the sign of the cross, and headed into the darkness with his faith and trust in God alone.

TO BE CONTINUED…

www.ingramcontent.com/pod-product-compliance
Lightning Source LLC
Chambersburg PA
CBHW060530180626
46817CB00002B/499